# Midnight Winters

# DANI HART

# Midnight
# Winters

# Dedication

Dreams can only fall short if you let them.
This is for my readers.
If you hadn't embraced this series,
it might have never been completed.

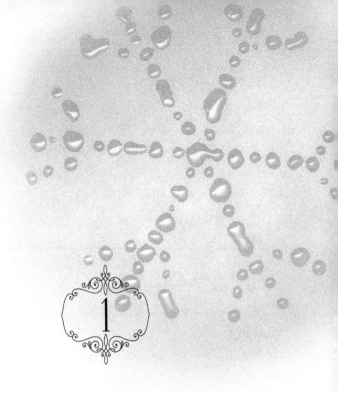

# 1

## ELIJAH

HER SADNESS COULD FILL a hundred buckets and still overflow, seeping into the hollows of my heart. That kiss, as desperate as it was, loosened The Order's noose around my neck, but also solidified the suffocating darkness I would travel to free myself from the hell that had been my life ever since Abigail Rose fell into my arms. When I had turned from the closed door that shrouded her pain in secrecy, a young girl with jet-black hair peered at me with an odd look. I thought her name was Jasmine, but it was hard to remember all the recruits. They had become an army of faceless warriors, but this one pierced me with accusatory eyes. Did she know what I was guilty of? What I was? Impossible. She was just a kid sucked into an endless battle at the wrong time. I felt sorry for her. For all of them. They signed on thinking they had a chance. That they were fighting for the greater good, but those lines had crossed, tangled, and intertwined so many times that the path had been all but erased and there were no absolutes anymore. Good or bad. Wrong or right. They floated in between here and there and swirled with doubt, confusing me. What side would I land on?

I slammed my fist into the punching bag again, feeling the satisfaction vibrate under my skin, sweat dripping off my skin like a fresh downpour. That kiss flashed between impacts, her eyes a fountain of maple from the trunk of its source pouring into me, flooding my soul.

Lies upon lies, the truth so hard to see anymore. And that kiss making it harder. She was supposed to be just an assignment. A repaid debt and then back into hiding, but I dug my grave deeper instead and the fall into it would be infinite and I would see all my regrets descending beside me, taunting me and whispering to me that I should have turned away when I had a chance. Now I would end up like Penelope in the end. The noose pulled taut until I broke. Choose my life over hers. And I knew what I would do. It's what chained me to The Order once again. To protect her. To die for her if it came to that.

The bag swayed with another punch.

I unwrapped the protective gauze around my hands, my knuckles still cracked under the pressure of my anger.

Abigail was on to something with Penelope and her brother, but I knew the truth. I knew why Penelope wanted me dead. I was the reason her brother was in that prison. I had tracked him for The Order. I took pleasure in it. Every single one of those monsters bore the face of the one that had taken my mother. I would have killed them all if I could, but The Order liked to collect them, and I knew better than to ask questions. Only The Order had lied to me. Zander wasn't just any monster. I could feel it. He was different, but it was too late. He had been changed.

The hot water felt good on my sore muscles as I washed off in the locker room shower. I had been training hard since Abigail decided to come to The Order training facility. I knew I would need to be in prime shape if either of us stood a chance. I cranked up the heat, leaning into the shower wall as it stung my skin, hundreds of needles puncturing the sensitivity I had developed because of Abigail, my love for her pushing the needles deeper into the marrow of my bones, siphoning the cancerous cells that split and grew into a forest of hatred after my mother was taken from my arms.

Abigail will be tested beyond her limits here, and I have already heard the venomous distrust of the recruits. She will have no allies. No friends. Getting permission from the council to be her partner, a shadow, is imperative. I made my formal request to the council and they accepted to meet with me tonight, but that wasn't the hard part. They could deny me because of our connection, which we made apparent at the tribunal, so every word and sentence I spoke needed to be carefully crafted. If I could make them see that our connection was an asset rather than a hindrance, then they might favor me by her side knowing I would do anything to protect her. Everything The Order had been planning hinged on Abigail's abilities. I remembered studying the prophecies of the Visionary when I was a Potential, and it mentioned that there would be one that would be above all others. A person who would encompass everything and everyone. A true weapon against immortals. No one suspected it would be a girl. In history past, Chosens had all been males. Strong and agile. From what I had seen of Abigail, she was off balance and frail. The Order still questioned if she truly was a Chosen, and they would go to extreme lengths to prove it without a doubt. Knowing what tests she would undergo made the tendons lasso around my muscles, playing a game of tug-of-war. I was able to protect her outside of these walls, but not in here. Everyone was at the mercy of The Order's discretion. If Abigail was not The Chosen, she wouldn't survive what The Order had in store for her. Only The Chosen could endure those tests. For The Order's sake, she better come out the other side of this unscathed or my wrath would bring an end to their empire.

I slipped out of my building, a temporary housing unit for members between missions, tucked at the bottom of the hill behind Building Twelve. It was unmarked and, therefore, off limits to anyone else. It was one of the very few buildings using fingerprint technology, and only when you were expected would your fingerprint be active. It was almost curfew for the recruits, so it was dark and quiet on the grounds. Jack was running the track just as he seemed to do every night. He was itching to go on missions, but I knew he didn't have what it took to be in one-on-one combat. The Order had recruited him because of his connection to Abigail, not because he garnered any gifts. He was smart, and The Order planned on training him as a field doctor.

Jogging up the hill to the main building helped expend the nervous energy stifling my concentration, only to tense up again when met by Polly's replacement upon entering the building. Tawny was younger and pretty, but didn't exude the warmth that Polly had. I was angry that The Order had removed Polly after Abigail's father was dragged out. I tried to plead for her, but in the end, they knew she could be a liability around Abigail. She had known too much and had become too close to James over the years.

"Mr. Winters, they are ready." Tawny stood up and smiled demurely.

"Thanks," I gruffed, ignoring her not so subtle advance.

As we approached the door that sealed Penelope's fate at the tribunal, my fists clenched. I had learned to hate The Order, and being back in this room would push me to my limits.

Tawny pressed her thumbprint on the keypad and held the door open as I passed through. Her perfume-drenched body made me nauseous, and only after she closed the door, leaving me alone in front of the elevator, did I dare to inhale. The elevator chimed, and I stepped in.

I walked the infamous hall again, only alone this time, noting there were no doors leading to other rooms. Just blank white walls, two vents, and a large return. The crawl space would be too small for me, but Abigail could fit. My fingers twitched on cue reaching for the memory of Abigail's hand as I stepped into the tribunal room and into the spotlight at the center.

"Good evening, Mr. Winters," one of the silhouettes off to the right announced.

I tried to memorize the cadence and pitch of each word he spoke, picturing a stocky man in his fifties. They didn't know my gift stretched into sound waves. James kept it between us as he trained me relentlessly on it. Sound waves reverberated around the source, making an outline of colors. The details were absent, such as clothing, but the shapes pulsed vividly.

"What matter is so urgent that you needed an immediate presence?" the man asked curtly. His eyebrows fell inward and his voice had stayed even, but his body language told a different story. He was annoyed.

"I'd like to request that I partner with Abigail as she goes through the buildings." Silence was followed by hushed whispers.

"And why is that?" a plump older woman asked.

"I know her weaknesses better than anyone. I can help break her of them."

"But you care for her." A comment from another

woman, young and petite. I continued to catalog each council member carefully.

"I have been tracking Abigail for three years now. I know everything there is to know about her. Her enemies. Her friends. I can make her stronger."

Silence again and then more whispers.

"Do you think you have the ability to make her hate the one thing she loves most?"

The question rubbed like coarse sandpaper against my chest. *Wes.* He is what they wanted most. For her to hate him and his family, because then they knew she was capable of destroying all of the immortals if she had a good enough reason to, but only if her heart turned against them.

"Without a doubt," I answered confidently.

More whispers. This time, I followed the sound waves around the balcony, each shape manifesting dimly. None of them stood out physically, except for one man. He was tall and burly. I could definitely pick him out of a crowd.

"We have voted, and your request has been granted, under one condition."

I gnashed my teeth together. Another debt to be paid, but wasn't Abigail worth it?

"You must bring in Wes Hunter immediately."

A low rumble hummed in my lungs, and the cracks on my knuckles bled as I squeezed my fists closed. Abigail would hate me if she ever found out. She would never forgive me. And that's exactly what The Order wanted.

They wanted her to hate us both, so she wouldn't hesitate when they asked her to choose them above all else.

"Mr. Winters?" the tall, older council member who started the tribunal pressed.

"Fine," I bit out and then left, storming out of the elevator, my insides raging with insuppressible fury. The intensity of their request blurred the world, and the fists of a hundred men pounded against my skull. I knew it wouldn't be easy. I knew they would want something in return, but this? How the hell was I going to do this without earning Abigail's undying hatred for a lifetime? A very long lifetime. I shoved the door to the lobby open with so much force the hinge buckled and Tawny flew under the counter. I snickered. She wouldn't last a week here.

Red glistened on the dew-slicked rooftops, the moon full of the blood of my victims, reminding me that I was a murderer, a beast groomed to kill other beasts. I wondered if the moon would rupture like a balloon filled beyond its capacity. What was one more? My work would never be done. Not until the world was rid of the murderous filth that littered our streets and preyed on our kind. They were here because of fools dabbling in dark magic centuries ago. And now their numbers were greater, and pure humans were on the brink of extinction. I believed in what The Order was trying to do. I even believed in their methods, although I would have preferred killing immortals and supernaturals rather than locking them up, but something had shifted within The Order. I left because of it, and now here I was again, supporting a cause that had been distorted, finding myself at their mercy again.

Jack was heading my way as I stomped my way down to the armory. Maybe he would sense my mood and—

"You look like you're in a mood," Jack said as he slowed his jog next to me.

"And you have horrible survival instincts," I grumbled.

"You headed to the armory?"

I ignored him, my patience waning, but he still followed close behind. I scanned my thumbprint at the door of the armory and pushed it open when the lock released. When Jack tried to follow me in, I pushed my hand into his chest. "Where do you think you're going?"

"Aww, come on, Elijah. I've never been in there," he whined like a pathetic teenager.

"Because you don't belong in there. Now, go," I seethed.

He studied me for a moment and backed up a few steps. "You're going on a mission, aren't you?"

"Why else would I be here?" Jack was getting tiresome.

"Take me with you."

I threw my head back, releasing an epic laugh, and then stopped abruptly and responded, "No."

"Why? I've been through all the training, and I was good enough for them to make me a commander."

"You babysit recruits. That hardly qualifies you for battle." I crossed my arms, waiting for a sound rebuttal.

"That stereotype is exactly why I need to go with you.

To prove I'm capable. I'm a Potential for the Elite program, and this would look good."

I had seen Jack fight in his final test against an immortal, but they had been imprisoned and half-starved. Hardly a real challenge. If I brought him with me, he could be killed but, really, what did I care? "Fine, but you have to do everything I say, without question."

Jack's eyes lit up.

"And lose the smile. You won't need that where we're going."

The door slammed shut behind us, the LEDs flickering on ahead as we walked down a long hallway and turning off behind us.

"That's not creepy or anything," Jack said, untrusting.

"If someone were to get past our security, it would ensure we still have the advantage in the dark." I shuddered at the thought. If anything with bad intentions were to find a way in here, we would all be dead. This is where the safe was that housed magical objects collected over the centuries, including Abigail's charm that had brought me back from the dead. Only, the safe contained a fake charm now since I switched it out to return the original to Abigail where it belonged. Magical objects had a way of finding the people they were meant to be with, and that charm didn't end up with Abigail by mistake. I'd be dead if she didn't have it.

The exterior building buzzed with some sort of universal energy. The Order wouldn't admit that it was magic since that went against our code, but they had done a lot of things in recent years that crossed the line. We were barreling down a path that wasn't much better than those we fought against.

However, in case someone was to get past the magic and lead-lined walls, the armory had many fail-safes, so it was doubtful anything would survive this hallway, but nothing was out of the realm of possibility.

I scanned us through two more doors, bypassing the usual weapons of guns, arrows, and knives. I went straight for the Elite weapons assembled by weaponry and engineer specialists. The same ones that the Elites were brandishing the night they had come for Abigail. They were armed and ready to take down anything that got in their way, only the Hunters had managed to escape, something that was damn near impossible against an Elite. Wes had offered to save me that night and I feared he would have. That he would change me into what I hated the most, but Abigail was the one who had saved me. She understood me. She put what I would want before herself. And the thought that Wes had the ability to care enough about her to save his enemy had confused me. It caused me to second-guess my years of blinding hatred and perpetual unhappiness. Now, I had to capture Wes, virtually sentencing him to a life of torture. I wasn't sure how I felt about it.

I snatched up a device that looked similar to a Taser gun, only much more dangerous. Non-humans weren't affected by electrical impulses, so this had been fashioned to inject them with a serum, temporarily shutting down their seemingly human functions, giving us enough time to apprehend them. It had been what Penelope used on Abigail when she kidnapped her. It was thought to kill humans, so the fact that Penelope was brazen enough to use it on her was infuriating, but it also proved she knew all along that Abigail was a Chosen. *The* Chosen. And the only way she could possibly know that was if the council had told her.

"Dude, don't point that thing at me." Jack put his hands up defensively and moved out of range as I checked the Taser.

"Relax. It's not loaded." I opened a box that contained the miniscule needles filled with serum, gathered a handful, and secured them in a little pouch, tossing them into a large army backpack.

"Those are the backpacks the Elites carry. Are you an Elite?" Jack looked stunned.

I scoffed, but didn't answer. I was beyond an Elite. There wasn't a name for what I was. No other human was as strong or as smart as me. The Order tested my abilities in the trials to the point where I was damn near death. James finally stepped in when they wouldn't listen to my father. The pain still pulsed through my veins, a permanent scar on my childhood. I wanted to make them pay for what they had put me through, but in the end, I understood this battle was bigger than me. Bigger than an orphaned boy with no hopes or dreams. They had given me a purpose and, although my faith in it had faded, it made me what I was today. A weapon. And until Abigail, a well-guarded one. No emotions, no pain. But then I had seen those honey-dipped eyes, and my walls crumbled.

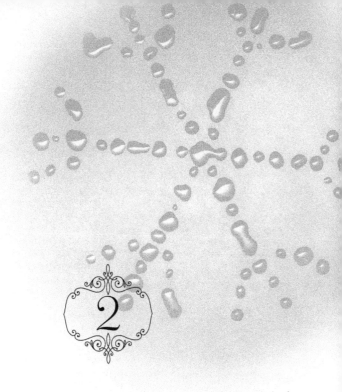

I PREFERRED THE SOLITUDE THAT my missions usually provided, and the light repetitious tapping coming from the passenger seat reminded me why. "Can't you just sit still? You're a Potential, right?"

"Wannabe, actually. I haven't been approved yet."

And he wouldn't be. Instead, they would try to sway him with his importance as a medic. He would mumble out a few words in his defense, but would quickly submit just like everyone else. "Lesson number one, stop wearing your nerves for everyone to see." I glared at his hands tapping on his knees, and they stopped immediately.

"I've never been on a mission like this. I mean, there was Abigail, but that was hardly a mission."

Just the mention of her name stirred up feelings I wanted

to ignore. That I needed to ignore so I could complete this mission. Whether I liked it or not, she loved Wes. I witnessed it firsthand while tracking her for her father. But, then, didn't she look at me the same way when she crouched over my dying body? I thought she had, and then the kiss in her room. It was desperate, yes, but there was more. There was something deeper.

"You won't like this one," I grumbled. The two-hour drive passed quickly. Jack remained nervously quiet, giving me time to work out different ways to take Wes without hurting him. He was strong and fast, and as far as anyone knew, he was the first hybrid this century. Mating with humans was forbidden. Wes was lucky The Order hadn't already seized him, especially after the car accident that exposed his supernatural side to Abigail. But The Order was bound by code. They had rules to follow and if they had apprehended Wes without solid proof, it would have started a war they weren't equipped to win. Not then, at least, but now they were because they had Abigail.

Jack sat up quickly, staring at the *Sandpoint, Idaho* population sign. "Why are we here?" he asked, alarmed.

"To collect Wes Hunter," I replied shortly.

"What? Are you crazy? Abigail will kill you." Tension coated his words. He was afraid.

"You wanted to come, so just do what I say and, hopefully, she'll never find out." Famous last words.

"Dammit, Elijah. You should have told me. You might not care what Abigail thinks, but I do."

I jerked the steering wheel hard, and the car went off the highway, our bodies bouncing with the car as it navigated the gravel shoulder. I slammed on the brakes and Jack was flung forward, the seatbelt locking and abruptly pulling him back.

"What the hell, Elijah! Are you crazy?" Jack unlocked the belt and scrambled out of the car.

It was like caring for a toddler. I unlatched my belt, growling under my breath, and stomped around the car to Jack. "Get back in the car."

Jack paced, crunching gravel under his steel-toed army boots. "You should have told me!" Jack jabbed his finger accusingly in my direction.

"You don't get to pick your missions as an Elite, Jack. You get orders and you complete them. I don't like this any better than you, but I have my orders."

Jack shifted his weight from one leg to the other as he carefully studied me. He was smart. He knew there was more. I could see his mind working through all the possibilities.

"This is about Abigail, isn't it? She's in danger if you don't do this?" Jack stopped pacing and his eyes dropped remorsefully.

"Yes," I confessed. Jack was an emotional creature. If he knew this would keep Abigail safe, he would shut up and get back in the car.

Jack kicked up gravel and cussed under his breath. "This sucks."

Dejected, I leaned on the hood, rubbing my face free of guilt. "Welcome to The Order."

"They won't kill him, though, right? Just imprison him like the rest?" Jack shifted uneasily.

"I don't know, but if they're still following their own rules then, yes, he would be indefinitely imprisoned."

Jack stepped into me with his hand held out. "For Abigail, then."

I shook his hand doubtfully and we got back on the road to Wes' house. I parked a block away in a cul-de-sac, and we walked the rest of the way to his house, hiding in a thicket of bushes out front. I pulled the backpack off my shoulders and tossed it onto the ground.

"They're in there," Jack whispered. Interior light crept between the shutters, and a shadow danced across the window.

I hesitated, regretting the deal I had made, but I knew I didn't have a choice. Either I brought Wes in or Abigail could be hurt. Possibly even killed. I didn't know how strong she really was. I could deduce all I wanted from rumors about The Chosens of the past, but I wouldn't stake her life on them. I unzipped the bag, pulled out the Taser, and popped two needles in.

"Two?" Jack looked over. "Are you sure it won't kill him?"

"We're about to find out."

"So, what's your plan to get him alone?"

"You."

"What? Is that why I'm here? Bait?"

"Yes," I said evenly. "Did you actually think I needed you for your strength and skills?" Neither of which he had in comparison to me.

Jack grumbled, "What do you want me to do?"

"Knock on the door, tell him you have news about Abigail, and walk him down here."

Skeptical, Jack stood up. "And you somehow think he's just going to trust me?"

"Why not? Abigail did. He knows your friends."

He took a few steps out of the brush, but then turned back. "Do you even care if he sniffs a rat and kills me?"

"He won't." It was why I hated Wes so much. He would never do anything that would risk Abigail's trust. Maybe I envied him for that, but it's what made him weak and the reason I knew I would bring him in successfully.

Jack trudged across the lawn to the front door, looked over his shoulder in my direction, and then knocked. I lifted my ear toward them and concentrated on blocking out all the other sounds around me. They were muffled, but I caught Wes agreeing to follow Jack. I tightened my grip on the Taser. Guilt for what I was about to do attacked me fiercely. Abigail would never forgive me.

When they were just on the other side of the brush, I stood and glared at Wes, pointing the Taser at his chest. "Jack, leave."

"Wh—?"

"Now!" I gritted through my teeth. Wes didn't look

surprised to see me, and he didn't try to run. He was poised and ready to fight.

Jack stomped in the direction of the car. Once I was confident he was out of earshot, I addressed Wes, "You need to come with me." A solid, even statement.

Wes looked at the Taser. "She's in danger, isn't she?"

"Yes, but only if I don't bring you in."

"That's all you had to say. Let's go."

I didn't bring the Taser for Wes as Jack had assumed. I lifted it, catching a glimpse of surprise register on Wes' face just before I shot past his shoulder. A loud thump filled the night.

"Stop!" Wes yelled, but it was too late. Ben was behind me with is his arm around my neck, trying to crush my windpipe. His sister, Zoe, launched at me from ahead, but I was faster with the Taser and she went down next to her father.

"Ben, let him go," Wes commanded, but Ben didn't budge. He crushed his arm tighter, choking the air from my throat. The Taser might have been empty now, but it still packed a powerful electrical punch that could stun a large animal. I shoved it into Ben's arm as waves of white flooded my vision. I knew it wouldn't hurt an immortal much, but it was enough to shock him into releasing his grip, giving me the advantage I needed. I struck him in the face and kicked him hard in the gut, making him fly into the trunk of a large oak. His body cracked against the tree, shooting off splinters. He recovered quickly, rushing me and taking me to the ground. His murderous black eyes accompanied a snarl and exposed sharp teeth. He bit into my neck, sending a searing pain throughout my body. I growled painfully as I pushed him off enough to get his teeth out of my skin. *Not vampires, my ass.* Ben's weight was suddenly pulled off me, and Wes stood between us.

"Enough, Ben, I'm going."

I stood up quickly, grabbing my neck, assessing my injuries based on the amount of blood left on my hand. Luckily, it wasn't much. I shook it off and readied myself for the next attack.

"The hell you are," Ben hissed. "Look what he did to our family." He waved over to Zoe and William unmoving on the ground.

"They'll be fine in a few hours," I grunted, still working through the burn Ben's bite left behind.

"Benjamin, this isn't a negotiation. He wouldn't be here if Abigail wasn't in danger."

Wes stepped closer to his brother, turning his back to me, giving me the upper hand. I bent down slowly and readied another needle while they were distracted.

"They'll kill you," Ben growled.

"And that's my choice to make. My life for Abigail's is not a bad exchange."

I recoiled at his loyalty for Abigail and questioned if I was I doing the right thing.

"He could be tricking you." Ben launched past Wes, but I was ready this time. I shot the Taser, the needle grazing his shoulder as he tried to dodge it. Ben hissed as he grabbed the cut left behind, stunned I had bested him. He stumbled as the poison entered his bloodstream. Like a spindle prick, it didn't take much.

"Brother," Wes said as Ben fell into his arms. "I'm sorry, but this is something I have to do."

Ben looked up at Wes, unable to respond.

I stood above him, taking no pleasure inflicting him with such pain. "I'm not tricking him. If I don't bring Wes in, they will keep me away from Abigail during her trials. I barely survived them. I need to be there with her."

Ben groaned as his eyes closed, unable to fight the poison any longer.

"Yes, you do," Wes agreed as he picked up his brother easily. "Help me?" He looked to where his sister and father were lying.

We carried them into the house and, after they were secured, Wes came quietly to the car. My intention was never to fight Wes. I knew he would come for Abigail's sake. It was his family's relentless loyalty that had worried me. I was hoping it wouldn't come to confrontation, but it had. Jack was leaning on the car, popping off the car, eyes wide as we walked up casually.

"Ride in the back," I ordered. He grumbled something to himself, but obeyed without a fight.

The drive was uncomfortable and silent until Jack began snoring in the back.

"Not a quiet guy, is he?" Wes joked as if he wasn't just

kidnapped and about to encounter the worst days of his immortal life.

"Never," I answered. "I owe you an explanation."

"No, you don't." Wes looked out his window. "She's only been gone a day, and I already feel dead inside."

My grip tightened on the wheel. I felt sick hearing an immortal, a vampire, speak that way about Abigail. She didn't belong with them. With *him. She belonged with me,* I thought.

"They will hurt you," I said.

"I know."

"They may even kill you," I pressed, wanting to gauge how far he would let this go.

His head dropped, and he turned to me. "I know."

Dammit. I wanted to hate him, but he was making it difficult. "Why do you love her?"

He turned away again. "Because she's my anchor to my humanity. She is the only thing that keeps me from turning into the monster you think I already am. It's always been her."

"Because you're a hybrid you think that you have some link to humanity?"

"No," he shook his head. "Because I have the capacity to love someone as I do Abigail."

The truth pierced me over and over again. I wanted to choke him. To take every needle in my center console and stab him with them. I wanted him dead, but not because he was a monster, but because he loved a girl I could never live without. *And she loved him.*

"I didn't ask for this life, you know. When my father told me what I would become, I didn't believe him. Not even after he showed me what he really was."

"What made you finally believe?" The more I knew about my enemy, the easier it would be to kill him.

"Abigail. The week before eighth grade she almost drowned in the creek behind my house. The current was too strong where she fell in. A storm had just rolled through, and she was getting pulled downstream. I was scared as I ran along the side, yelling for her to swim to the edge, but when her head went under I knew she couldn't. Everything my father told me about what I would become raced through my head, and I launched myself into the creek and carried her out. It was so easy. The water felt like nothing more than a tug on my pants, and Abigail felt as if I were carrying a small animal. It was then that I knew I would become something she couldn't possibly love. I ran away that weekend. My siblings found me and convinced me I could be different. That *they* were different. So I came back and did everything I could to hide what I was, but then the transformation started, and the accident," he paused, "and, well, you know the rest. I never did thank you for saving her from me. If you weren't there, I don't know what I would have done."

"Nothing," I replied. "You wouldn't have hurt her."

"How do you know?"

I saw him study me out of the corner of my eye. "Because you loved her even then."

A small smile crept on his face. "How long had you been tracking her before the accident?"

I shouldn't tell him anything. I didn't owe him anything, and I didn't want to give away too much, but if he was willing to give up his life to keep her safe then I owed him something. "A year."

"So, you knew about me then?"

"Yes. I knew about all of you."

He seemed satisfied with the conversation as it died for the last bit of the drive. I could tell he knew more about me than he was letting on.

The snoring ceased in the backseat as Jack wrestled to life. "How much longer?"

"It's time." I pulled to the side of the road. Wes looked at me confused, but Jack had already plunged a needle in his neck, and Wes fell limp. I caught his head and rested it against the seat. We couldn't let him see where we were going.

"Sorry I crashed," Jack said, ashamed.

"You have a lot to learn, kid." I pulled back on the road.

I rolled into the back of the facility, stopping short of the gate. I killed the lights and got out of the car.

"So, you're really going to do this?" Jack stood at the open passenger door, staring at Wes.

"I don't have a choice."

"This is a choice, Elijah. I just hope you can live with the consequences."

*Me too.*

I grabbed Jack's shoulder and concentrated hard, ignoring the angry words spilling from his mouth as my fingers dug into his skin. I filed through his most recent memories, of kidnapping Wes all the way to the mention of me going on a mission, and stole them. Jack became dazed and stared at me through glassy eyes.

"Go to your building and sleep," I instructed.

He moved to the security pad, scanned his fingerprint, and went through the entry gate of the facility, disappearing around the armory building.

Kidnapping Wes Hunter wasn't part of the big picture, but The Order had outsmarted me. They had fed on my weakness, my love for Abigail, and they won. Having Wes in their possession would give them leverage over her because they knew she would do anything to save him. All that mattered now was keeping Abigail safe. She was the answer to all of this. She was the key.

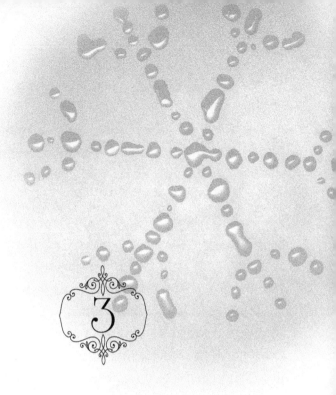

3

Wes' head popped up, his eyes black with rage. "Where are we?" he hissed.

"The Order of the Crest." I dropped my hand from where my chin was cradled for the last hour while Wes slept. "We need to talk before I turn you over.

"I get it. You don't trust them," Wes said smugly.

The hate I felt for all of *them* was hard to keep hidden, but the one thing that had kept me alive was not showing emotion. Not giving them anything. "If they have you, they have control over Abigail. That is all this is."

"It's about time you finally understand how much we mean to each other. Even The Order understands."

I open and closed my fist several time to try to keep

it together. "She deserves someone with a heartbeat," I seethed.

"What, like you? Does she know everything about you, Elijah? You might have an organ that beats against your ribcage, but you are closer to my kind than hers."

I envisioned stabbing him with the poisoned needle I was clutching in my fist, but that would only delay me getting back to Abigail.

"You can't hide how closely intertwined our families are, Elijah. No matter how much you despise us."

"You should really learn when to shut up," I growled, closing my eyes and trying to think of anything aside from smashing his face. Now that the sun was rising, the car was suffocating, and I could still smell traces of Abigail on his skin.

"What do you need from me?" Wes bowed his head in defeat.

"I need to know who turned Zander Cross." He couldn't deny it was one of his own, and he gave it away with his silence.

"My brother."

"Why?" I pressed.

"You would have to ask him. We were less than thrilled when he risked his life to save a human."

The way he glossed over saving a human's life like it couldn't possibly be worthy of saving is why I could never falter in my hatred for his kind. I pushed open the door. This conversation was over.

"Are you even going to tell me why this Zander kid is so important to you?"

"No," I replied curtly as I stepped out of the car.

"You either have a death wish or a hell of a lot of confidence that my family won't kill you."

"Like you said, we are closely intertwined." I shut him down. I had never been around an immortal for this long, and it was taking everything in me not to lose it. His voice wasn't making it any easier.

"Elijah, stop," Wes begged.

The muscles in my back tensed. "Dammit," I hissed under my breath and got back in the car.

"Let me go with you. I promise you'll have me back here before evening falls again. I want to hear what my brother has to say. And there's a smaller possibility of them killing you."

My hands gripped the steering wheel, my knuckles white under the strain. This would delay me getting back to Abigail, but this would go smoother with him there. "Fine," I spat.

When I pulled into Wes' driveway, Ben, Zoe, and William appeared on the sidewalk, poised to fight.

Wes jumped out of the car and spoke to them softly and quickly. They stared at me maliciously as I got out and walked in their direction, keeping a safe distance and holding several needles in my fist.

"So the dramatics of earlier last night were for nothing,

I see," Zoe said smugly as she crossed her arms over her chest.

"I wouldn't say that. I got to put you down."

Ben growled and Wes caught him just before he launched at me. "I assumed Wes would know why you turned Zander Cross. My intention for last night still remains. Wes is going to The Order."

Ben pushed against Wes while William held back Zoe now. Their low growls were vicious enough to send chills down my spine. I had seen firsthand what they could do and how they could make a person suffer when they wanted.

"The hell he is," Ben challenged loudly.

"Brother, stop. Abigail's life is in danger. I will go, but I promise I will be fine." Wes squeezed Ben's shoulders. "Elijah needs to know why you saved Zander. He says it's important to Abigail's life."

*Saved? What a joke,* I thought, but when Ben's eyes met mine, I was certain he knew why it was important. His body relaxed, and he broke his stare to whisper something to Wes. Wes dropped his hands and stepped aside.

"If I tell you, you need to promise my brother's safe return." Ben made a few calculated steps toward me.

"You know I can't guarantee that. It's The Order. But I will promise I will do everything in my power to try." Making deals with the Hunters was like diving voluntarily into a pit of fiery lava, feeling every bit of flesh melting off my bones.

Ben's head jumped from me to Wes, then to Zoe and

William who nodded in approval, and then back to me. "Fine," he hissed.

Suddenly he was in front of me with his hand out for me to shake. He was trying to intimidate me with his speed, but I didn't even flinch, and he shrugged defiantly. My fist was still clutching the needles, and I held them firmly to my side, not that I would shake his hand anyway.

He dropped his hand, smirking, and then headed to the house, followed by his family. I trailed behind, stuffing the needles carefully into my boot. I was not about to walk into the lion's den unarmed. Wes stood by the door and closed it after me.

"You sure you want to do this?" Wes asked.

"Are you?" I retorted.

The expansive view of the backyard was visible from the front door. I carefully took note of the kitchen off to the left and a hallway that led to some rooms, and to the right was a recreational room. We walked straight through a sitting room and onto the back patio where the Hunters all sat quietly at a picnic bench. I sat next to Wes, across from the others.

Ben started. "Zander Cross is special. Like you." Ben locked bitter eyes with me. "I don't know how much you actually know about your bloodline, but you aren't the only one of your kind."

My fingers wrapped around the bench seat, the wood splintering slightly under my grip. "I know enough," I bit out in a low rumble.

"I don't think so," William added. "If you knew everything, you would see that we aren't the enemy. The Order is."

"I didn't come here to be brainwashed. I know what The Order is. My only purpose is to secure Abigail's safety."

"Understood," William replied with a nod.

"Do you know what happened to Zander and Penelope's parents?" Ben continued.

"No."

"They died in a fire at the same house Abigail was held hostage, but their death wasn't an accident. They were on an assassination list produced by The Order. Their whole bloodline was to be eradicated. The kids were saved and placed in the foster care system, making it impossible for The Order to reach them without raising suspicion, but when Zander turned eighteen and adopted Penelope, they became easy targets. The Order went after Zander first. Zoe and I were passing through the town he lived in, and the smell of his blood hung in the town like a thick fog. We followed the scent and found him in an alley, bleeding out. From the stench that clung to his body, we knew he wasn't just any human. It's the same scent that surrounds you." He flicked his head in my direction. "I couldn't just let him die, so I saved him that night. I cured him." His accusatory eyes pierced mine. "But then you captured him." He looked pained.

Zoe placed her hand over Ben's, and William patted his back. It was ironic to watch monsters consoling one other.

*Murderers.* "It's funny how you think turning someone immortal is saving them. I'd rather die." I looked at Wes, acknowledging that night he almost *saved* me.

"If Abigail wasn't there that night, we would have turned you, Elijah. Whether it was your wish or not," William interjected.

They all stared at me, waiting for a reaction, for anything, but I said nothing. I understood they were alluding to some connection we supposedly shared, but I wouldn't give them the satisfaction of having me at their mercy.

William spoke, "The Order was afraid of Wes because he is a hybrid. The first hybrid in a century. Before The Order was founded there were many hybrids, but The Order had deemed them abominations and had them wiped out. It started the Great War between immortals and humans, killing thousands on each side. After many decades, The Order presented the immortal Lord with a peace treaty. There were two stipulations: no hybrids, and keep themselves hidden from the humans. Most immortals and other supernaturals felt humans were inferior, so they had no problem agreeing to the terms. But then at the turn of the twenty-first century, they discovered a man in a small village in northwestern Spain that came down with a rare disease and believed him to be the carrier of the next plague. The symptoms were strange to humans, alerting The Order. They apprehended him and found his DNA strand was altered. He was human but displayed the gift of telepathy. He killed himself before they could study him any further.

From what we've learned, The Order has been collecting humans with gifts and either using them for their own purposes or killing them. All we can figure is that Zander and his family were a threat to The Order."

"How? And, if he was like me before you turned him, then why didn't they kill me and my father?" I challenged his story, finding it hard to believe.

"They don't want peace," Zoe interjected. "They want to kill all of us."

"They're extremists," Ben added.

"And why would I want to stop them?" I scoffed.

Wes took over. "I'll give you two reasons why you should care. One, your blood reeks the same as Zander's and, two, so does Abigail's. We know she is the one prophesied to have the ability to kill us. That's why we moved to Sandpoint and why we had Wes befriend her."

I seethed at Wes' deception to Abigail, the tension in my fingers breaking the bench seat. I dropped splintered pieces onto the ground and glared at them, stopping on Wes. "I will kill you." I wanted to kill all of them, right here, leaving no traces of their existence.

William put up his hand. "That's how it began, but we all became fond of Abigail, and that's when we realized this could go a different way. We could have killed her at any point, but we didn't. Instead, we made it our mission to show her we aren't the monsters she would be made to believe. That we have as much of a right to life as anyone else."

"But you aren't alive," I said matter-of-factly. "You are the product of some dark magic gone awry hundreds of years ago."

"And from that dark magic an evolution began, which is why you are who you are. Without our existence you would not be here. At least not in the form that sits before us now. So, don't you see? We are all related in some way, no matter what the origin."

The presence of immortals had pushed human evolution so they would be equipped to protect themselves, and The Order believed if all the immortals were destroyed, over time, evolution would reverse and humans would become pure again. I believed in their mission, even if I wasn't purebred myself. I had seen what immortals and supernaturals were capable of and how they viewed humans low on the food chain. Their immortal powers made them far superior.

"It's time to go," I said to Wes. I stood up and readied to leave. I learned what I had needed to. Zander was a Special before he was turned. Or maybe he still was and that's why The Order hadn't killed him. I was just grateful I hadn't marked him that night, or else his story would have ended a lot sooner, because there was no chance in hell that I would live with the presence of an immortal in my head.

William stood. "Elijah, your parents were Specials, too."

My muscles tightened in my jaw and I glared over to William. "My father would have told me." When we went to The Order for help, he was as clueless as me about immortals and other beings."

William sat back down. "As far as we have been able to discern, you are the first to be bred of two Specials. That's why you are so powerful."

"So, *not* human." Wes emphasized.

Ben and Zoe were watching me carefully as William still sat calmly as if we were having an afternoon lunch.

"How do you know any of this?" My jaw twitched violently as I gnashed my teeth together.

"I met your father soon after he joined up with The Order. He was sent to apprehend me, as The Order calls it, but I had information about your mother, so we made a deal. Information for my family's freedom."

"My father would never make a deal with monsters."

"Why do you think your father tried to escape The Order with you when you were thirteen?" William pressed.

They were sidelining the conversation, but I needed to hear what they were saying. Even if it wasn't true, it was more than I had heard in years. Everyone stopped talking about it when The Order had claimed the immortals had killed my mother. The night before my father died he tried to convince me to leave. He had wanted out of The Order. He was desperate and angry. That was the first time I was ever afraid of him. I had refused, and the next day he was sent on a mission with Abigail's father, James. He never came back. He was killed in an ambush by immortals. "Go on," I gruffed.

"I told your father what I have shared with you. I assume they had a tracker on him because The Order had him killed the next day. I don't think he even had a chance to tell anyone what I told him."

I wanted to believe they were lying, but The Order's questionable behavior over the years made it plausible.

"I liked your father. We talked a lot that night. He told me about you and about his faith in The Order. I told him that you were on the list of Specials to be apprehended." He paused and his eyes reflected remorse for my loss. "Had I known he was in trouble I would have done everything in my power to help him, but I was too late."

William went inside and came back quickly, clutching something in his hand. I jumped up, instinctively ready to fight with my one hand ready to retrieve the needles from my boot and the other in front of me in a warning fist. The others stood up quickly, placing themselves beside William.

"Relax. I just wanted to give this to you. It was on your father's body when I found him." He reached out his hand and dropped a chain with a key into my own outstretched hand. The engraving on the key was that of The Order—an infinity symbol with one side shaded dark. I remembered seeing it around my father's neck the night he wanted to leave, but he was acting so crazy I didn't ask him about it. I had never seen it before then, but this was definitely the same one he was wearing.

I clutched it in my fist, my body tensing with an accusation of murder. I hissed, "This could be proof that you killed my father." It would only take me a fraction of a second to throw these darts into each of their necks. They were fast, but I was faster.

Everyone accept William tensed, prepared to defend themselves.

"Why would I insinuate my involvement? Your father was a good man. He believed that key was important. He would have wanted you to have it. I can't make you believe me. I'm asking for you to trust me. *Us*." He motioned to his family. "We have the same goal here, Elijah. To save Abigail and to stop The Order."

I studied them carefully. How their bodies shifted when they were on alert and how their eyes darkened when they were angry. I knew a lot about immortals, but I had never had the chance to study them in their own environment. "I still need Wes to come with me."

Wes stepped forward. "And I am still willing."

Ben growled and walked away, Zoe trailing after him. William smiled weakly, placing his hand on Wes' shoulder, and without another word, followed after Ben and Zoe into the forest.

"Let's go," I mumbled as I pulled the chain over my neck and tucked it under my shirt. "I have a stop to make first."

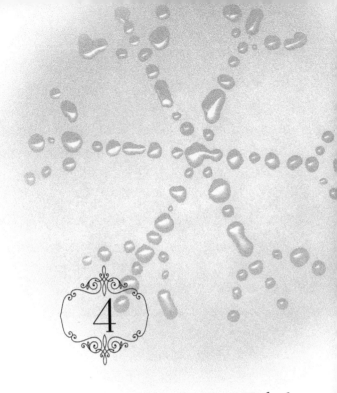

**W**ILLIAM'S WORDS CLAWED AT ME like a feral cat. He had liked my father. I had already been with The Order for almost five years. Five years of training. Five years being taught to hate immortals as if my mother's murder wasn't reason enough. Five years of worshipping my father for his missions. He would boast about his captures, and when one of his captives had died during apprehension, a thrill would fill his eyes, like an animalistic hunger had been temporarily satisfied. The same hunger had me begging relentlessly to go with him on missions, and after some time, The Order relented, but not to apprehend anyone. Not at first. I was to track. My father and James would bring me an imprisoned immortal of little importance, I would brand them, and then they would release him. After some time passed, the hunt would begin. My first few attempts took days to find my prey, but I got better. I learned to feel the energy they dropped like breadcrumbs, and then I would get that same hunger within my eyes as James and my father killed it. It was against our code and the treaty to keep peace, but The Order justified the kills by claiming my gift needed to be kept hidden, so those inflicted by my presence had to be taken care of.

And who cared about a stupid monster, anyway? *Penelope had*, I thought.

I was responsible for Zander's apprehension five years ago, after Ben turned him. I was fifteen and had become an expert tracker, among other things. Only this time, Zander was spared and dragged into The Order to be tortured. I didn't understand why James wouldn't let me mark him, but now I did. Because he knew Zander would be kept alive and that would torment me endlessly.

After my father died, The Order trained me in magic, telepathy, strength, agility, and anything else they could think of. Every gift they had discovered in humans, and every ability an immortal revealed they tested on me, and I always came out ahead. I was gifted with just about everything, but The Order reminded me that the difference was that I was human and I had a responsibility to *my* kind. To humans. To keep them safe. To keep them on top. The Order was using me because they needed me. Now that they had Abigail, I wondered how much longer until I was no longer an asset, until they added me to that assassination list. After the trials. After she proved her worth. That would be the day they would have me executed.

I lied when I told Abigail she was my first mission, because all I wanted was to forget what I had become, what The Order had done to me. It was the reason I went into hiding. And then James found me and begged me to watch her. I couldn't say no, but it brought me back into a war I no longer wanted to be a part of. For Abigail, I would fight. I had been inexplicably drawn to her, and when I carried her bloody body from Wes' car that day, it was like my whole world had shifted. For her. There was no logical reason, just this overwhelming dread if I lost her. If the world lost her.

"Abigail's? Really?" Wes huffed from the passenger seat.

We were parked in her driveway, the engine still running. "Yep. Scared?" I smirked devilishly.

"No, but this ought to be interesting." Wes reached for the door handle.

"You're staying here." I stepped out of the car and started for the front door, still reeling over what the Hunters had revealed to me. As my boot pounded on the front porch step, I felt it. The energy here was off. The smell was wrong. I went into autopilot, urgency pushing away the anger as I quietly lifted my boot off the porch, backed up slowly, and went around to the side of the house, looking for a window to peek into. A tracker had been here. They left traces of their energy behind. *Amateur.* And I knew exactly who she was.

As I turned the corner to the back of the house, a fist collided into my face, knocking me off balance, but I recovered instantly, grabbing the offending appendage and staring right into Penelope's eyes. Her face grimaced under my grip. "How did you get out?" I growled.

"How do you think?" She threw her head down and wrapped her teeth around my wrist, puncturing deeply.

I didn't flinch and she let go, spitting out my blood. "Acting more like a vampire every day, P."

The anger raged in her muscles, and she swung her leg at my feet, but I was solid.

"Drinking the Kool-Aid, I see," she accused.

I used my grip on her fist to swing around her, pinning her back to my chest, and I asked again, "What are you doing here?"

She thrashed around, barely moving under my grip. "You're a real jerk, you know?"

"Tell me why you are here, and I will let you go." I pulled her tighter to my chest.

"Why do you think, Eli? The Order sent me to kill Abigail's parents and, in return, they would let me and Zander go free."

I wanted to crush her, enjoying the sound of every broken rib, puncturing her heart as they splintered. "Where are they?" I asked slowly, barely containing the fury taunting me to kill her.

She choked, clawing desperately at my arms. "You're crushing me, Eli."

I could feel the panic radiate off her and the whistling of her lungs as they struggled to take in oxygen.

"Please, Eli. I wasn't going to hurt them. I was coming to warn them."

"Why should I believe you?" My grip only tightened.

"A—Abigail," she managed to cough out.

I released her and she crumbled to the ground, clutching her chest and gasping for breath.

"Abigail what?" I hissed.

After a few more shallow breaths, Penelope began to recover. "She could have had me killed, but she didn't. At the tribunal." She winced in pain, gathering her breath. "And neither did you, so when they gave me the ultimatum I accepted it, knowing if I didn't they would send someone else. At least this way I could warn them."

*Dammit!* I knew she wasn't lying, which only meant another tracker would be coming shortly. I held out my hand and she grabbed it as I pulled her up.

"Gee, thanks." She brushed off her pants. "So, now what? Do you know where they are?"

"No, but if I did, I wouldn't tell you," I snarled. I flinched when she touched my shoulder. "Don't do that."

"You never minded before. That is, until your obsession with Abigail."

I stepped away from her. "It's over, Penelope, and it has been for a very long time. A lot has changed."

"I can see that. Since when do you keep *their* company?" She tipped her head past me to Wes.

"I told you to wait in the car," I hissed at Wes.

"I heard the scuffle and was hoping to catch the fight," he responded smugly.

"The Order gave me my own ultimatum. Him for Abigail." I focused my attention back to Penelope and explained.

"What do you mean?" She acted like a jealous ex-girlfriend.

"I requested to be Abigail's partner." I didn't elaborate further. The less everyone knew the safer for Abigail, and besides, I didn't trust anyone.

"Jerk," she said, knocking into me as she went back around the house.

"Lover's quarrel?" Wes chimed in.

"Shut up." I could lay him out right now and be done with it, and I would if I didn't think Abigail would hate me for eternity. "Why don't you make yourself useful and try to find out what happened to Abigail's parents."

"What?" Wes plowed through the back door, and I went around the house to find Penelope.

She was pacing in the driveway already recovered from our scuffle. Watching her now, with her arms crossed, and the anger replaced with uncertainty, I felt guilty for being so insensitive. When I went back to the training facility after James asked me to watch Abigail, I had befriended Penelope because she was so lost. Her parents were gone, and she had just learned of her brother's death. She had no one and neither did I. We had found a way to comfort each other when there was no one else. Then over the next year, as I watched Abigail, something had drawn me to Abigail like nothing I had ever felt before. And after Abigail's accident, I was fully consumed by her. I didn't know how to deal with Penelope, so I didn't. I just disappeared like everyone else in her life.

"Hey, P, we need to talk." She stopped, her eyes meeting mine and her heartbreak piercing me with accusations of betrayal. It was a look I had become familiar with around the facility after I stopped associating with her. Eventually, her look was filled with anger, and we pretended the other didn't exist. It was easier that way.

"Why? You didn't care what I thought or how I felt for two years, Eli. What's the point now?" She shook her head.

I had lost almost all of myself after my dad died, and Penelope was the first one to help me feel something again. If it hadn't been for her, I wasn't sure if my heart would have been as open as it was for Abigail. I owed Penelope. I took a step toward her, and when she didn't step away, her eyes begging for a past long forgotten, I pulled her into my arms and held her while she sobbed.

"I loved you, E. You were all I had. How could you do that to me?" She choked the words out as if she held on to them for far too long.

I held tighter still, trying to calm her trembles.

"I'm sorry," I whispered, and I meant it.

I pulled her face up to mine, my thumbs wiping away her tears, her eyes flooding with a hope I couldn't give her.

"I can't go back. I can't turn off what I feel for her. Even if she doesn't feel the same for me. I care about her and, for whatever reason, that outshined what we had. I care for you, too, P, but it was easier to ignore you. It gave me a valid reason for what I did to you. You didn't deserve it, and for that, I am truly sorry." I kissed her forehead and hugged her close again, and she didn't resist.

Wes came out the front door. "There are no signs of struggle, so they must have known The Order was coming for them. Do you think they're in Seattle?"

I shook my head. "I doubt it, but I can track James. It'll just be harder because he's no doubt blocking so other trackers can't find them." We needed to get to them first.

Wes rolled his eyes over to Penelope and then back to me with a questioning tip of the head. I shrugged him off. No doubt he was enjoying this.

"The Order is looking more and more awesome every day," Wes said sarcastically.

I growled, "It didn't used to be like this. You know as much as me that they were needed. The ones with blood lust were killing children and stealing parents. They stole my mom."

Wes shook his head. "You still don't see it. Even after my father explained it to you. After he told you what you and your parents are. The immortals didn't kill your mother, Elijah. The Order had your mother taken because of what she was. What you are. You were on the assassination list just like Zander and the rest."

Penelope was watching us intensely. She still had no idea what she was or what happened to her brother. What *really* happened. And I needed to be the one to tell her.

"Not now," I bit out to Wes. It had occurred to me after William told me about my father and our bloodline that The Order could have been behind my mother's disappearance, whether it was to kill her or to lure my father and I to them, I wasn't sure. Either way, the possibility was festering under my skin like an open wound. I needed to find out what James knew. I would find out what happened to my parents and show the kind of pain my heritage could inflict. "We need to go," I urged. Wes and I went to the car, but Penelope stood back. "You should come with us."

She fidgeted as she contemplated. "Fine," she grumbled. "It's not like I have anywhere else."

"I think we should go to their place in Seattle. They may not be there, but I know James. He more than likely left clues to where he might have gone. It'll be faster than my tracking." I drove out of Sandpoint with Wes in the seat next to me and Penelope in the back. When her hard edges softened, she was undeniably beautiful. She was a good person, too. She was just trying to survive any way she could. "Have you seen Zander?" I asked Penelope carefully

"No. They had me in a different part of the prison, by myself. I begged, and that's when they presented me with the deal." She shook her head. "They're sick."

We drove in relative silence the rest of the way to Seattle. I parked a few blocks away from the house in case we were followed. Wes walked a few steps ahead, so I took the opportunity to talk to Penelope.

"Look, P, I know things went crappy for us, quick, but I need to tell you something and I hope you'll forgive me one day."

Her eyes were already filled with remorse. "I already know, Elijah. That's why when The Order asked me to kill you, it wasn't as difficult as it could have been."

"So they were behind it." I flexed my fists trying to keep the anger at bay. "I didn't know who he was or who you were. It was a mission, and it was my last. At least until Abigail, and that was only because I owed James."

"I'm glad you didn't die." She nudged me, her way of accepting my apology.

"It was lucky. Abigail didn't even know what she had. Magical objects are so rare." I was glad I had stolen it from The Order and gave it back to Abigail. The only way they would know I switched it with a fake is if they tried to use it, which is forbidden.

"I know about our bloodline, too. The Order told me when I graduated from the training."

I was surprised she knew so much. "What else did they tell you?"

"That it was their mission to eradicate all the immortals and other unnatural beings so human evolution would cease. So we could be free of the burden of our gifts. It's why I stayed with them for so long. I believed in their school of thought. I just didn't realize to what lengths they would go to get there. And when I found out about why they killed Zander, I knew my days were numbered."

"Who told you about Zander?"

"One of my prison mates. He was a chatty fellow." She sighed. "I thought I had found a family with The Order, and you, but I've made enemies on both sides. In the end, I fear I'll be killed no matter which side I choose."

I understood the loneliness she felt. When I left The Order, I roamed the world doing nothing of importance, steering clear of anyone. "What if we didn't have to choose a side? What if we could make our own?"

"Really? And be lone rangers?" She teased.

"Sure. Why the hell not? I believe they're called rebels." I winked.

"So, you would kill someone from The Order?" she inquired.

"If they gave me a reason, in a heartbeat."

"And what about your new friends?" Her eyes lifted to Wes walking ahead.

"They aren't my friends. They are a means to an end." Although my hatred for the Hunters had lessened, it hadn't blinded my personal mission. I would do anything to keep Abigail safe, and that included keeping the Hunters away from her.

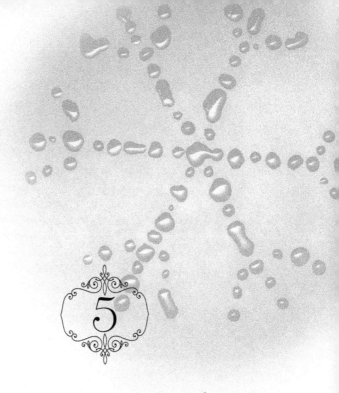

W E DIDN'T FIND ANYTHING at the Seattle house. It was
starting to feel like we were on a wild goose chase.
James would do whatever it took to keep his wife safe, so
I wasn't surprised. I wasn't sure how much he knew about
everything, but I had to assume he didn't know the whole
story because he never would have let Abigail go.

Penelope sat next to me on the back porch. It was after
dark now and we decided to stay the night. Wes was still
around. I didn't really worry about him taking off. Abigail
meant too much to him to risk leaving.

"This is all a big mess, isn't it?" Penelope played with
her hair.

"I like the pink."

"Thanks," she replied shyly.

"Yeah, it's a big mess, but it has been for a long time. That's why I left, but I can see that was a mistake. At least if I had stayed I might have prevented some of it."

"That's a huge burden to carry, Eli."

"It's hard not to believe it, though."

"Where did you go for all those years?"

"Everywhere. Anywhere." A few memories flashed in my head. Many I wanted to forget.

"Eli, if you hadn't met Abigail, do you think maybe you and me—"

"I don't know." If I was being completely honest with myself, before Abigail, I didn't think I'd ever care so much for a person. "Did they hurt you in the prison?"

She looked away, but not before I caught the hurt in her eyes. "You could say that," she choked out quietly.

I put my arm around her and pulled her close. "I'm still here for you, P. I'm sorry I ever left."

"Thanks."

Wes joined us. "So, what's the plan?"

The energy shifted and Penelope felt it, too. Wes must have heard something because he was gone in a flash into the forest beyond the backyard.

"It's James." He had let down his block so we would know he was here.

Wes and James walked out of the tree line together.

"Is Abigail okay?" James asked immediately as he approached. He looked worn-out with dark circles under his eyes and wrinkled clothes.

"She's fine. She's going through Building One right now, so I have time before I need to get back." I shook his outstretched hand.

"Care to explain the company you're keeping?" He looked to Penelope, then Wes, and back to me.

"The Order wants Wes in exchange for me staying close to Abigail, and they sent Penelope to detain you and Lucinda."

James didn't hide his anger. "I should have known they would turn on me once they had Abigail. They played me."

"Don't feel too bad. They played us all. Is Lucinda safe?" I asked.

"Yeah," he grumbled as he sat on the porch.

"What happened to you?" It was obvious that he had been in hiding and in a fight.

"Someone gave me up after I was excused from the council. You name it and they came after me. I've done more than my fair share of apprehending and collecting enemies over the years."

Wes chimed in. "Why would they give you up?"

"Simple. They want me dead. The less people alive that are connected to Abigail the more they can control her."

"She's stronger than that," I added.

"We better hope so, because they have officially declared war with anything that is not pure human."

"And Abigail?" Wes asked.

James nodded. "She's the only one who can kill an immortal." The brevity of the revelation brought us all to silence. "After the last Chosen was killed, a visionary foretold that this particular Chosen would be able to kill immortals with one touch."

"She's touched me plenty and I'm still here." James and I glared at him. "Not like that," Wes clarified. "I just mean we've hugged and held hands, and it's never made me feel sick or anything."

"I don't know how it works. The Order doesn't either. The trials are set up specifically to the recruit. Abigail's will be tailored to finding out how her gift works."

"Wait, so you're saying they are going to have her face immortals?" Wes' temper flared. "They'll kill her."

"That's why Elijah is making your trade, so he can be there to make sure she doesn't get hurt. Once she discovers how to use the power, she'll be more powerful than all of us combined. And that makes her invaluable until all the immortals are killed. Then they will dispose of her because she isn't a Puritan."

Penelope had stayed quiet, but spoke up now, "When I was in the prison, there was this special cell. One of the prisoners said it was for The Chosen. I didn't understand why they would imprison a Chosen, but now it makes sense. I don't think they intend to kill her. I think they are going to keep her alive as insurance."

"So then we just bust her out," Wes blurted.

James' shoulders dropped as he shrugged. "It won't be that easy. There are thousands of Order members around the world that believe in the Puritan philosophy. They will just keep coming for her. We need to find as many influential members as possible and convince them The Order has become too extreme and they are putting everyone's lives in danger. The Order was not founded to be at war. It was founded to bring peace and save as many lives as possible. This is not the same Order of the Crest my family helped build."

"Finding the members won't be easy." He was talking about tracking the leaders of large factions of The Order. Each state is divided into four sections and has one principle leader and four subsidiary leaders under them. This goes for countries, too. And the twelve council members ruled over everyone and stayed relatively local to the facility.

"The principles report to the council members twice a year, in January and July," James informed us. "They will all be at the facility at the same time. If we have enough people, we can split up and cross paths with them after the meeting."

"That's still two months away." Wes was agitated. "Are we comfortable leaving Abigail in their care for that long."

James stood up, scratching his head, noticeably distressed. "To be honest, the training facility will make her into a more than a weapon. She'll be a warrior. She will train night and day and learn how to utilize her gifts. If anything, they are preparing her for the war. They just don't realize it will be against them."

"But you heard what Penelope said about the room in

the prison, and Elijah has already mentioned how dangerous the trials are," Wes pleaded.

"We don't have much of a choice. Tracking all of them down could take just as long. They move locations once a month and live under pseudonyms. We would need more than Penelope and Elijah to track them down," James explained. "But what we can do in the meantime is prepare. All members have this symbol branded on them somewhere." He pulled up his sleeve to show the half-shaded infinity symbol on his shoulder. "When a member is in need, all they have to do is display their symbol and members will reveal themselves. The three of us can start there."

Penelope and I nodded in agreeance.

"What do you need me to do?" Wes inquired.

"You need to bring the proof that your kind is worth saving. And any other supernaturals you might come in contact with. If we are going to get Order members to turn on the life they committed to, we are going to need to be very convincing of your worth." James pulled his sleeve back down.

"I need to get back to the facility before Abigail moves on to Building Two, which could be tomorrow or a few weeks from now, but I don't want to take my chances. Let's meet back here in one week to evaluate where we are before Wes and I go."

"I hope you guys know what you're doing," Wes shook his head and disappeared into the dark.

"It's not safe here. Let's stay downtown," James instructed. "We can hit the local bars before bed. I'm going to get some things." He went inside.

"You might want to consider a wardrobe change, too," I said, messing with him.

"It's been a long time since I went barhopping," he joked back.

Penelope was pacing around the backyard when James left. I had never seen her wound up like this. She was always so over confident.

"What happened to you, Penelope?" I went over and stood in her pathway.

She chewed on her thumb and peered up through her lashes with a dark truth daring me to ask more. "Aside from starving me? They pulled my thoughts from my head, which you know is like having someone pound a mallet on your head while you have a migraine. That went on for a couple of days until they were satisfied that I hadn't turned on The Order. Then they depleted me of my abilities every day to insure I couldn't escape. I'm surprised they haven't found a way of taking them permanently yet. Then they showed me my parents being burned alive, over and over again. And you killing Zander. That one was on repeat for hours." I stepped into her, but she stepped away and put her hand up. "Don't, please. I feel weak enough as it is. Just let me heal."

James locked up the house, and we made our way downtown. It didn't matter what day of the week it was,

Seattle's nightlife was always busy. James pulled into a parking garage close to Ballard Ave, host to many hotspots. He pulled up his sleeve and Penelope walked with her bare wrist out, putting their tattoos on full display. Mine was not as easy to flash unless I took off my shirt, which I was almost certain wasn't proper etiquette.

"Have you done this before?" Penelope asked warily.

"Once," James admitted. "It was a long time ago."

I wondered if he was referring to when he helped me escape The Order.

Walking into the first bar was a bust. It was plenty busy, but no one approached us. Same with the next two.

"Maybe we need to come on the weekend?" Penelope asked doubtfully.

Just as we were heading back to the car, a large guy fell in step a block behind us. Then two more guys joined him. We kept our eyes ahead and kept walking casually. This was how it worked. No one talked until in a secure location. The parking garage was the perfect cover, free from cameras and minimal cell service. By the time we got to the basement floor, there were at least a dozen men and women following.

The lighting was dim and the air stale, suffocating. The three of us faced the group that had kept a sizeable distance. Muscles flexed and teeth gnashed under the tension. Penelope stood tall next to me, clenching her fists and ready to fight. I fought to control my temper. James stepped into the center.

"This is not a fight." His hand was poised for surrender.

A young woman met him in the middle. "You are wanted," she stated plainly, unafraid.

"Unduly so. The Order is covering their tracks."

I rolled my stiff neck, the veins on my forehead pulsing. "Don't take your eyes off the group," I whispered to Penelope. She nodded once.

"The Order only does what is needed to keep everyone safe," she challenged, heat in her eyes.

"If you know I'm wanted, then you know who I am. You know I was a council member until recently. Aren't you curious why they would dismiss a member of the council for the first time since The Order was founded?"

She stepped into James. "It means you broke one of the rules. *The* rule." Her eyebrow arched.

He couldn't deny that he's killed, because he had, and there was surely a detector in the crowd. If he lied, this talk would turn into a bloody battle, and I wasn't sure if Penelope was up to it yet. I was stronger than everyone in this garage, but combined they could prove to be a challenge. I still had the darts in my boot, but that would only take down a few, and there were more than a dozen.

"I won't lie." James scanned the mob. "I have killed, but only upon the council's request. That's why I am here." He turned to me and Penelope. "Why we are here." He turned back to the woman who emerged as a leader for the group. "The Order isn't running by the code anymore. They've become extremists. They call themselves Puritans. They are no longer interested in upholding the treaty between humans and others."

The woman crossed her arms, considering what James said. "Why do we care? We all hate immortals and the others. It's about time we got rid of them. They must have a way to finally defeat all of them."

The group rumbled approvingly.

"They do," James confirmed.

What the hell was he doing? I took a step toward him, but he put up his hand to call me off.

"My daughter. She's The Chosen."

Whispers erupted between the group and wary looks eyed us.

"That's quite a plot twist. Good for you and her. But why get rid of you then? Were you trying to go against them?"

James looked past her to the group and addressed them. "How many of you have a gift?"

They exchanged glances between each other, but no one said anything.

"If I'm accurate, there are at least a few of you, which means you are not a Puritan. Once the immortals and the other supernaturals are eradicated, they will dispose of every human that has a gift. They believe in human purity. They want to reverse the evolution process that began when the population of immortals and others rose."

I wasn't sure if James was reaching all of them, but he had surely grabbed the attention of the Specials. I knew exactly who they were. Three women and one man, plus, the woman who had stepped forward as the leader of the group, which could only mean she was a subsidiary. Not smart, outing herself so easily.

"Why should we believe you?" she questioned cautiously.

James stepped right into her face. The Specials of the group started forward, and Penelope and I did the same. We were in a tight circle now, ready for the moment that told us the talking was through.

James studied her before answering and then cocked his head curiously. "But you already knew, didn't you?"

Her body shifted just enough to give away her discomfort from being discovered. I gave Penelope a warning glance and readied myself to pull out the darts.

"But why?" James inquired. "You're not a Puritan. They may save you for last, but no matter what they promised you, they will kill you."

Her eyes squinted as she took in his truth.

"They promised the principles and subsidiaries immunity."

The Specials behind her exchanged nervous looks, the fight releasing from their stances.

"You're a fool if you believe them. My family has served on the council for three generations. My grandfather was a founding member, and yet they turned on me the second they realized they had the weapon they had been waiting for to rid the world of everyone whose DNA showed any magical traces."

She uncrossed her arms and her back relaxed into an unsure slouch. "You are proposing that they will kill thousands, and that they have the means to do it?"

"Yes. They will do whatever it takes to create a Puritan world."

"But why would they turn on their own?"

In a consoling tone from one betrayed to another, James answered, "That's what extremists do. They use anyone they can to get their message heard, and once they are in a position to tip the scale, they strike. They are striking, and we need your help to stop them. To save my daughter."

"We'll help," a man in the group with the other three Specials called out.

The subsidiary looked back at him for a moment and then back to James. "How do you plan on stopping them? This is just a fraction of the members around the world. A fraction of a fraction," she clarified.

"Because we will have my daughter, and without her they are nothing."

"If The Order falls, what will keep us safe from the immortals and others? The treaty stopped a war. What's to say we won't be repeating past mistakes?" Concern filled her voice.

"I don't know what will happen, but the visionary said that Abigail is the key to ending the war. The Order chose to interpret that as killing all the non-Puritans, but I believe it's to bring peace. After three hundred years, I believe she will stop the war."

James even had me convinced for a minute, but I wasn't completely invested in the visionary's tale. I just wanted to keep Abigail safe, and if that meant siding with the enemy, I would do it. Only for her.

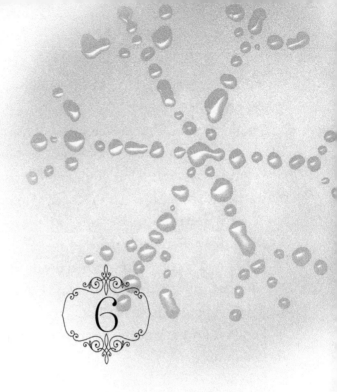

# 6

"THAT WENT WELL, RIGHT?" Penelope asked James as we drove away.

"As well as could be expected. They are at least listening, so hopefully they'll spread the word."

I could feel James look over to me. I hadn't said anything since he shook hands with the subsidiary because I couldn't stop thinking about Abigail. "I need to get back soon." Something wasn't feeling right and, as a tracker, I learned to listen to my instincts. Abigail and I had a unique bond. I could feel everything she felt, so when she was in pain it radiated through me like poison on the fast track to my heart.

"What do you feel?" James inquired earnestly.

I glanced over my shoulder to see if Penelope was

listening. She was staring out the window, so I thought maybe not. "She's scared."

"Wait, what?" Penelope blurted. "You can *feel* her? That's not a tracker thing unless you're touching her..." Her words trailed off. "But you're not just a tracker," she finished once she figured out the truth. "Holy crap, Eli. You can feel everyone you are tracking? All the time?"

A low hum vibrated in my chest.

"The bond is only severed upon death," James clarified.

She gasped. "That's why you killed. For Elijah." Recognition poured from her lips.

I shifted uncomfortably. I hated that James was taking the fall for me.

"He was only thirteen. It was too much for a kid to handle. We had no choice."

My father helped kill them before he was murdered, but it was mostly James. Another reason I ran away and why he helped me. We knew one day it would catch up to us. But every day I walked around with an invisible hand around my neck, choking me, reminding me of the blood on my soul.

"That's intense," Penelope whispered through a sorrowful breath.

"You can't go back without Wes," James reminded me. "And I was hoping you'd help me with something, if you think Abigail will be all right."

As long as she followed the rules and kept her head down, she would be safe. The Order wouldn't jeopardize her allegiance while they had it freely. The fact that they had a cell especially for her meant they intended to keep her alive either way. My fear was they would break her, brainwash her, but she had a mission right now. To find her little brother and that would keep her focused and obedient.

"I got a lead on my son, and I'd like you to come with me."

"Your son?" Penelope practically showered us in spit she was so shocked.

"Thought you knew everything about Abigail, didn't you?" I said dismissively. "Are you sure you want the backseat spitter to come with us?"

"I can hear you, you know," Penelope huffed.

"At this point, I think we are all we have," James spoke a harsh truth.

Both Penelope and I were orphans, and James was on the run. "Of course. I owe you my life. Who's the source?"

James didn't answer right away, which was never a good sign. Either I wouldn't like his source or I wouldn't like where it was taking us.

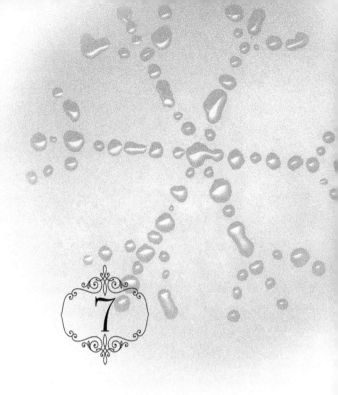

## 7

## ABIGAIL

I WOKE UP WITH A SICK FEELING in my stomach and my clothes soaked through from a restless dream. How could Polly have been on that bus when I was six years old? How could she still look the same? And how had I not recognized her? Did my father have that memory snatched, too? According to my watch, I still had thirty minutes before the alarm went off, which meant forty minutes before I was expected in lineup. It was plenty of time to confront Polly in the main building. My heart pounded in my ears as I jumped out of bed and dressed in my white uniform and white shoes. I scavenged through my red Chucks to make sure the charm that saved Elijah's life was still safely trapped inside the hidden fabric. It wouldn't be safe with my belongings for long, so I planned on burying it at the tree when I could steal away today.

I fixed my hair on top of my head, brushed my teeth, and then raced down the hallway. It was dead silent as I flew out of Building One. An orange glow covered the grounds as the sun rose above the mountain peaks.

For one year, this place would steal my freedom, and while I thought it may break me, I tried to focus on how it would make me stronger. I would learn how to fight and defend myself. And when I was ready, I would get revenge for my father's banishment, and I would find the brother they stole from us. We were brought to The Order of the Crest to learn how to keep humans safe from immortals, but who would keep us safe from The Order?

I raced up the hill to the main building where I met Polly for the first time. I was out of breath when I pushed through the doors, partially because of the adrenaline, but also because I was sadly out of shape. I expected Polly to greet me with her overzealous smile but, instead, there was a young woman seated behind the desk.

"May I help you?" the blonde woman asked politely.

I looked around the sterile lobby. "I am looking for Polly."

"She no longer works for The Order. Is there something I can help you with?" Polly's replacement didn't show any signs of distress over Polly's removal, so she either didn't know her or didn't care.

"She was just here yesterday, and she didn't mention leaving."

"Yes, well, she received some bad news last night and needed to leave. I'm sorry. I can get her a message, if you'd like?" She placed a pen and notepad on the counter in front of her.

"Sure. That would be great." I wrote my name on the paper, but I didn't have a phone number to give her.

"I just need your name." She smiled and took the paper back. "Was there anything else?"

"No, I guess not." I turned to leave, but then stopped and asked, "Actually, yes. What's your name?"

"Tawny."

When she didn't say anything else, I left. She was friendly in a not-so-friendly way. Short and to the point. I still had twenty minutes until lineup, so I ran the track. The air was brisk, and leaves crunched underfoot, signaling winter was closing in. There was no escaping once the surrounding mountains turned white.

As I passed the first recreational building, Jack whizzed by me without so much as a nod. I pushed my muscles to the max and yelled as I started to catch up. "Jack."

He slowed down and turned to me with a smug grin.

I stomped up to him and punched him in the face. "That's for my dad."

"Ow." He winced.

I didn't wait around for a reprimanding. I jogged back up the hill to Building One and got into line.

Ten minutes later, kids shuffled out of each building and lined up at full attention. When Jack approached where I was standing, I stifled a laugh as I took in his freshly swollen eye. He glared and then walked down the line.

"For some of you," Jack spoke loudly and locked eyes with me, "this is your first day. Take my advice and keep your hands clean, your mouths closed, and your eyes on completion. The training in each building will prepare you for the next. It will get harder, not only physically, but mentally, as well. Be prepared for blood, sweat, and a lot of tears. If you don't experience all of those at some point, you aren't doing it right and will most likely fail. Any questions?"

Some kids looked around, but no one spoke up. Except me. "I have one," I said smartly.

"I had a feeling you would, Miss Rose."

If he thought this was brazen, then he didn't know what was coming. This was just the start of a whole new Abigail Rose. "What happens if you fail?" Eyes jumped from me to Jack. I wasn't the only one wondering.

"Great question, Abigail. For those who know the answer, please tell Abigail what happens if you fail."

A boy around my age stepped forward.

"Yes, Matthew, please," Jack encouraged.

"Failure is not an option," Matthew announced as if this message had been drilled to him over and over.

"Exactly. Failure is not an option."

I was perplexed. "But you said it's possible to fail."

"No, I didn't. In fact, you can't fail, because your team won't let you fail."

"Team?" I asked.

"Yes, team. You will be placed in teams, and if you fail, they fail, and no one wants to be the one to take down their team, do they?"

I was never good at working in groups. Not in school or in sports. I was a loner. I was like Elijah, but I wasn't being given a choice here.

Jack stalked over and stood directly in front of me. "Any more questions?"

I shook my head. "No."

"Good." He led us around the corner of our building, unlocked a metal door, and held it open as the line filed down to the basement. I was last in line, and Jack grabbed my arm to stop me.

"I'm going to let this morning slide because of what you went through yesterday and because of our history, but if you disrespect me again there will be consequences," he seethed. "Are we clear?"

"Like an untouched lake," I replied curtly.

Entering the basement of a secret facility was not as I had imagined. We descended wooden floors into a large furnished room complete with a fireplace in the corner. The room was full of sofa chairs, couches, and bean bags. The seasoned recruits made themselves comfortable while the few of us stood uncomfortably.

"You can sit," Jack announced.

Looking around, there was a solo chair off to the side. I sat down and stared at all the silent faces. There were two places we were not allowed to speak unless instructed to do so: the dining hall and anytime during training. A door opened, and several women and men dressed in business attire and white coats filed out, calling recruits one at a time. When a woman with her hair in a tight bun finally called my name, I reluctantly rose from my chair, following her down a long hallway. The walls on both sides were lined with open doors that revealed small rooms set up with folding tables and chairs. A recruit sat at each table with a white coat. We entered a small room at the very end of the hallway.

"Please take a seat, Abigail," the lady in the white coat instructed.

There was a small table like the other rooms and a file with my name on it. We both sat, and she ignored me while looking through the file. Finally her eyes met mine.

"I'm Doctor Lizelle. I will be performing your psych evaluation. Once I feel it's complete I will dismiss you to the next building. The more open you are with me the faster and easier this will go."

An evaluation? What could they possibly hope to find out about me? That I hate high school and miss my parents?

"Do you have any questions?" she inquired.

I shook my head no.

"Great. Let's get started, then. Tell me about the first memory you have of Wes Hunter."

It felt as if she had punched me in the gut and all the air was trapped in a breath I couldn't release. "W—why do you need to know about Wes?"

She laughed nonchalantly. "Because he's a part of your life, and this evaluation is about you."

Suspicion snaked its slimy tentacles around my rib cage. "Why not ask me about my parents, then? They have been in my life longer than Wes Hunter."

Her eyebrow rose with a smug grin. "You're very intuitive, Abigail."

"That's what I'm told." I looked around the room nervously.

Lizelle closed my file. "Look, I'm not the enemy here. None of us are. We are trying to keep humans safe from immortals, and you are going to play a big role in that. In order for trust to be established, we need to know everything about you, including your soft feelings toward immortals. You can't care for them and then expect to be able to kill them if the circumstance requires it."

"Kill?" My head snapped back to her. "I thought immortals couldn't be killed?"

"No, that's not true. They can be, but it's very difficult. What I was implying is that you will need to have a clear head when faced with a dangerous threat. Can you honestly tell me you can do that if Wes or one of the other Hunters tried to harm you or another human?"

Wes, Ben, Zoe, and William's faces spun around the room. "They wouldn't do that."

She stood and walked around, her heels clicking on the wood floor. "Oh, really? What if it were to save you?"

"Then it would be justified," I said confidently.

"So, you're saying that another human's life is less important than yours?" she challenged.

"If that human was trying to kill me? Yes, absolutely. They would be a murderer."

"I didn't say that a human was trying to harm you."

She was confusing me and distorting words. "The Hunters would never hurt a human."

"We'll see." She smirked as she walked back to the table and sat. "That'll be all for today."

"What?"

"You are excused," she said more forcefully, not bothering to glance up from my file as I left somewhat perplexed.

I strolled back down the hallway, all of the doors closed now to the other rooms. Sobbing pushed through one door and shouting from another. It felt more like I was in an apocalyptic insane asylum than the beauty reflected above the surface. I rubbed my arms in an effort to comfort myself, but as I left the hallway and back to my chair in the corner, the empty room chilled me to the bone.

I sat alone for hours. I busied myself with walking around the room several times, trying out every seat in the room, and picking at the skin around my fingers after trying to leave the basement only to find the door was locked. The room crawled with such silence, it startled me when doors started opening and recruits began filing out of the hallway. I was met with blank stares, horrified looks, and bloodshot glares. The ones who tucked their head between their shoulders bothered me the most. The first day and they had already been broken. What type of place was this?

The basement door slammed open, and the sun spilled down the steps. Hopeful eyes popped up, but no one dared move.

"You're dismissed," Jack announced.

The energy to escape reached out to all of us. I ducked my head as I passed Jack, but his hand wrapped around my arm, stopping me abruptly. "Hope your day went well," he said snidely.

"What happened to you?" I yanked my arm free and raced up the stairs, not waiting for an answer.

The sun was blinding as I emerged from the basement. Jasmine waited a few steps away.

"Hey." Jasmine smiled brightly.

"Hey," I responded less enthusiastically.

"That bad?" she asked.

"That obvious?"

"It gets easier. The first day was hard for me, too. They went right for the jugular," she tried to reassure me. "And you don't go every day. Today was my day off."

"What was it like for you?" I implored Jasmine. Her smile faded and her eyes dropped. "Never mind. You don't have to answer that."

"Do you want to walk?" she asked.

"Sure." I followed her down to an empty spot on the grass where we sat.

"They asked me about my parents." She pulled up blades of grass and twisted them in her fingers.

"I take it that's not your favorite thing to talk about?" It broke my heart. My parents were so loving, and I couldn't imagine not having their support.

"My father killed my mother in a drunken rage when I was nine." Her eyes stayed fixed on the grass she intertwined in her fingers.

"I'm so sorry."

"It was a long time ago, but it still hurts to talk about. My mother was trying to protect me and he didn't like that. I barely escaped alive. A couple of neighbors pulled him off of me. I was in the hospital for a few weeks and then shuffled around foster homes. They weren't all bad, but they weren't my mom. They weren't my home." She sniffled back sobs and held out her wrists. Large raised scars adorned both. "The Order found me before I bled out. They saved me."

I restrained my horrified reaction. "Jasmine, I…"

"It's okay. Everything happens for a reason, right?" She didn't seem entirely convinced.

"You're very brave and very wise for your age."

"Thanks." She dropped the blades of grass and brushed her hands together. "So, what did they ask you about?"

Jasmine felt safe to me, so I shared freely. "My immortal boyfriend."

Her eyes lit up. "Really? You have an immortal boyfriend? That's so cool."

I was surprised by her reaction. I thought everyone in The Order hated them. "Aren't you supposed to be repulsed like everyone else?"

She leaned in and whispered, "I met an immortal once. I ran away from one of the foster homes and was living in this abandoned building for a while. He found me starving and brought me food every night. He was kind. He even scared off an attacker. I don't think all immortals are bad."

"Neither do I." I smiled as I thought of Wes' last touch on my skin.

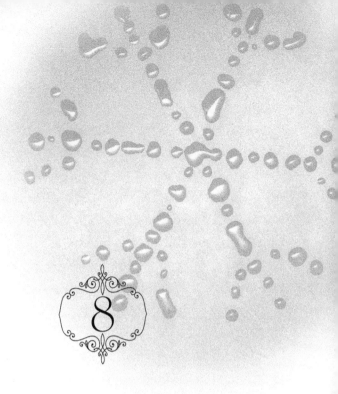

W E HUNG OUT ON THE GRASS until lunch. Jasmine told me about her mom, and I told her about my parents. The rest of the conversation with her was light, and she even laughed when I told her how Jack kissed me in front of his parents. She liked hearing about his more embarrassing moments, because he wasn't very friendly to any of the recruits. It had me wondering what changed him so drastically.

Entering the cafeteria was less daunting than the first time, but still oddly fascinating. The arrangement of colored uniforms and eerie silence reminded me of a zombie apocalypse. Kids shoveled food on their plates in an orderly line and took their seats, eating quickly and then leaving, completely unfazed. Jasmine said I would get used to it, but I highly doubted it.

The rest of the day was recreation time. While we were encouraged to socialize and partake in activities around the grounds, we were not required, so I rushed back to my room, grabbed the red shoe and extracted the charm, squeezing it in my palm securely as I ran out of Building One and over to the tree of solitude where no one could watch me. I froze momentarily, remembering the last time I was here was with my father. It was extremely hard to be in this place without him.

"Hi."

I turned and met Elijah's eyes. "Hi." I wasn't sure what to say after our intimate exchange yesterday. I hadn't meant to do it, and I was consumed with guilt for losing control. It wasn't fair to him.

"Can I join you?" he asked.

"Of course." I squeezed the charm tighter in my hand. I could have just told him I was burying it here, but something still told me I couldn't trust anyone. Not even Elijah.

I sat down next to Elijah who was leaning against the trunk of the tree. The circles under his eyes had grown deeper overnight, and he seemed more emotionally distant. Maybe he regretted the kiss, too. Relief should have shaken the guilt free from my chest, but I was surprised that a light dusting of sadness was present instead.

"It's a little late in the season for the little guy." A ladybug crawled off a blade of grass onto his finger.

"A rebel," I said approvingly.

"Yes, but it will die if it doesn't conform soon. The elements will kill it," he added and put it back down.

"Are we still talking about the ladybug?" I studied his face. The familiar enchantment that had befallen me from the moment we first touched buzzed in the background. Our bond. The bond he had bestowed upon me without my permission, but by my father's request. The feeling was fabricated, but it was still tough to resist at times. Like yesterday.

He sighed. "You came here for a reason, Abby. To find your brother. If you resist this place, you are only hurting yourself."

The truth ached in my bones. "I know," I said softly.

"I'm sorry you have to go through this." He paused dreadfully long. "It's not going to be easy."

I thought about the interrogation. "Yeah." I scoffed.

"I take it your first day didn't go well?"

"Nothing I can't handle. Others have it worse."

"Do you want to talk about it?"

He placed his hand on mine, and my whole body sizzled. "No." I pulled my hand from his touch. "Elijah, we should talk about what happened yesterday."

He shifted uncomfortably. "I'm sorry I let that happen. You're in a vulnerable place right now and I should have –"

"It was a mistake. I love Wes." I sucked in a shaky breath. "It will always be him," I said softly, turning my head because I was a coward. I was too afraid to see the havoc my words were wreaking on him.

Elijah wrapped his arm around my shoulders and pulled me in close. "I know," he whispered in my ear, taking me back to the bridge of our second encounter. The night he whispered in my ear that I needed to be afraid. I *was* afraid then. Of him. And I was still afraid, but for everyone else now.

"I have to get back," he said, pulling me back to the present.

The tingling poured off my body and was swept away as he stood to leave. "Hey, Eli?" He turned around. "Do you know what happened to Polly?"

"No," he said remorsefully and then disappeared down the hill.

I found a deserted spot on the hilltop by the main building that overlooked the facility and watched as the sun set behind a valley of rolling hills. I pulled my legs in tight to my chest, attempting to warm myself against the evening chill.

"You're going to freeze out here." Jack was standing above me, holding out a blanket. "Peace offering?"

I smiled cautiously. "What's the catch?"

"No catch," he responded. I raised a suspicious brow. "Okay, maybe one." He smirked.

"I knew it," I snapped.

"It's not what you think. I just wanted to say I'm sorry and ask for your forgiveness."

"Really?" I was still waiting for there to be more.

"Yes," he admitted. "Are you going to make me stand here all night, or can I sit with you?"

Without a word I looked back to the twilight sky. Jack wrapped the blanket around my shoulders and sat quietly.

"Why are you here, Jack?"

"Here as in sitting next to you, or here as in here?" he asked with a sweeping arm motion.

"At The Order. How did that even happen?"

He sighed loudly as if the weight of the world was crushing his lungs. "I thought I was special when The Order came to me. Like they saw something in me, but then when they sent me back to watch you, I realized they were just using me. I was angry. I *am* angry, and I took it out on you."

I felt sorry for him. He was dragged into this mess because he happened to move to my town and his sister became my best friend. "Is Kendra one of us?" I had been wanting to ask him since I got here, but I was afraid how he might answer. If she was a Special or a part of this in anyway, it would crush me. I trusted her like a sister, and I just couldn't bear knowing that my whole life had been one big lie. Her innocence was the thread holding me together.

Jack looked over alarmingly. "No, Abby, I swear. She knows nothing about this."

"I believe you." But even though I felt he was telling the truth, it didn't seem like a coincidence. Nothing seemed to be a coincidence. My father told me that The Order rarely told members much about their missions, including who were members. I wouldn't put it past them to have whole families in The Order completely unaware of each other's involvement.

I shook my head and looked back over the hills. "How did we get here? So far away from home. From reality."

"I don't know. Seems like yesterday we were hanging in Kendra's room listening to playlists."

"It was forever ago." I laughed.

He laughed, too. "I guess you're right."

"Did you have a choice? I mean, did they give you a choice about joining?"

"It wasn't really a choice. The person who came to me made it seem like I won the lottery. I was desperate to find something to do that would make some kind of a difference in the world."

"What do you mean? You were going to be a doctor. Saving lives, Jack. That's making a difference."

"I thought so, but I was dumb, Abby. I got sucked into partying and, before I knew it, I was already so behind in my classes. I was failing out, and then The Order approached me. I thought it was an easy way out. Man, was I wrong." He shook his head.

"Yeah, kind of. There's no easy here, no matter what angle you look at it from."

"I still can't believe supernaturals exist. It's mind blowing. There are days I wake up from night terrors. Sweating and my heart racing. I'm terrified, Abby."

Even after what an ass Jack was to me, my heart wavered.

He wasn't meant to be here. It was his association with me that spun his world out of control. "You would have been a good doctor. Remember that time I fell down the steps at that old abandoned house?"

He laughed. "How could I not. You were spooked by that blind cat."

"It was not blind. It was staring straight at me," I shrieked defensively.

"All right then, we remember it two different ways."

"You jumped right into action, securing my ankle and helping me hobble home. You even made that makeshift cane out of that stick."

"Oh, yeah. I totally forgot about that."

Reminiscing about things before reality shifted was nice. I felt normal for a fleeting moment. There was no going back for either one of us now. This was our present reality and, most likely, our foreseeable future.

"Thank you for having mercy on me."

"You get one free pass with me, Jack." I winked. I wondered how much he knew about the Specials. "Have you ever met any Specials? Besides Elijah."

"No. I don't have that kind of clearance yet. I've heard a lot of rumors, though. Ones that can erase a whole life of memories and replace them with fake ones, others that can tell the future, and I even heard that some can run so fast it's as if they are transporting from one place to another."

"And they're human?" I questioned.

"Of course. There's no way The Order would work with supernaturals."

"You've referred to them as that two times now. They are immortals," I corrected him.

"Not all of them are, Abby."

I was so confused. My father only mentioned immortals. "Well, then what are they?"

"Think about every mythical creature imaginable and it probably exists. I've never seen them, but the potentials talk about their existence."

"The potentials?"

"Recruits like me that go through the buildings and then request to be considered for the elite program. There's a whole library of books on these creatures that they have to memorize before they can be considered a potential. Then, if they pass that, they can move on to the next level. I'm not sure what it is, though, because potentials never come back to the facility once they move on."

"And that doesn't raise any red flags for you?" The Order was taking the secret society mentality to a whole new level of extreme.

"No, why?"

"Seems like this place runs on a whole lot of blind belief." Twilight turned into evening, and the temperature dropped dramatically. I shivered. "We should go."

"Yeah. Can I walk you to your building?" Jack yawned out the words.

"I'm good." I smiled and handed him the blanket.

"Thank you for coming to me. It'll make this whole thing seem a little less uncomfortable with you as my friend instead of my enemy."

"For me, too."

After a few awkward moments passed I said goodnight and started off to my building.

"Hey, Abby?"

I stopped and turned back to him.

"Don't lie to them. Just tell them what they want to know. It's a test. The psych evaluator can see your memories and read your thoughts. All she has to do is make eye contact."

"Thanks," I offered weakly. There really were no secrets in The Order. I would remember to keep my eyes on the desk from now on and hope all she could see was the knowledge she was seeking and nothing more.

When I got back to the building, it was like a ghost town. The curfew was ten o'clock, but it seemed everyone went to their rooms well before that. Being social wasn't really my thing, but living among programmed humans was going to be hard to get used to.

I slid onto my bed and stared out the window, thinking about all the mythical creatures I had read about. Obsessed about. I loved reading, and mythology and paranormal were my favorite. I had asked the Hunters about vampires and they laughed it off, but they didn't deny it either. They just corrected the stereotype derived from ancient legends. And what of the other mythical creatures of Greek mythology and fairytales? There were so many. How could they all possibly exist so secretly? Did The Order really have that much power to keep them under control? In the shadows hidden from the world? From humans?

I needed to find the library. Maybe it would tell me more about the magical charm that brought the dead back to life and maybe even my grandfather's key. It wasn't a coincidence that he gave me that jacket. He wanted me to find that key. It was an old brass key with silver showing through on the parts rubbed too many times. It looked like a toy key for a children's treasure chest, but I highly doubted my grandfather harbored old pirate's booty. The thought of him sitting in front of a chest filled with gold coins and necklaces made me smile, though. I missed him. I missed so many people, and on the top of that list was Wes. I didn't know if in a year from now if Wes would be in the redwood forest where we said our goodbyes, made our promises, but I wanted to believe he would be. I needed to believe, because seeing Wes again was the only thing that would make this nightmare bearable.

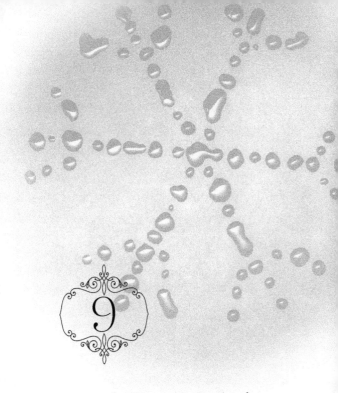

IBURIED THE UNDEAD CHARM at the Tree of Solitude after my talk with Elijah yesterday. It was a huge relief, because this place was creeping me out with every second that ticked by. I would probably need to hide my grandfather's key too but, for now, it was in my white uniform pocket. I planned on using my recreational time at the library today in hopes it would tell me more about it. As I sat across from Lizelle, I paid mind to Jack's warning about not looking her in the eyes. It was more difficult than I thought.

"Is there something wrong, Abigail?"

I could feel Lizelle's eyes bearing down on my head as I picked the skin around my fingers. "No," I lied. I peeked up as she wrote something in my file.

"How are you getting along with the other recruits?"

"Fine. Everybody is … great." I wasn't sure how much to share with her, so I shared very little and kept out names.

"I heard you and Jack were less than friendly yesterday. I know you were close back home."

I picked particularly hard around my nail when she mentioned home. It brought back too much. "We worked it out," I answered plainly.

"That's good to hear."

*Was it?* I rolled my eyes to myself.

"You and Jasmine seem to be getting along. She's a tough case."

I could feel Lizelle's suspicious eyes on me again, so I stood up and walked around the room. If she suspected Jack had told me about her gift, I didn't know what would happen to him. "How much longer will I be in this building?" I changed the subject.

"Eager to leave me?" she asked without disdain.

"This is just really boring. My dad mentioned training … with actual weapons."

I heard rustling of papers and saw that Lizelle was packing up.

"Yes, lots of weapons," she said almost too happily.

"Are we already done?" My body stiffened. This was only the second day. Something was wrong.

She stood up and faced me. I kept my eyes on her lips, avoiding her stare. "It seems that's all you needed. Good luck with your weapons, Miss Rose." She spun on her heels and left.

I couldn't believe what just happened, but I was more afraid of why it happened. Jasmine had been in this building for several weeks, and I heard some never make it past it. What had I done right?

Jack appeared in the doorway when I failed to leave the room for a long while.

"You planning on staying in here all day? You've been released." He smiled proudly like I had just won something big.

"I ... uh ... I'm not sure what just happened." I raised my hands, completely lost.

Jack laughed, which was somewhat reassuring, but seemed quite out of place at the moment.

"When they fail to see a reason to keep you here, they release you. They either know everything they need to know or they are convinced they will better learn what they need to from your training in the other buildings. It's really not a big deal."

He said it so nonchalantly. Like I was crazy for being anxious. But I was. And scared. Lizelle's demeanor was different today. As if something had changed overnight. Something bad.

When I still hadn't moved, Jack came over, throwing his arm of my shoulders and pulling me with him out of the room. "You're worrying about nothing. If something big was going on, I would know about it."

The Order was built on secrets. I doubted Jack would be privy to anything having to do with me, The Chosen, but I kept that to myself. I didn't want to be the one to burst his bubble. He was an ally in here, and I had very few of those at the moment.

"You're done? Really?" Jasmine squealed excitedly for me when I told her the news. "That's amazing. I can't wait to get out of this building. All we talk about is my parents."

"So, you think it's a good thing?" I chewed on my thumb while ridding the ground of grass where I was pacing.

"Absolutely. You worry too much. We are here because they want us to be here. They want us to succeed. And you are the freakin' Chosen. How could this be anything but awesome?"

I wanted to believe this was a good thing, but the war raging in my stomach was telling me otherwise, and at some point I knew I would find out why. "I am going to head to the library for a bit. Do you want to come?"

Jasmine jumped up. "Hell yeah."

I laughed at her child-like joy. If she could go what she went through and still find small pockets of bliss, then so could I. We headed across the grounds and down the hill. The library was not quite all the way down the hill, but it was tucked away from the other buildings. It made me wonder if they were purposely trying to discourage knowledge seekers.

As we entered, we were immediately met with the enriching smells of old text books. The building was oddly deceiving from the outside, looking small, but inside was not a disappointment. There was one story above us and three stories below us. Several spiral staircases led up and down and the walls were covered in books. Each floor had tables in the center to study. I think the most unnerving part for me was that the floors and ceilings were made of some sort of reinforced Plexiglas so you could literally see all the way down and all the way up. There was no privacy. No hiding. This was going to be more challenging than I had anticipated, because I knew full well that the knowledge I was seeking was in books that would not be easily accessible.

"Holy books!" Jasmine exclaimed. She stepped forward onto the infinity glass without hesitation.

"It's magnificent," I agreed, unmoving, with less trust in a floating floor keeping me afloat.

She giggled as she observed my trepidation and held out her hand. "Come on."

I steadied my eyes forward, taking care not to glance down as I took her hand. "Why couldn't they have normal floors," I muttered.

"Are you looking for anything in particular?"

I thought about my grandfather's key in my pocket. I wasn't even sure where to begin. I headed to the center table where there were a set of computers. Jasmine decided to wander haphazardly while I pulled up the *search* on one of the computers. I tapped my fingers lightly on the keyboard for a moment and then typed *keys* in the search and pressed enter. A plethora of books popped up. The amount was so overwhelming that I knew I needed to narrow down the search. I pulled the key out of my pocket and thought hard as I turned it in my hand. The mark of The Order was engraved in it so maybe if I searched Order keys? I typed it in the search and pressed enter again. The results were less harrowing, but still almost fifty books came back. What else? My grandfather was a devout council member and my father was also a council member, so maybe it was specific to that title. I typed in *Order council key.* One book came up. It was untitled and there was no cover image, but it did give a location.

"Did you find what you were looking for?"

I jumped, clearing the search, and clicked out of the screen quickly. I didn't expect Elijah to be in here, and I knew he would not agree with what I was doing.

"What's that?"

Elijah was staring at the key I had left by the keyboard so carelessly. I slipped it off the table and put it back into my pocket. "Nothing. It was just a trinket from home." I stood up, but Elijah blocked my way. He stood so close I could feel the judgment radiating from his skin. Or maybe that was the bond. It was so hard to distinguish, because whenever he was this close my body flushed and my heart raced. *Ached.* He must have felt it, too, because he took a big step back and, instantly, a cooling sensation washed over me. I shook off the moment and straightened.

Elijah's eyes scanned the room and then he spoke in a soft voice, "Let me help you, Abby. I want to help you find your brother."

The sincerity of his words was overpowering, but I

couldn't let him go down this road with me. There was a chance that if I were caught, they would let it go because of who I was, but not for Elijah. He couldn't get caught sneaking around. I couldn't lose him, again. It could be the bond that had me so infatuated with his safety, but it didn't matter, because it was there. And it nearly split me in two last time.

"No," I said simply as I scooted by him. I wouldn't lie to him and I wouldn't drag him into my family mess. He had been through enough and he has already done so much for us. "Eli, you are released." I watched him carefully as I spoke the words. I saw the light twitch of his lips and the flash of pain cross his eyes, but what hurt the most was the feeling that transferred from him to me, wrapping around us like a rubber band, holding me to him until I could barely stand, a thousand broken hearts screaming for mercy. "I'm sorry." I slipped by him without looking back. This was the first step and it felt like an earthquake destroying hundreds of lives.

The computer said that the book was in a section that didn't exist. I stood between section *E* and *G* in the historical corner wondering where the hell they hid *F*. It had to be here, or why else even list it at all.

"What are you staring at?" Jasmine bounded over.

"I found a book, but it says its right here in section *F* of historical, but it's clearly not. It skips *F* like a forgotten letter of the alphabet."

"That's because it's forbidden. Get it? *F* for forbidden."

Was I really this dumb? "Duh," I chastised my stupidity. "But if it's forbidden, why even list it at all?"

"The better question is, why are you looking for something that's forbidden?" Her voice rose in intrigue.

I sighed in defeat. "Well, I didn't know it would be forbidden." I wondered how much I should share with her and resolved that if I couldn't trust her, then I couldn't trust anyone, and then I truly was alone in all of this. Only one way to find out. I pulled out the key and showed it to her. "My grandfather left this for me after he died. I was hoping something in here would tell me what it was for."

She took it from my hand and looked at it closely. "It has the mark of The Order, so it's definitely meant to be here. You don't think it's one of the keys that opens the safe of magical artifacts, do you?"

"I don't know. Maybe? It would just seem odd for them to not take it back after he retired."

"That's true," Jasmine agreed. "Did you ask Elijah?"

My body heated with the mere mention of him. "No, and I kind of told him to go away." Guilt thickened my words.

"He's a guy. He'll be back." She laughed.

"Are you sure you're only thirteen?" I raised an amused eyebrow. Truth be told, Elijah and I could never be rid of each other even if we wanted. Our bond was for life.

"So, now what?" Jasmine asked.

"I don't know." And I really didn't. I didn't have a plan

and it was frustrating. We left the library empty handed. Well, at least I did. Jasmine checked out three books.

"You want to come to my room for a bit?"

Jasmine's answering smile could reach the stars. "Really? Yes!"

We stopped by her room to drop off the books and then headed to mine. When I opened the door, I was stunned to see a red uniform on my bed with an envelope.

"You're leaving already?" Jasmine's voice dropped lower than a bass drum.

I opened the envelope and read it. I was to move into Building Two before curfew. "I guess so."

"That's awesome, Abby. Congratulations." Her shoulders slouched in opposition.

I went to her and gave her a side hug. "You'll be over there with me soon. You'll see. And it's not like we are going to hang out less."

"Really?" She raised her big brown eyes to me.

"Of course. Friends for life." I put out my pinky finger, and she hooked hers with mine, and we shook on it.

I pulled out a deck of cards from my duffel and showed her how to play solitaire.

"Why did you come here?" Jasmine asked curiously.

"What do you mean?"

"Did you have a choice?"

I watched her for a moment. I never considered that, maybe, I wasn't the only one who was coerced into being here. "It was my choice. What about you? Did you want to come?"

She shrugged her shoulders. "I didn't really have anywhere else to go."

Her situation was disgusting, so this place must have seemed like heaven to her. "I didn't really have much of a choice either. There's someone I love very much out there, but there's also someone I lost that I love very much and would like to find."

"And you think being here will help?"

"I do." And as soon as I found my brother, we would run far away from The Order and never look back.

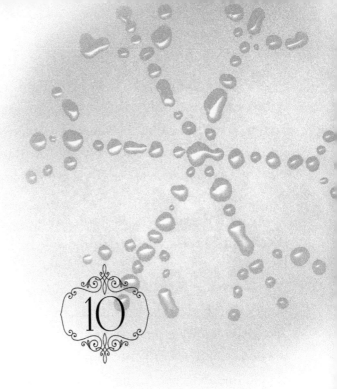

## 10

WEARING BLOOD-RED FIRST THING in the morning was not exactly what I had in mind when I agreed to come to The Order. It was disconcerting, to say the least, but as soon as I entered the first training session in Building Two, I understood why. Or, at least, I had my theories. It was to hide the blood.

We were ushered into the basement of the building, enclosed by concrete walls and floor. The cold trapped in the cement reached out and kissed my bones, sending shivers through my muscles. The crimson recruit next to me, glared with a sideway glance. And she wasn't the only one. As I looked down the line, every boy and girl glared in my direction, their bodies rigid at attention. Boots stomping on the ground drew my attention, and a nasty-looking woman in a leader's black uniform stopped right in front of me, with a scowl that could easily scare away a pack of starving werewolves. The thought prompted a smirk, which did not go unnoticed. A hand suddenly slammed across my face, leaving a sting in its wake and a sharp pain in my neck.

"Something funny, Miss Rose?"

Tears filled my eyes as my hand nursed my swelling cheek, but I kept my mouth shut, while others stifled their laughs.

The woman in black glared up and down the line at the others who had broken formation at my expense. "Drop and give me fifty push-ups, and if I see your stomachs hit the floor you'll be doing fifty more."

No one objected as they immediately dropped to the floor, including me. By the twelfth push-up, my arms were shaking, and by the thirtieth, they felt like they were going to give out. The threat of having to do fifty more, and my cheek still throbbing from the unexpected assault, kept me going. On my fiftieth push-up, I hugged the concrete, welcoming the chill on my bruised cheek.

"Get up," the woman seethed in my ear.

I held in the grunts of pain as I stood up and at attention with the others. If they didn't all hate me before, they sure did now.

"Now give me fifty suicides, wall to wall," she said loudly in my face.

I was already feeling nauseated from the push-ups, and the basement was at least half a football field long. I couldn't imagine doing one right now, let alone fifty, but the slap that bounced off the walls pushed me forward. I ran with the others, but I quickly fell behind, and to make matters worse, she made the others do push-ups until I finished. The hatred I felt in these four walls was like nothing I had ever experienced before.

I barely made it back in formation when I finally finished. I was dizzy and barely holding back the bile in my throat. Sweat soaked my clothes, and the chill shook my limbs violently.

"You are dismissed," the woman announced, but added, "except for you," as she stood toe to toe with me. It took everything in me to hold my head up. When the room was free of prying ears, she leaned in just a little and echoed my conversation with Lizelle yesterday, "Weapons come tomorrow." She straightened and released an eerie chuckle, then left. As soon as the basement door slammed, I ran to a trash can in the corner and threw up.

"I see you met Helga."

Jack took my chin in his hand and turned my head to examine my cheek.

"Is that really her name?"

He grinned. "No, but it's fitting, right?"

I smiled carefully, every movement of my face bringing on a new surge of pain.

"She didn't break anything, so consider yourself lucky."

Jack had found me huddled on the floor of the basement and brought me to the infirmary. It was similar to the one

Elijah had been in, but this one was above ground. The white of the sheets looked even more sterile against my red uniform. Jack took a soft ice pack out of the freezer, put it in my palm, and directed it to my cheek. Even the soft graze caused me to flinch. "Is she always that mean?"

"Yes, but you'll get used to it, and once she finds a new target, you'll be in the clear."

I shuddered, thinking how long that could be.

"Believe it or not, she has a method to her madness." He leaned back on the counter with his arms crossed. "And, now your cheek matches your clothes," he teased.

"Ha-ha." I threw the ice pack at his stomach which he caught dramatically. My arm ached almost as bad as my cheek from all the push-ups. "I don't think I'm going to be able to walk tomorrow." That would surely bring on more beatings from Helga.

"Good thing I got you a few days off to recover then." He winked.

I was relieved for a moment until the glares of the others popped in my head. Getting special treatment would only have them hating me more. And I could only imagine what fury Helga would inflict when I returned. "It's okay. I'll manage."

Jack shook his head with a disapproving air. "It's your funeral."

And was it ever. I could barely move when I got up the next morning. My body fought everything, and I bit back screams when the others would bump into me purposely during our laps around the basement. I was so sick from the constant pain I feared I would end up in the infirmary permanently. Helga left me alone for the most part. She chided me about being weak, but didn't punish me or the others like yesterday. No, she left the torture to the recruits, turning a blind eye to the boy with white hair that jabbed me in the gut, and the girl with the jet-black hair who pushed my cheek as she raced by, knocking me off course and running into another recruit who tripped me and laughed as my knee smashed hard into the concrete. If I had any doubt that they hated me before, it was definitely gone now.

I was shocked when a hand reached down to help me up. Bright blue eyes stared down at me. I hesitated, not sure if she was tricking me or not.

"A white flag," she said, raising her other hand in surrender.

I took it and stumbled to my feet, bearing most of my weight on the leg that didn't get crushed in the fall.

"Do you think you can finish the last lap?"

I followed her eyes over my shoulder to Helga who was huffing like she was about to blow. "I don't know," I admitted fearfully, and then the girl wrapped an arm around my waist and took my arm and put it over her shoulder. "Why are you helping me?"

"Because you took the target off *my* back."

I felt sorry for her even though I had become the new target. "Thank you."

She helped me around the rest of the basement and then to a set of benches where everyone had gathered.

"My name is Ray," she said after gulping down some water from her jug.

"I'm Abigail." I chugged some water, too.

"I know. We all know."

I looked over the other recruits as their eyes bore into me. "What is your problem?" I addressed all of them.

A tall boy who looked to be a few years older than me stepped forward. "You."

I tried to stand up to lessen our distance, but I immediately regretted it when a pain shot through my knee.

"That's why." He pointed to me. "You're weak and will get us all killed."

The other recruits nodded in support.

"I just got here," I shouted.

"Yeah, so? We were told you are The Chosen, that you are stronger than any other Chosen of the past, and that you will be the one to end the war, but look at you. You are pathetic."

Self-doubt flooded me, drowning my lungs and restricting my words. I didn't have a response because he was right. They all were. I was weak and would probably get them all killed.

Ray leaned over and whispered, "Don't let them see you cry."

I heeded her advice, but I didn't say another word. I waited until everyone was gone, including my new ally, before I hobbled out of the basement and back to my new room in Building Two. It wasn't in the corner, and I doubted my father had stayed in here, but it was next door to my one ally, Ray. I wasn't willing to admit it before, or maybe the magic was wearing off, but I was scared and lonely. I did my best to sit on the twin bed, pulling my knees to my chest and allowing myself something I couldn't earlier. I cried. And not silent tears of pity. Full-on sobs from a source deep inside that I wasn't even aware of, a place that existed in everyone, but was touched by very few. And it hurt like hell. I wouldn't let the others see me break, but I was split in half, one part with my family and the other part with Wes. I would never be whole again. Not while I was here. Not until I found my brother and we were all together again.

I thought about the bridge where I said goodbye to Wes. His promise to see me again right where we stood when I was done here, but the truth was becoming more evident and reality more flawed. It would take a miracle to make that moment happen. Or maybe it would just take me becoming what they all thought I already was—a warrior.

I stretched out my tired legs, feeling my busted knee crunch along the way, pushed myself off the bed, and pulled open the closet door. I had put my red Chucks on the same shelf as the other closet, but I wasn't going to hide them anymore. I wasn't going to hide who I was anymore. If they wanted a fighter, that's what I was going to give them, only on my terms.

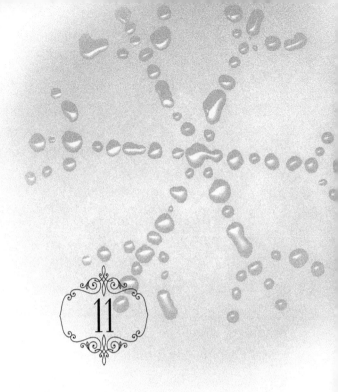

# 11

"CUE THE DEATH MARCH," JACK teased as I exited Building Two. He was leaning on the wall by the door and his eyes immediate fell to my feet. "What the hell are you thinking, Abby?"

I shrugged him off, held my head high, and started to line up until his hand grabbed my arm yanking me back and around the building. "Jack," I hissed. My body was still killing me and his hand felt like a vise around my overworked bicep.

"What are you trying to prove?" His fear for me settled between the lines of anger around his eyes.

"Everything, Jack. I have to prove to everyone that I'm not just a seventeen-year-old weak-ass girl." The self-doubt was changing into unadulterated anger.

"Now is not the time, Abigail. This is your first week. Don't let those jerks get to you."

"But they have, Jack, and they're right. I came here thinking this would be easy because I was The Chosen. It was a mistake. I have to show them that I can do this. That I am not weak."

"By wearing tattered red shoes?" He was exasperated.

"Yes," I replied stubbornly, nearly stomping my foot, "by wearing *my* shoes!"

"This is only going to make your time here harder."

"It might, but I'm already losing myself, Jack. I need to remember who I am." *And why I'm here,* I thought to myself. He had no idea I had come to find my little brother. No one here did, except Elijah.

I glanced at my watch. "We have to go." Jack was still unsure. "I'll be fine." I gave him a quick hug and then rounded the building. A row of red was standing at attention. I fell in at the end. The girl with jet-black hair that had bullied me yesterday shifted her eyes to my feet and then turned to the boy next to her and whispered. Within seconds, all eyes were gaping at my red shoes. Ray broke from the line and took her place next to me. The line shifted robotically to fill in the gap to escape punishment from Helga.

"I hope you know what you're doing," Ray said kindly.

I sighed, nervous now. "I don't," I admitted. There was a small part of me that hoped my shoes would go relatively unnoticed because they were red.

Helga marched down the hill and walked the line, inspecting each one of us. When she came to me, my heart was pounding, and I swallowed down my breakfast that had risen in my throat, threatening to expel on Helga's shoes. She stood stiffly, her eyes drifting from my eyes to my shirt. Sweat beaded in every crevice of my body as her eyes slid down my pants, landing on my shoes. My hands clenched into fists as I braced for another slap, hoping it would be my good cheek. I squeezed my eyes shut instinctively and waited. The only sound now was her hard breathing and the drum that had replaced my heart. It was so loud that when Ray whispered, I had completely missed the absence of Helga's breathing.

"You can breathe now." Ray's words reached my ears.

I opened one eye first, and when I confirmed that Helga was actually gone, I opened the other and released my fists with a big wave of relief. The girl next to me huffed defiantly, a promise that I wasn't going to get away with anything.

Helga split us into groups, tossing me and the boy with white hair a large, thick walking stick. He spun his stick effortlessly in the air while approaching me with a sly grin. The stick could have been any object as far as I was concerned, because I had never played swords as a child or spun a baton as a drill team member. I had never really done anything athletic, but I gripped that stick like it was the only thing that was going to keep me alive and I stepped forward with the confidence of a naïve child.

"Let's see what the almighty Chosen has been hiding," the boy taunted.

He spun, swinging the stick around and taking out my feet. I landed hard on my side, my arm taking the brunt of the fall.

"I guess those aren't lucky shoes." He laughed, and the others joined in, except for Ray who appeared terrified.

The fall hurt worse than the beatings the other day. My body hadn't recovered, and every touch felt like it broke a bone, but I pushed my body up, refusing to show any more weakness. As I was about to straighten, the stick came down hard on my back, and I fell to the ground again. The sting pulsed through every bruise, causing my eyes to water from the pain. The laughter was loud but muffled as I tried to catch my breath. I wanted to get up, but I also wanted to give up. I didn't have a chance in hell if everyone was against me.

I popped my eyes up as a loud crunch burst through the air. The boy with white hair was rolled into a ball on the ground, holding his stomach and gagging for air. Elijah stood above him, holding the boy's stick. Helga looked on from another group behind him.

"Fair fights don't exist when you fight non-humans, but we are civilized, and cheap shots against each other will not be tolerated. If you have something to say to Abigail, do it now or deal with me later."

The pain from the impact to my lungs subsided slightly, allowing me a chance to make it to my feet. I stood as straight as my splintered body would allow, and I waited. Eyes glared with hatred, but no one spoke, and I feared they never would. Elijah had hit the boy so hard he had to be carried away to the infirmary. I knew how strong he was, so I wouldn't doubt if he didn't come back to training while I was in Building Two. My training for the day was certainly over, but I refused to leave. I watched as the other groups trained with the sticks. Some were graceful, having been in this building for several weeks, while others would fall to the ground, having just entered, like me. That gave me hope.

Elijah stood close by, but not close enough for the physical bond to be felt and I was surprised at how disappointed I was by that. Even if he were right next to me I didn't think I could distinguish the vibrations of him from my tingling wounds. Jasmine knew he wouldn't stay away long, and I was grateful. It was evident that I needed him in here, whether it was good for either of us or not.

"The shoes again?" Elijah's eyebrow rose curiously. He wanted to help me up the basement stairs, but I refused and was now hobbling slowly up, far behind the others.

"Is that a problem?"

He chuckled. "No."

Instead of the infirmary, we retreated to the Tree of Solitude, away from prying eyes, and curious ears. I slid down the trunk of the tree, painfully, letting out a rush of air when I was safely sitting.

"You are going to get killed in here if you don't keep your head down," Elijah offered.

I stared at the small, disheveled patch of grass where I buried the charm. It was small enough for the absent patch of grass to go unnoticed when passing by, but sitting right next to it made it seem like a meteor hole. "Honestly, I think it's just the opposite. I think the isolation is what started all this."

Elijah rested his arms on his bent knees, looking out into the valley of hills. "Yeah, maybe."

"Why were you down there?"

"I convinced the council to let me watch over you."

"You, what?" I shouted, pain replaced with anger. Or maybe it was embarrassment. "I'm not a child that needs a babysitter." I would have gotten up if I didn't think I'd fall over.

"Oh, really?" he said calmly, his eyes rolling over my pathetically weak body. "Look, I know you're The Chosen, but that doesn't mean you woke up with the strength of a two-hundred-pound man and the speed of a cheetah. You need to train. Hard. And these little shits aren't going to give you a chance to get stronger if I'm not here. Jealousy is your worst enemy, and you have hundreds. When you are ready, I promise, I will give you space."

We sat quietly for a while. There were so many things I wanted to say and all starting with an apology, but they never made it past my lips. Eventually, my watch timer alerted us to dinner, so many words left unspoken, which seemed to be the theme of our friendship.

I decided to skip dinner, my body just too weak to make it up the hill, but Jasmine noticed and brought it to me.

"Is this against the rules?" I asked as I ate a biscuit.

"I don't care. You need to eat." She paused and commented on my shoes. "Nice shoes."

"Thanks." I wiggled them. "I couldn't get them off." I laughed and then stopped when the pain jabbed my kidney.

"Can I?" Her fingers wrapped around one of them.

"Thanks." I held my breath as she pulled them off carefully.

"Good thing it's the weekend."

We had the weekends off from training, but we were still expected to partake in recreational activities. "I think my activity will be not moving this weekend," I joked, trying not to laugh at myself whilst the pain returned.

"Yeah, probably a good idea." She pulled off the other shoe and walked to my drawer, taking out a fresh pair of pajamas and placing them on the bed. "I forgot to tell you that I graduated from Building One, so I'll be seeing you on Monday."

For a moment I was excited for her until I realized she could become the next target of torture from Helga.

"What's wrong?" Jasmine asked when I didn't say anything.

"Nothing. That's great. Helga's vicious, but I think the others will like you." *As long as you stay far away from me,* I thought. Nothing good would come from her associating with me, and I wasn't about to let anyone touch her. She was only thirteen. She shouldn't even be here. *Neither should my brother, wherever he was.*

"What made them finally release you?"

She giggled mischievously and then said, "I told my therapist to shove it."

I stared at her, shocked for a second, and then burst out laughing. It hurt so bad, but I was so damn proud of her. She was so sweet and quiet, and all they wanted was for her to stand up for herself. We laughed for several minutes until my ribs bruised so badly I was beginning to gag.

"I'm sorry. I didn't mean to make you hurt," she apologized profusely.

"Don't ever apologize to me or anyone else. Show those jerks how strong you are and they won't mess with you."

She stood up. "I should let you rest. Do you need anything else?"

"No, I'm good. Drop by tomorrow?"

"Okay." She smiled widely and then left.

I changed into my pajamas and slid under the white sheets, wishing away the pain and thinking about Wes and my red shoes.


*"Abby."*

*A whisper slithered through the darkness. I became keenly aware of three things. First, I was asleep. Second, I wasn't alone. And third, I might die.*

My feet fumbled with sheer terror as I ran into nothingness, falling to the ground, dried leaves manifesting under the grip of my fingernails. Popping my head up, a thick forest of trees appeared around me, and the sound of lapping water reached me from afar.

"Abby."

Fear surged through me, filling me with adrenaline to run toward the water. Somehow I felt I would be safe there. Safe from whatever was chasing me—hunting me.

Jumping over fallen trees struck down by lightning and cutting my bare feet on sharp rocks and scattered twigs, I ran as fast as my heart was racing. I pushed my burning muscles to the max. I wouldn't go down without a fight.

The rippling of gentle waves amplified as I neared water, seeing the light of the moon just ahead, my predator not far behind. Thrashing through the last of the trees, I fell down a tall ditch bank, rolling hard over storm debris and cutting my cheek, my arms, and every exposed part of my body. It felt like I was falling down Alice's endless rabbit hole, possibly falling to my death, but then my palms sank into dry sand.

I recognized this beach. It was Sandpoint City Beach. I hadn't been here since—

"Aaaaabbbbbbbyyyyy."

The hunger was more pronounced as my name stretched along a timeless moment.

Scrambling to my feet, I headed to the water, glancing back several times to see how far away my predator was. The water would save me. I was sure of it. My instincts screamed for it. Finally, the icy water covered my feet and then my knees until

*I was treading in the black lake. The surface glistened like ice crystals, my reflection revealing a gash on my forehead.*

*I spun around, breathing hard as my arms tried effortlessly to keep my head above water. I scanned the beach and stopped dead on a pair of eyes glowing at the top of the cliff, fixated on me. I couldn't look away, and in those few seconds I saw my hunter, and he was no longer my savior. He was my enemy, out for blood. My blood.*

I clutched my throat for air as I sat up in bed. The nightmare had returned, which could only mean one thing—Wes was near.

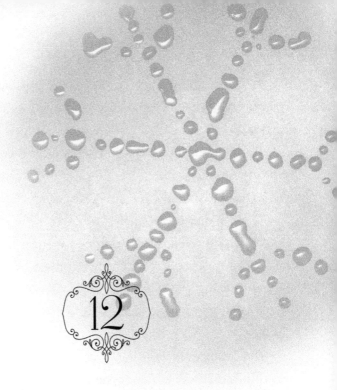

I COULDN'T LET GO OF THIS gnawing feeling that something was wrong with Wes. Having that nightmare again after all this time just didn't make sense. And it had changed. Instead of Wes saving me, he was trying to kill me.

I managed a shower, although it took twice as long with all my bruised body parts. Luckily, it was early Saturday morning and everyone was still asleep. We had two days to sleep in until eight, and here I was at five, taking a shower. That nightmare had scared the hell out of me, and there was no way I was getting back to sleep.

The grass was crispy underfoot, covered in a layer of frost, as I limped down to the building where Elijah was staying. It was fingerprint locked, but I was hoping if I was close enough, he would feel me out here. A minute later,

Elijah raced out, still in the process of putting his shirt on over his bare chest. I forced my gaze away as a blush heated my skin.

"What's wrong?" His eyes scanned the grounds before landing on me.

"That's just freaky." I shook my head.

"You're upset. I can feel it. What's going on?"

"Nothing. Well, something or I wouldn't be here." The sun wouldn't rise for another couple of hours and it was below freezing.

"Come inside," he said as he ushered me through the door.

The lobby was inviting, with a fireplace and couches, much like a resort lobby. None of the other buildings were anything like this. "Wow," I said, somewhat envious.

"Yeah, right?" Elijah walked over to the fireplace and lit it. The fire roared to life and immediately started to warm the small room. "Sit," he offered.

"Are you sure I'm allowed in here?" I welcomed the soft cushions. My muscles were not only sore, but also aching from the cold.

"Of course." He sat next to me, but keeping a safe distance. I laughed at it. "Why are you laughing?" He smiled.

"It's just this," I waved at the ample space, ensuring we didn't touch, "is kind of ridiculous, don't you think?"

He dropped his head, scrubbing his hand down his face. "I'm only trying to respect your wishes."

"I know. I didn't mean to make it so awkward. I just didn't want you to feel obligated to stick around. I'm safe here. No monsters can get me. This place is built like a fortress," I joked.

"Nothing's getting in … or out," he added.

His tone was haunting.

"Actually, I was hoping that you could get out." His eyes darted up to mine. "Before you say anything, it's not about what I said to you in the library. It's actually kind of lame now that I'm trying to explain it." I paused, trying to find the words without hurting him. "For a long time after the car accident I had this recurring nightmare. It was always the same and it was terrifying. Then it stopped for a really long time, until Wes came back to town. Then it stopped again." I chewed on my lip and looked down at my hands, wondering if I sounded like a crazy person and continued, "I had it again last night." It was slight, but I caught an unnerving expression cross Elijah's face when I peered up. "What is it?" I pleaded.

"What? Nothing. It's probably nothing, Abby." He stood up and poked the wood in the fire.

"I don't think it is, Elijah. There's something else." Every muscle in his back froze. "The nightmare changed. It's always been the same, but this time …" I let my words trail off, not ready to commit them to reality yet. *Wes was trying to kill me.*

Elijah shoved the poker back in its holder roughly, shaking the stand. "It was just a dream. Don't read so much into it." His words were bitter, but there was something mixed in with the disdain. *Guilt.*

I pushed myself off the couch and straightened as best as I could. "Is there something you're not telling me? Is Wes okay?" My heart was racing with the possibility that Wes could be in danger.

Elijah finally turned around and when he saw my concern he placed his hands on my shoulders and said, "I'm sure he's fine, but if it'll make you feel better I'll make sure."

"Really?" My pulse steadied and tears of relief filled my eyes.

"Yes." He squeezed my shoulders and then released them. "You should go back to your room. I'll come find you when I know something."

I couldn't help it. I jumped into him and hugged him hard. He didn't have to help me anymore. He could have said no, but he didn't. He hugged me back, taking care not to hurt me, and then walked me out. When I turned back one last time, the way his eyes reached out to me daggered my gut. Something was definitely wrong.

Instead of going to my room, I went back to the library. I wasn't sure if the doors would be unlocked this early, but they were, to my surprise. I stood in the historical section between sections *E* and *G*, still mystified that they would even bother skipping *F* at all. I mean, it didn't take a genius to notice it was missing, alerting anyone to something that might be hidden. It was careless, really.

"Noticed the missing letter, too, huh?"

I nearly jumped out of my skin. It wasn't even light out yet and the library was dead silent, so I assumed I was alone. I turned to face Ray. "What are you doing in here?"

"I could ask you the same thing," she replied smartly. "I haven't been able to sleep ever since I came here. The library is the only thing open all night, so I end up here a lot. What about you?"

"I couldn't sleep either. I was actually pretty surprised to find the library open. Seems like everything is locked tight after dark."

"They don't publicly announce it or anything, but they encourage the Potentials to study often, so they give them twenty-four access. Technically, it's still curfew for us." She winked. "So why are you staring at the missing section? It's not like it's going to just appear out of nowhere."

I sighed. "There's a book I wanted to read and it was listed in historical, section F."

"You know that forbidden section doesn't exist, right?"

She seemed to know a lot about things here. "How do you know that?" Her cheeks turned crimson to match her red uniform.

"I was dating a Potential and he told me things before he left."

"How long have you been here?"

"Six weeks. I met him the first day and we just kind of clicked. It's lonely here, so it's nice having someone." Her voice dropped.

"When did he leave?"

"A few days ago."

"I'm sorry."

"It's okay. I knew it was coming when I met him. He'd been here for a little over a year. Once he finished the training program, he applied to be a Potential. I had no doubt he would be accepted. I'm hoping once I get out of here I'll see him again."

I understood all too well how she was feeling. I missed Wes terribly, and I wasn't sure if I would see him again. "So, how does a section not exist, but exist at the same time?"

"Magic," she said evenly.

I was taken aback. "Magic is against Order laws," I said a bit confused.

"Rick, my boyfriend, said that The Order hasn't followed the ancient laws in a while. They justify it if it's used for the common good. For the war against non-humans."

"Seems a bit hypocritical."

"Yeah, but do you really expect us to win a war with just Specials? Our gifts are great and all, but I don't think I could kill a pack of them. We have to even the battlefield."

"I guess you're right." She was, but it still bothered me how much everyone hated non-humans. They weren't all bad, but I was only one voice in a sea of belligerent shouts. I would never be heard. Just used as a weapon.

"I wouldn't bother with the book. It doesn't exist. Only those with a special key can break the magic," she said as she walked away.

*A key.* Holy crap. I was looking for a book about the key

that could only be found with the key. And I had it. I raced down the aisles, saying thank you to Ray as I ran out of the library. I heard her reply "You're welcome?" faintly behind me. My legs burned like logs on fire, but I had to get back to the key and hide it. If anyone knew I had it, if anyone saw it … I shuddered at the thought.

I burst into my room, locked the door, and scooted under the bed, tearing back a piece of fabric from the box spring. I reached inside until I felt the hard metal and gripped it tightly in my hand. When a knock suddenly pounded on my door, I nearly dropped the key.

It was sunrise.

"Line up in five," a boy's voice deafened the hallway.

It was Saturday. Why were we lining up? An uneasy feeling rolled through my stomach. I slipped out from under the bed and tucked the key in my pocket. Knowing now how important this key was I needed to bury it with the charm as soon as possible.

I stalled a few minutes, so it looked like I was getting dressed, and then I rushed out into line next to Ray. Everyone was looking around as if they knew what was coming. I leaned over to Ray and whispered, "What's going on?"

"I don't know, but it's not good."

No other buildings were lined up. It was isolated to Building Two, whatever it was.

Helga marched angrily out of the building, glaring at each one of us.

"I was rudely awoken to hear that one of my recruits was out gallivanting before curfew was lifted." She stopped in between Ray and me and then continued pacing the line slowly. "I will give you one chance to come forward or else all of you will suffer the consequences."

My legs wobbled from the effort of staying upright for so long. My body had no time to rest, and now it looked like it was going to suffer more before it had a chance. Just as I was about to step forward, Ray grabbed my arm and pushed herself forward.

"It was me. Only me. I was by myself at the library."

I stared at the back of her head trying to fathom why in the world she would take the fall. We should share the punishment.

Helga stomped quickly to her, growling. "Do you think you are above The Order laws?"

"No, ma'am," Ray responded crisply.

"One week in isolation."

Shocked whispers carried down the line.

"Quiet," Helga ordered.

Bodies stiffened immediately. I didn't know what isolation meant, but it had to be better than a beating, right? Looking at the expressions on the other's faces had me worried.

"The rest of you may be dismissed."

Everyone retreated swiftly, while I hesitated after a few steps.

"Do you want to join her?" Helga challenged me.

I looked at Ray, and she shook her head quickly, her eyes pleading with me to leave.

"No, ma'am," I repeated Ray's words and then headed back to the building, but I didn't go all the way in. I watched as Helga pulled Ray down the hill and out of sight.

"I know it was you."

The girl with jet-black hair was standing close by with her arms crossed. I had learned her name was Ebony. At least that's what people called her. "She wasn't alone," I admitted.

"Pretty crappy friend to let her take the fall by herself."

I wanted to come up with some quick-witted response to put her in her place, but she hit the nail dead on. I should have stepped forward. Maybe the punishment would be less.

"You wouldn't have lasted half a day where she's going. Not all broken like you are. Lucky she has your back, because no one else does." She spun around and headed down the hallway, disappearing into her room.

I didn't want to think about what she said, about me not surviving "all broken." What the hell did they do to people here, and how was it legal? Maybe I was in over my head. Hell, I knew I was. Every day I learned something new about this place and it was never good. And, more importantly, my instincts had been screaming foul since my dad walked me into this place. I was trying to hold on to what he said, that this place was a sanctuary for him and he learned how to survive because of their teachings, but I also could see the fear in his eyes and the trepidation in the tone of his words. He was afraid for me when he left. He knew things had changed here, and that's why they kicked him out. He was confident I'd be safe because I was The Chosen, but what if it turned out I wasn't? What if everyone was wrong?

I needed to get the key, get to the library, and see what The Order was hiding. Maybe then I would find out where my brother was and get us the hell out of here. I just hoped Ray would come back in one piece, because I owed her, and I would make sure to repay my debt.

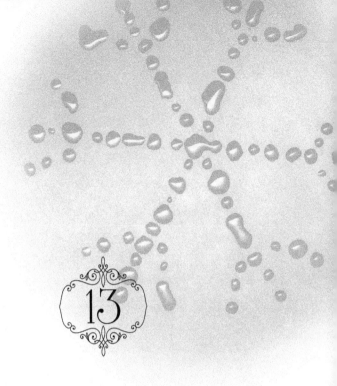

13

THE COLD SHOULDERS WERE more prevalent now, or maybe
I was just paranoid after what happened with Ray, but
it sucked nonetheless. Thankfully, Jasmine was still talking
to me.

"I heard what happened this morning. Is it true?"

Jasmine found me at the Tree of Solitude, sulking in self-
pity. So much for giving them a fighter. "Depends what you
heard."

"That they took Ray to isolation and that maybe you
should have gone, too?"

"Yep, you heard right, but we weren't really together.
I just saw her at the library briefly. I didn't think it would
be a big deal, and she said she goes there all the time in the

middle of the night. Seems odd that the first time she gets caught is when I venture out."

"Do you think someone is out to get you?" Jasmine pulled another blade of grass and tied it to the string she was making.

"Oh, I don't think, I *know*. It's like everybody hates me here, and I have no idea why. Other than being born into something I have no control over, I've laid low. This place is worse than my old high school. At least people there just left me alone. I've never had so much attention in my life." Not since I stopped being friends with the cool girls. I missed Kendra. She would know how to cheer me up.

"I know it seems like everyone is against you, but I can assure you it's just the opposite."

"What do you mean?"

"A lot of people don't know we're friends, so they talk freely around me. They don't *hate* you, Abby, they are in awe of you. Yeah, some come off as jealous but, really, they are excited to see what gifts you have."

"They have a funny way of showing it." I scoffed.

"I think they're just growing impatient."

I picked up a few blades of grass and started to knot them together like Jasmine. "Can I tell you something?" I couldn't believe I was going to tell her this.

"Anything. You can trust me."

"I don't have any gifts." I was surprised how blank her expression stayed. "Aside from great instincts, if you can even call that a gift."

"Nothing has manifested? Speed, agility, disappearing into thin air?"

"That's a thing?" Disappearing would come in handy a lot around here.

"Yeah. Don't you know about the history of The Chosens?"

I had been here a week and been to the library twice and it hadn't crossed my mind once to look into what exactly I was or what everyone thought I should be. "No," I replied quietly, and then Jasmine squealed excitedly while clapping and bouncing all at once. It was all very loud and jarring, and a bit embarrassing.

"Abigail, you're a freakin' warrior!"

And as if her display wasn't enough, she grabbed my shoulders and started shaking me.

"Oh, my God. I have to show you." She grabbed my hand, pulling me to my feet as she simultaneously started to drag me to the library.

"Slow down, Jas. Broken, remember?" My muscles were screaming expletives at her.

Jack was headed toward us, laughing. "What are you two up to? No more trouble, I hope?" He gave me *the* look. You know, the one parents give you.

"Apparently, a thirteen-year-old is going to teach me all about me," I almost sang.

"Have fun," he said as he headed back up the hill, but then called back. "Hey, do you know where Elijah is? I can't find him, and I really need to ask him about something."

My whole body smiled. He went to check on Wes for me, but I couldn't tell Jack that. "No, I'm sorry. I haven't seen him."

"If you do, can you tell him I'm looking for him?"

"Will do," I promised and then caught up with Jasmine who was waiting impatiently in front of the doors.

She went straight for the historical section. The key was still in my pocket because I had every intention of coming back here when the library was empty. Jasmine stopped at the C section and grabbed a very thick leather-bound book. *How obvious*, I thought.

Jasmine sat crisscross on the ground with the book open on her lap. "Only the last three Chosens are written about. All guys. The first one had the gift of speed and strength, along with the instinct thing. It helped him sense when energy was off." I sat next to her, peering at the words.

"That creepy feeling like spiders running up your arm," I added.

"Yeah," she said like I had defined a feeling she had never quite understood. "Exactly like that, only now I'm going to think spiders are attacking me every time I'm freaked out." Her body shivered.

"I'm sorry. My grandfather described it like that and it just kind of stuck."

Jasmine continued, "The second Chosen was the one who could disappear, or go invisible, or something. They never really knew exactly what it was. It says he was skittish of people and rarely talked. They thought it might have had something to do with his family being murdered by non-humans."

"You think?" I blurted uncomfortably. How horrible that would be. It was my worst fear.

"The last Chosen had all the things the others had, plus being able to move objects with his mind. How cool is that?"

I thought about the progression of gifts. "Each one gained the other's gifts," I said aloud.

"Yeah, which means you can do all of those things."

"But I can't. I mean, I haven't yet." To think I could make things move without touching them should be the coolest thing, but it terrified me. What if I moved something by accident and it hurt someone?

"That's why you're here. This place was designed to help Specials find their gifts and use them. It'll happen. Just wait."

I hated this place. The recruits were mean, the council was dangerous, and the weather sucked. "Can I see the book?" She handed it over and popped up.

"There are so many great books on the history of The Order, too. Your great-grandfather and grandfather are mentioned quite a bit."

"Oh, really?"

"Totally. All I did the first week was read. I'm not very social, if you haven't noticed." She brushed her fingers along the spines until she found the book she was looking for. "I think they were in this one a lot." She handed it down to me.

"Thanks." At least this one wasn't leather-bound. It was a dark navy hardback with The Order crest engraved in the center.

"I'm going to look at the training section. I don't want to go in blindly on Monday."

That's right. Monday she was entering Building Two. "Look up stick fighting. At least I think that's what we're doing."

"I love martial arts," she exclaimed and then bounced off.

"I wish I had just an ounce of that enthusiasm," I murmured to myself. I put the books on the ground and crawled to the end of the aisle to make sure she was gone and nobody else was around, and then I crawled quickly back to the missing section. Where the hell would a key go? I searched the wood shelves, but found nothing and I was beginning to feel really stupid. I had to be crazy to be buying in to all this magic crap, but if immortals existed, which I saw firsthand, then anything was possible.

I spun around, unsure what to look for next. I could take all the books off the shelves, but that would be tedious, and it being a recreational day, this place was busy. Anyone could walk over here at any time and see me. Then, what would I tell them? Just doing a little dusting? If the spider tickling feeling inside wasn't blaring loudly, I would have left, but I knew I was on the right track. I just didn't know which way to go.

I pulled the key from my pocket. "I wish you could

talk," I said to the key and, suddenly, a light glowed brightly behind a group of books between sections *E* and *G*. "No way," I exclaimed.

"What?"

I spun around quickly, hiding the key behind my back. Jasmine was trying to peek over my shoulder. "Just all these books. It's incredible." My voice broke. I wish I had my dad's gift for lying.

"I know, right?" She waved a stick fighting book in the air. "Found it. Want to study together. Kick a little ass on Monday."

I laughed. "Probably smart." I slid the key back in my pocket as I bent down to pick up the two books I dropped earlier.

We sat at the tables. Jasmine read her book while I flipped through one about the founding council members. My great-grandfather, Liam, and three other men founded The Order of the Crest based on the philosophy that all creatures, whether dead or alive, had a right to live so long as they lived an honest life, following all the rules of the land they walked. I had no idea my great-grandfather helped establish The Order. Why would my father keep that from me?

"Learn anything new?" Jasmine peeked over.

"Yeah," I said quietly, not sure what to do with this information. I couldn't call my dad and Elijah was gone, so I turned to Jasmine. "Did you know I was a member of the founding family?"

"Of course. You're royalty, Abigail."

I feigned a smile, but my body tensed. I was not only a member of The Order, but I was also responsible for the murder of so many like Wes. In a screwed up way, I was responsible for his mother's death.

"It's doesn't have to be a bad thing, Abby." Jasmine noticed the sour look on my face.

"How's that?" I could barely speak.

"Because you can change things. You can make a difference."

I looked down at the book, reading the other names. "I'm sure I'm not the only offspring of the founding men: Brecken, Anderson, and Daniels."

"I wish we knew who the council was," she huffed in frustration.

Everyone was kept secret. I was surprised they even committed the founders to print. If anyone outside of The Order got their hands on these names, their whole lineage would be at risk. I thought about Penelope and how she went rogue. What if there were others?

"Don't you find it strange that they listed their names in here?"

She shrugged. "I don't know. I guess everyone wants to be remembered for doing something big. You can't be remembered if no one knows."

"You are wise beyond your thirteen years, Jasmine." I was enamored by how mature she was.

"Why, thank you." She bowed her head and giggled innocently.

And, for just a second, I looked at Jasmine differently. It was just a flash, but I felt it, something strange. But I shook it off because this was Jasmine, the shy little thing who'd been to hell and back and the only one to give me a chance without question. She deserved more, and I was willing to accept that I was surrounded by magic and my instincts could just be misfiring. *Hopefully.*

I read more about the founders. All but one had married, and only one had kids, so the possibility of there being a present generation of Breckens was high. The book didn't list any names beyond the founders, so finding a founding family member wouldn't be easy, but also not impossible. You could find out just about anything in the blink of an eye with an internet search these days.

After over an hour, maybe longer, I slammed the book shut. I had been listening to Jasmine's tips on stick fighting in between and felt a little better about Monday.

"Want to go practice?" she asked slyly.

"Seriously?"

"Yeah. They want us practicing, right? Be the best we can be?"

I smiled at her. "Sure, but where are we going to get sticks? It's not like they just leave weapons lying around."

She shut the book, tucked it under her arm, and jumped up. "I know where some are."

She wore proud like a gold medal, but it also concerned

me that she knew where an arsenal of weapons were, but I scooped up my books and followed her out of the library. She headed down the hill, to which I blindly followed, and then around a building that buzzed with a prickly energy. "What's that?" I asked Jasmine who was a few steps ahead.

"Magic." She smiled.

"You can feel it, too?" I stared at the building like it might crack from its foundation and fall on me like the witch in *The Wizard of Oz*.

"You'd have to be completely out of touch with your senses to not feel that." She tossed her book under a tree and went to an iron gate.

I didn't realize there was a back door to the facility. "Are we allowed to be down here?"

"Sure, why not? The running track passes right by here." She pointed over to the path only a dozen or so yards away. She wrapped her hands around the bars of the gate and started to chant something quietly.

"Jasmine, what are you doing?" But before she could answer, the lock disengaged and she rolled the gate open just enough for us to pass through.

"Come on." She waved.

My pulse picked up speed and my chest ached for me to go back to my room, but I didn't listen. I tossed my books next to hers, took a quick look over my shoulder to make sure we weren't seen, and slipped through the narrow opening. Jasmine closed the gate and the lock activated.

"What are you doing? What if you can't get us back in?"

My hands were shaking. Only hours ago I reassured Elijah how safe I was inside the facility, and now I was locked outside with no weapons and no gifts, just Jasmine.

"Calm down." She laughed mockingly. "The security is nothing for me."

That didn't make me feel safer. "Do they know you can just come and go as you please?"

"No," she said nonchalantly, "and I'd like to keep it that way. Who knows what they'll do to me."

That little voice was pounding on my chest, begging for me to listen, but I couldn't. If I relied on my fear all the time, I would never get stronger.

"What do you think was in that building? It's gotta be pretty important if they have it protected by that much magic."

"Weapons and non-humans." She stopped abruptly and looked up into a tree.

"What?" I half-shouted.

"Shhh … do you want to get us caught?" She started climbing up the tree trunk.

"Jasmine, what the hell is going on? How do you know what's in there?"

She didn't answer, and she quickly disappeared into the leaves.

"Watch out," she called down.

"What, why?" But it was too late. A large stick dropped from the tree and I had to jump out of the way for it to not hit me on the head. And then another one followed, dropping at my feet. Jasmine climbed back down and smiled widely with her hands on her hips. "Should I even ask?"

Her hands dropped, as did her smile. "I know about that building because I was a prisoner once."

I knew there was something off about this whole situation. I took a step backward, contemplating if I could outrun her, but even if I could, how would I get back into the facility?

"Not like that." She chuckled. "Remember how I told you there was an immortal who helped me when I was living in an abandoned building?"

"Yeah." I listened carefully while my mind was still racing with escape plans.

"At first, they assumed he had turned me, so they detained both of us. After some less than fun tests, they determined I was untouched and enrolled me here." She looked at the building with sadness in her eyes. "He's still in there."

And my heart instantly broke. Not only for the pain radiating off of her, but also for almost not believing in her. "I'm sorry."

"I try not to think about it, but I swear, at night when I'm sleeping, that I feel him, like he's reaching out to me to help him."

The uncanny coincidence rippled through me. *Wes.* "Were you two close?" I asked carefully. She referred to him as a man and she was only thirteen, but she lived as a homeless kid, so I wasn't sure what she had to do to survive. It made me nauseous.

"Not like that." She wrinkled her nose. "Gross. He was like an older brother."

I felt the relief pulse through me. "I'm so sorry."

"But he's why I know not all non-humans are bad. Some are just the opposite. It makes me sick that The Order doesn't see that. They used to. This whole place was a sanctuary for good non-humans, and now look what it's become—a place to murder them." She choked back tears with her disgusted words.

"I wish there were something we could do. Show them that they aren't all out to kill."

"*You* can," she said confidently as she threw me a stick. "Because, not only are you The Chosen, you are a Rose. *The* Rose. The one *we* have all been waiting for."

Chills raced down my spine as glowing eyes stared back at me. Jasmine wasn't a gifted human. "You're a witch!"

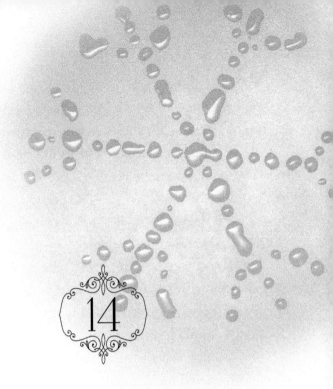

# 14

OUR STICKS SLAMMED TOGETHER, the crack igniting the forest around us; birds flew out of trees and ground creatures froze in fear.

"I don't see myself as a witch," Jasmine corrected as she flung the stick underneath her arm like a true master of martial arts.

I tried to do the same and fumbled, dropping it. I scooped it up quickly, fearing she would best me. I shouldn't be out here and I shouldn't be doing this. I had put myself in danger like a complete idiot. *Fragile and naïve little Abigail.* That's what Natalie and my other used-to-be best friends would say. It didn't matter what she saw herself as, she was a witch by any definition. She jabbed the stick at my rib cage, knocking the breath from me. Sweat was beading on my forehead already and I struggled to get back to my feet.

"Why do you look as if you're facing your killer?" She stood still, jabbing her stick into the ground next to her.

I was clutching my side and trying hard not to throw up. The pain was unbelievable, and all my strength had melted into the grass. "Why—" I sucked in an easy breath to settle the stabbing pain in my side and slowly tried again. "Why did you bring me out here?"

"To show you how to fight," she said plainly. "You seriously thought I was going to hurt you?" Her confidence turned sour and her words filled with concern. "Abby, I'm so sorry. I should have told you."

She sat down next to me, keeping her stick close by. "Yes, you should have."

"Look, no one knows who I am, except the council. I'm not just a witch, Abby. I'm a visionary."

Her confession was astounding. "What?"

"Yeah. My father was one, but he couldn't get a handle on the visions, which made him unstable and then, eventually, he went crazy and killed my mom. I was too scared to tell him I had visions, too, but my mom knew. She tried to help both of us, but you see how that worked out."

"I'm sorry." That's all I had been able to say to her because I didn't understand what she had gone through. I had no wise words of comfort.

"It's funny because I felt the safest when I was with the immortal. Then he disappeared and everything just seemed so hopeless." She rubbed at the scars on her wrists.

"Is that why you tried to kill yourself?"

"I don't know. I just missed him and my mom. I had nobody."

"You said your immortal friend disappeared, but he was caught with you?"

She wiped away a tear. "He said he felt I was in trouble, so he came to check on me. He said he left for my safety, but I could see how bad he felt when he found me bleeding out. He cut open his arm and lifted my head to it, but then I blacked out. I woke up in the infirmary, the underground one. I was there for a month. When they explained where I was and what I was things made more sense, but I didn't dare ask about Caleb. That's his name."

"You mentioned they did tests on you in that building?"

"After the infirmary, they took me there for the tests. I couldn't see Caleb, but I felt him. His presence was so strong that I could feel it in my bones."

It sounded so much like my nightmares and how they told me when Wes was near.

"I'm sorry I scared you," she said apologetically.

"I understand. I never know how much to share with people anymore. So, you can see the future?"

"Sort of. It's weird. It's more like a feeling and then I'll get these dreams, but they are pretty vague. Like the night my dad killed my mom. I had a dream about something bad happening to her, but not by who or what, but then when I was hiding in the closet, I felt that moment in the dream. I knew she was going to die and I didn't do anything about it."

She choked on tears, trying to wipe them away shamefully.

"Please don't do that." I took her hand. "Don't blame yourself and don't be ashamed for crying. You were nine. What the heck could you have done?"

"I could have warned her, told her to be careful."

"But you didn't even know what was happening until it was too late. Jasmine, you are here for a reason. You have to know that, right?"

"It just sucks because I owe The Order for saving me, twice, but I hate them for what they're doing to Caleb and other ones like him—good ones. I've learned so much about my powers because of this place, but it's so hard to not break him out of there and run away."

"You really think you can break into that building?" I wondered.

"I don't think, I know. Who do you think put the magic around it?"

I was amazed. The power I felt buzzing off that building was immense. "Jasmine, that's insane. What else can you do?"

"I can bypass any security system, undetected. I can shield just about anything with a protection spell, and I can remove magic. Most visionaries just have visions but, for whatever reason, I have these other powers. I am human, but a witch would be a pretty accurate label for what I am."

"You can't tell anyone, Jas. According to the ancient laws, you are pure evil and completely forbidden." That alone made me extremely nervous as to why The Order had not only saved her, but was training her.

"I know, trust me. I have read pretty much every book on The Order. I know all the ancient laws, everything that happened that led to the peace treaty, and the Great War that's still raging."

Jasmine was impressive on so many levels and all that knowledge was dangerous. If The Order wasn't viewing her as a threat, they were undoubtedly preparing her for something big, and they wanted to ensure she was on their side. "Can you do me a favor?" Her desperate eyes peered over her lashes at me. "If you trust me, please tell me everything. No matter what happens or what they say, tell me."

"Do you not trust them?" Her expression turned worried.

"Honestly, no, and I care about you. I don't want to see you get used ... or hurt."

"I believe you." She smiled. "Thank you."

A pattern of crunching that sounded a lot like footsteps rang through the forest around us. We both shot to our feet, grabbing the sticks.

"Stay close to me," I whispered. She was way more skilled then me, less broken, and had a handle on some of her gifts, so it was almost comical that I felt such a powerful urge to protect her.

"I shouldn't have brought us out here. I'm sorry," she whispered back, our bodies brushing closely together.

I fought the pain and lifted my stick, gripping it tightly in my fingers. The crunching stopped and suddenly the world seemed to spin out of control. Adrenaline surged through me and I launched forward just as something jumped out of the brush, priming to attack as it rushed us. It looked human, but something about it was not right. I could feel its hatred and its intent on murdering us. It raced around us in a blur, confusing me, and Jasmine chanted something quickly, and the next thing I knew, it was in slow motion. I didn't hesitate. I swung the stick, knocking it to the ground, but breaking Jasmine's spell at the same time. It launched again, this time grabbing my arm, crunching the bones together like a bag of potato chips. I screamed out in pain, tears spilling down my cheeks, until the grip lessened. I stared into the thing's eyes, the brown irises turning black and bleeding into the white, but what really kept my attention was the venomous anger fading into fear and pain. Its grip lessened more and it fell to its knees, its expression now pleading for mercy. My own pain and fear disappeared, and a darkness filled my heart. I released another scream, but this time in anger. Its fingers released my arm as it fell to the ground, rolling around violently and releasing a shriek so sharp and loud Jasmine and I dropped to the ground covering our ears. Then everything was quiet and the beast was gone. *Vanished.* Bewildered, I looked to Jasmine. "What the hell just happened? What did you do?"

"I did the time spell, but that wasn't me, Abby. That was all you."

Instead of appearing scared, she looked proud. "Me?" I couldn't get a grip on what had just happened, and the darkness that overcame me was crippling. Did I just *kill* it? The stick fell from my fingers and I wrapped my arms around my body and began to shake.

"Abby, what's wrong?" Jasmine touched me but recoiled her hand quickly, screaming and holding her smoking hand.

I wanted to call out to her, to comfort her, but I was paralyzed in this absolute desolation of light, leaving only thoughts of death and darkness. And it hurt worse than anything I had ever felt before. *Despair.* My body continued to shake as I lay myself in the soft grass. Jasmine's voice rang through me, but it was distorted and slow. My chest cracked as my body crashed and stretched like a demon possession. Then the black void was sucked out of me and I felt normal again.

Jasmine lay by my side, the fear of hell raging in her eyes, her cheeks soaked, and her cries loud. But she wasn't touching me. She wanted to reach out to help me sit up, but withdrew as recognition trapped her behind an invisible fence.

"I'm fine," I said as I sat up, the old wounds aching with every slight movement.

"Abby, what happened? Why can't I touch you?" She sat back in a more relaxed position, but still stressed.

"I don't know how to explain it." I shook my head, willing the right words to manifest.

"Well, try, because when I touched you I felt like I was dying."

"That's it." I pointed as if the words were laid out in front of me like writing in the sky. "That's what I felt. Like I was dying and then it was just gone."

"You don't think …" Jasmine's words trailed off.

We were thinking the same thing. That my touch was lethal. "But how? It doesn't make sense. I've touched you plenty of times … and Wes. No one ever spontaneously combusted."

"Because you never felt threatened by us. It's attached to your emotions, not your strength."

"That can't be good," I half-joked.

She laughed with me and then reached her hand out for me. I hesitated, but I felt that I wasn't going to hurt her, so I was relieved when she didn't burn up in a blaze of glory.

"I must have gotten in between whatever you and that thing were doing and that's why you hurt me."

"Yeah, I feel fine now." But it didn't change the fact that I killed something. Jasmine sensed my turmoil.

"It was trying to kill us. Don't regret a thing."

I stared at the dead outline of grass where the body disappeared wondering why it would dare come so close to the facility.

"We need to get back," Jasmine said.

She climbed the tree and I handed her the sticks, and then we raced back to the fence. She put her hands around the bars, chanted something quietly, and the gate opened.

We slid in, running to the track. The buzz of the building bit my skin as we passed. Rubbing the feeling off my arm, I asked Jasmine, "Can you describe what it feels like with Caleb?" We walked the rest of the distance up the hill.

"Well, when he was close, I felt safe, like this intense sense of peace. And when he was hurting, I felt that, too, but only when we are in close proximity to each other, like every time I pass that building."

She looked back, the mere thought of him taking her light away, briefly. It was exactly how I felt with Wes and it was strong right now.

"I had a dream about Caleb last night. He was in pain, but he had hope. It was so strange."

"Let's get him out," I presented.

"What? Are you crazy? If we get caught—"

I stopped her in her tracks. "I'm serious. He doesn't belong in there. We need to get him out. Tonight." I was just as surprised at the resoluteness in my tone as she was, but I had this overwhelming feeling that Caleb was in danger, and I wasn't about to ignore my instincts again. They tried to warn me about that beast and I didn't listen. I could have gotten Jasmine killed. I wouldn't let it happen again.

"Thanks." She smiled.

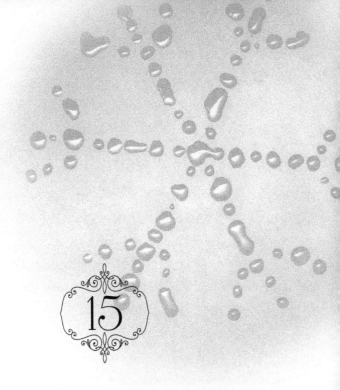

"I DON'T KNOW IF THIS IS a good idea." Jasmine shoved the few personal items she had into a backpack while I paced her bedroom.

"Look, I don't think you have any other choice. You seem to understand your gifts pretty well, and you know Caleb is in there. I'm telling you, Jas, something big is coming, and I think we're a part of it."

"Then, shouldn't you be coming?" She zipped up the backpack and sat hard on the bed.

"I can't." My stomach tightened. I hadn't told her about my little brother, the only reason I was here. I wanted to tell her so many times, but it was one of those secrets I was scared to tell.

"Why not? There's nothing here for you."

I chewed on my finger as I stood still now.

"What aren't you telling me?"

I stood my ground, remaining quiet.

"I'm not going through with this until you tell me, Abby."

This was my last chance to tell her and, besides, I probably would never see her again. I sat down next to her, gathering my thoughts. Where did I begin?

"My whole childhood I wished for one thing, a sibling. It never happened, but then I found out that I actually do have a brother. He's your age."

"That's great, right?" She was reacting to my somber tone.

"Yes, but The Order took him right after he was born, so I've never met him. I'm here to find him."

"Why would they take him like that?"

"It's complicated, but that's why I can't leave. Not until I find out where he is."

She took my hand. "I understand. I can stay and help you."

I shook my head vehemently. "No way, Jasmine. Caleb is your battle, and my little brother is mine."

We played cards and talked while we waited for nightfall. I figured the best time for her to sneak out was right before curfew, that way no one would be looking for her until morning. It should give her and Caleb a good head start.

"Let's get going." I picked up her backpack and handed

it to her. "So, you are positive you can turn off all those traps you mentioned, because I really don't want to get fried."

"I'm positive. My handprint will scan just like any other authorized person, which shuts off everything for three minutes."

I cracked open her door and poked my head out. The hallway was clear, so we slid out, walking briskly out of the building. The grounds were already deserted, like every other night. My only concern was the library now that I knew it was always open to the Potentials. They could be lingering around.

We jogged down the running path to look less conspicuous and, of course, I should have figured Jack would be out too. He jogged right up to us, out of breath.

"Hey, what are you guys still doing out? You only have a few minutes until curfew." He eyed the backpack on Jasmine.

*Shoot.* "We were just walking the path before bed. We've been at the library most of the day and borrowed a bunch of books." I patted the backpack.

"Okay. But, hurry. You don't need to be seen out after curfew again."

Once the darkness swallowed Jack, Jasmine and I broke out into a run. According to my watch, we had two minutes. When we reached the building, Jasmine put her hands up to the invisible, but very much alive, air that tingled with magic and chanted quickly. The buzz lifted like brushing cobwebs from my skin. Then she placed her hand on the scanner and chanted again. The red light turned green and she turned to me with a huge smile.

"See?"

I was definitely impressed, but we weren't in the clear yet. Not by a long shot. The lock disengaged and Jasmine pulled it open.

"Let me lead. I want to make sure all the traps are off."

That wasn't very comforting, but she had the magic, not me, so I followed closely behind and started the stopwatch. We stepped just inside and the door locked behind us. We only had three minutes to get to the end of the hall and I had no idea how long it was.

"I don't feel any traces of magic, so we should be good."

"Let's not waste any time."

She walked briskly, but cautiously, forward. "I can feel him, Abby."

My stomach churned because I felt Wes as well, but there's no way he could be here. He wouldn't be stupid enough to come here. Would he?

We pushed forward quickly, dim lights brightening the hall and then turning off as we passed. At the end there was another doorway. Jasmine got us through, dumping us into a weapon room.

"Where the hell are we?" I asked.

"This is where all the weapons are stored. Behind that door are the special weapons the Elites use."

She pointed to another door across the room. It gave me the heebie-jeebies. I knew firsthand what some of those weapons could do. Penelope used one on me that could have killed me, but it hadn't. "I don't see any other doors."

She waved me over to a spot where there was a completely out of place rug. She pulled it back, revealing a large trap door. Before she pulled it up, I stopped her. "Wait. There have to be guards on these prisoners. How are we going to get past them?"

She smiled wickedly. "Why, magic, of course."

I never wanted to be on a witch's bad side. "Let's do this then. You remember the Panic Plan?"

"Yes, but it won't come to that. Trust me."

Man, did I ever, but this all seemed too easy. If they knew what Jasmine was capable of there's no way they would let her just run around free like this. I mustn't be thinking this all the way through. I was missing something, but we had already come so far.

"What's wrong?" she inquired.

"Nothing. Let's just get you and Caleb out of here." I shook it off. Even if we did get caught, they surely wouldn't hurt two of their most prized possessions. Caleb was another story. As Jasmine started heading down the hatch, I swiped a hunting knife from a rack of knives, pulled it from its leather holster to make sure it would suffice in a sticky situation, and then shoved it in the back waist band of my red pants, covered by my shirt.

I waited at the top until she gave me the all clear.

"Guard is asleep." She beamed up at me.

I climbed down the ladder, taking in our new

surroundings. We were in a fairly large, bright tunnel. The concrete floor and walls kept it cool … *and creepy*. You could go either way in the tunnel: one way opened to who the hell knew where, and the other was gated about twenty feet away. The gate was open now, and the guard standing by was asleep on the ground. As we walked past him, I realized he wasn't just any guard; he was an Elite. My breathing quickened.

"Jasmine, he's an Elite. Are you sure he won't remember any of this?"

"One hundred percent." She walked forward confidently.

There was a large soundproof door closing off whatever was on the other side. It was equipped with a scanner, and Jasmine placed her hand on it, and the door clicked open. Immediately, a rush of moans and angry voices carried out. Lots of angry non-humans. Lots.

We slipped in and were faced with a long hallway with thick iron doors on either side. It looked as if the hallway went on forever. The sounds were muffled but they still seeped out of the rooms. Some were horrible moans of pain while others were delirious cries of laughter. And then there was the banging. So much banging. With each clap of sound my heart jumped. How many of them being held here were innocent, like Caleb? How could we just free him?

Jasmine suddenly stopped and turned to a door, placing her hand on the cold iron and closing her eyes. She was still for so long I thought I had lost her to some unknown realm, but then her head turned to me, her cheeks soaked with tears, and then she opened them.

"He's in here, but he's hurt. Bad."

"How do you know?" I asked.

"Our connection is weak as if he's on the edge of this life and another. We have to get him out of here," she added desperately and then sprang into action.

She chanted some words, much angrier than I had ever heard her speak. She stepped back and the door flung open. She didn't hesitate as she rushed inside. I was less enthusiastic about entering a locked cell, so I crept slowly through the doorway and had to cover my mouth to keep from screaming. Caleb was lying on the floor, his face bruised to the point of barely recognizable; his clothes were torn, and he was barely moving, even as Jasmine lifted his head and spoke softly into his ear. She rocked his head as she cried from the very depths of her soul and then she peered over to me.

"I can do a spell to make him light as a feather. That's the only way we're getting him out."

I didn't realize my hands were shaking until I let go of my mouth to speak. "Okay. What do you need me to do?"

"Just help me guide him out of here." She chanted again quickly and then picked up Caleb like he was nothing. I rushed inside and took one of his arms and threw it over my shoulder. Jasmine spoke some inaudible words and the door closed again. As we carried Caleb back down the hallway, I couldn't shake the intensity of which I felt Wes, so I called out.

"Wes?"

Jasmine looked at me questioningly. "Do you feel him?"

"Yes," I confessed, "but we have to get you two out of here." I frantically looked back and forth between Jasmine and the way we had just come and remorsefully added, "There's no time to look for him."

"No, Abby. You see what they did to Caleb. You have to find him if he's here. Go. I'll wait by the guard to make sure he doesn't wake up."

The conflict was so intense. The longer we stayed down here the more at risk we were of getting caught, but she was right. If Wes were down here I needed to get him out too, and I couldn't do that without Jasmine. "Shoot, all right. But if you hear anything, take the tunnel the other direction and find yourself a way out."

"But what about you? I can help," she whined.

"Don't worry about me. I'm The Chosen, remember?" I winked. I wasn't so sure that would keep me from being tortured like everything else down here, but I needed her to feel comfortable enough running without me.

"Just hurry and trust your instincts. That will lead you to him," she urged and headed out the door.

Instincts were all I had. I steadied my nerves and walked slowly down the hall, concentrating on what I felt, looking for any influxes. The hallway was long, and once I found the end of it, but not Wes, I was somewhat perplexed. So, on the way back, I tried the old-fashioned way; I shouted his name over and over, riling up the others. The bangs became erratic, and the moans turned to cries for help. The hallway was alive with pain, and it killed me as I walked past each door, ignoring all of them and shouting Wes' name louder. I listened hard for a response, but nothing. Near the end, someone responded calmly. I rushed toward the sound, placing my hands on a door, like Jasmine had done, but I didn't feel anything different. Nothing stronger.

"Wes?" I put my ear against the chill of the iron and listened, hoping it was him, but at the same time hoping it wasn't after seeing Caleb's condition. The room on the other side was silent, and then a whisper that was right where my ear was filled me with dread.

"No, but I can be," it hissed and then laughed wickedly.

I jumped away from the door, terrified. Wes wasn't here. I ran out to where Jasmine waited.

"Nothing?" she inquired as we moved Caleb to the trap door.

"No." Then the hatch started to open. "Are you doing that?" I asked desperately.

"No."

I looked down the other way into the blackness. "There has to be another way out."

"I can just use my magic," she replied.

"No." I shook my head. Something was telling me that whatever was coming down Jasmine couldn't just bewitch them asleep. I pulled Caleb and Jasmine down the tunnel quickly. We stopped deep in the darkness and remained still and quiet.

"I'll cloak us," Jasmine whispered.

"No." I put my hand on her arm. "He'll sense it."

"Who?"

Boots crashed down the ladder. The man's back was to us, and he was unnaturally still for a moment, and then his head turned in our direction. My heart pounded against my chest. It was Elijah. He would sense me like I sensed him. He would catch us. I looked over at Jasmine's terrified expression. Not us. He would catch me.

"Jasmine, listen to me. You need to go. Elijah won't turn me in."

"What? No," she shook her head.

"It's alright. This was our plan all along. You and Caleb go and I stay. It's just a little altered, that's all." I wasn't sure if I had convinced her, but then she nodded slowly.

"Thank you for everything, Abigail. We won't forget you."

"Stay safe and well hidden." I gave her a quick hug and nudged her along.

"Abigail?"

Elijah's voiced carried over to me like invisible ashes from a fire. It was low and cross. Not a good sign. I cringed at my betrayal.

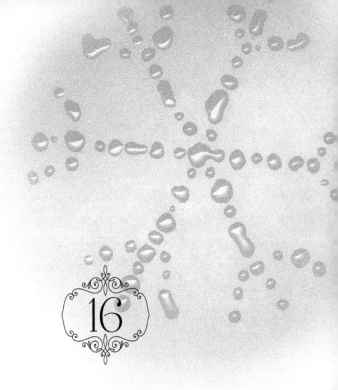

# 16

IDEBATED ON RUNNING AFTER Jasmine and denying the whole thing later when Elijah asked me about it, but then that wouldn't be giving her much time to get out of here. I needed to stall him. He was going to find out Caleb escaped soon, and he already knew I was down here because of our stupid bond. I took small, slow steps toward him. When I made it into the light, Elijah scowled.

"Are you crazy? Because you have to be to come down here when you're already on a very short watch list." He stood tall and stiff.

What was I going to tell him? Jasmine needed more time, so I couldn't tell him the truth. Well, not the whole truth, anyway. "I followed my instincts down the tunnel and it led me here." I pointed the way Jasmine went.

Elijah looked past me, skepticism flooding his eyes. "And how did you find the entrance to this tunnel?" He raised an eyebrow and crossed his arms.

He was testing me. He knew where this tunnel led. Logically, it had to be some sort of escape route, or even a way of getting non-humans in and out without disturbing the recruits, so I made an educated guess.

"Outside the back gate of the facility." I took slow, even breaths to keep my body calm, because Elijah would sense if I were lying.

"And how did you get outside the gate?" His concern was breaking through the anger.

This was an easy one. "Jasmine. She wanted to show me how far along her magic has come." It was hard to read his expression, but I imagined he wasn't thrilled that I knew Jasmine was a witch.

"So, she told you?"

There were still several feet that separated us, and it was filled with unease.

"Yeah, I know she's a witch. I told her about Wes, and so she brought me to this tunnel."

He took a step toward me. "How far did you go?"

A rustling behind him drew our attention. The guard was waking up. My eyes darted to Elijah.

"Go," he ordered as he waved me up the ladder.

I rushed up and he followed quickly, closing the hatch and scanning us back out of the building. He grabbed my arm tightly and dragged me to his building. He didn't say a word until I was in his room and the door was securely locked. He plopped me on his bed and began pacing. His face was blood red and his fists were clenching.

"Eli—?"

He put his hand up and stopped. "Don't."

Then a siren blared in the room. We both grabbed for our ears, sharing a painful glance.

"It won't stop until everyone has evacuated the buildings," he yelled over the deafening screech.

I nodded in understanding and followed him out of the room. The sirens were blaring through the halls and outside. Large crowds of recruits, Potentials, and leaders were clawing at their ears as they lined up at the buildings.

"Go to your line. We'll finish this talk later," he growled.

I had never seen Elijah so furious. It terrified me. I ran to my building, getting in line relatively unnoticed next to a boy I hadn't met yet. After several more painful minutes, the sirens ceased, and a troop of Elites marched down the hill to the building Elijah and I had emerged from. Jasmine had disabled the cameras for the few seconds when we entered the building, but they surely caught Elijah and me coming out. The plan was for me to stay with Jasmine so she could scramble the cameras until I was back in my room, but that plan got shot to hell. They would go to Elijah first, and then it would be my turn. They would suspect his involvement in Jasmine and Caleb's escape, and who knew what they would do to him. I was such a fool.

It was nearly pitch black until they turned on the

floodlights around the facility. Now it was as bright as a cloudless day, but our breath was visible in the night chill, and some recruits were beginning to shiver. No one dared deviate from attention, though. Helga marched back and forth, wearing a poker face as strong as my father's. There were a couple hundred bodies sharing the space between buildings, yet you would never know with how silent it was.

A shot rang out and my body jumped in response. I became a mess of emotions: scared, fearful, anxious, sad. Jasmine and Caleb had a really good start, so the shot couldn't have been for them.

"You heard it," Helga snapped. "Get back to your rooms."

I searched the other recruits for answers, but no one spoke. They all seemed to know what the gunshot meant. I followed them into the building obediently, but before I locked myself in the false safety of my room, a hand grabbed me. It was the boy from line.

"That was the all clear," he informed simply.

"Thanks."

"My name is Jesse."

Jesse had a sweet face. He couldn't be more than fifteen. His hair was sandy blond and eyes as green as a blade of dewy grass. His skin was tan, and he was a few inches taller than me.

"I assume you already know who I am?"

He chuckled. "The almighty Chosen who is going to save the world."

His tone was free from teasing, so I let out a half-laugh. "Yes, exactly." I shook my head. It was ridiculous. "But, please, call me Abigail."

"Get to your rooms," Helga shouted from the front door.

"See you around," he said and strolled to his room. His was three doors down from mine.

"Bye," I replied weakly.

When I got to my room, I locked the door and my head spun with different stories I could tell the council. All of them sounded unbelievable, and if they had a mind reader in the room they could force me to look in their eyes. All of my truths would be told then. Maybe staying here was a stupid idea, after all. But then I remembered my brother. I was no closer to finding him than I was a week ago when I first arrived. I knew it would take time, but I had already royally screwed up my plan for lying low. I got Ray locked up in isolation, helped Jasmine and Caleb break out, and sucked Elijah into this whole mess.

I sat on my bed, resting my back on the wall, hugging my knees tight to my chest. I pressed my eye sockets hard into my knees, trying to keep the rush of tears from breaking free. My dad would know what to do. He always had a plan. He never folded under pressure. Why couldn't I be as strong as him?

I heard the footsteps before the knock on my door. They were here to take me, but where? Solitary? Tribunal?

Lockdown? I shuttered at the thought. Being down there for those few minutes was enough. The knock came again, quicker this time. They would just unlock it if I didn't open it, so sitting on my bed, paralyzed with fear, was silly.

"Abby, it's me," Elijah hissed.

I bolted off the bed and fumbled to get the door unlocked because my hands were so shaky. My fear had literally paralyzed our bond. I didn't feel him even though he was only feet away. I should be afraid to see Elijah because of what I had done, but it was relief that threw me into his arms and the permission my body needed to shed those dreadful tears. "I'm so sorry," I choked out with my head buried in his chest. He pushed us inside holding me tight and closed the door.

"I know, Abby."

He rubbed my back and gave me a moment to compose myself. I wiped my nose and waited for him to lay into me. He sighed loudly, his face changing from anger to something else entirely. Fear?

"You've made a huge mess." He scrubbed the worry from his expression. "I need to know everything if I'm going to fix this."

All the lies I had concocted were erased like memories stolen from me as a child. No lie would be better than the truth now. "I helped Jasmine break Caleb out and escape."

The color in Elijah's cheeks darkened. He contained his frustration within his white-knuckled fists. "Do you not remember why you are here?" He blew up.

I was startled enough to jump back a step. "Yes," I shouted back.

"Then what the hell are you doing? You aren't invincible, Abby. They will break you here if they have to. You aren't an exception to the rule."

*What had I done?*

"You know what Jasmine is? She's an exception," I challenged.

"It doesn't mean they wouldn't break her, too. Don't you get it? They are collecting anyone that can help them kill off all the non-humans. Not just the bad ones, Abby. All of them. They are going for complete extinction, and they won't put up with this crap from you. They will torture you in ways you can't even imagine until you can look Wes in the eye and kill him."

And there it was. My heart sank to the bottom of the ocean. One day they would ask me to kill someone I loved possibly even more than myself, and I wouldn't be able to do it. In the back of my childish, naïve mind I knew it already, but I had blindly convinced myself that I could change things, that I could make The Order see that not all non-humans were bad, but they weren't going to listen. They were on a mission, and I was just collateral damage.

"I could never do it." My voice was hoarse from the emotional exhaustion. I fell onto the bed, feeling the defeat seep deep inside of me.

Elijah sat next to me and said, "I know."

"They're going to take me to solitary, aren't they?"

"No." He shook his head.

I looked over to him, surprised by his answer. "What did you do, Elijah?"

"Jasmine's not the only one who can manipulate security footage."

"What?" He never told me what his gifts were, but I hadn't imagined they stretched into witch zone. "Are you a witch?"

He laughed. "No, but I can do a lot of things witches can and some things they can't."

"Like what?" He shifted uncomfortably. "What are you keeping from me?"

He looked away. "This isn't the time to get into it. If anyone asks where you were coming from, you tell them you were in my room playing cards." He picked up the deck off the dresser and dropped it loudly.

Red flags flapped wildly in my chest. "Why won't you tell me?"

He stood up. "Because it's not important right now, that's why."

But I knew that whatever he was keeping a secret was because it involved me. There would be no other logical reason for him to get so upset. "Uh-uh. Not good enough." I wasn't backing down. "We are supposed to be in this together. You promised my father and me. No secrets."

His lips parted for just a second, and I actually thought he was going to tell me, but then they closed, and he left the room without another word, leaving me stupefied and scared. He was the last person left that I trusted in here, and he took that trust with him in one fell swoop.

When the Elites came knocking, I answered their questions in a daze. I told them I was with Elijah, playing cards. I think they believed me, but I couldn't find it in me to care. Tonight things had changed drastically, again, and I knew if I were going to survive, I was going to need to make superficial allies and get stronger. I couldn't let anyone break me. Not Elijah or The Order. I had lost focus to help Jasmine because I let my feelings for her situation get in the way, but I couldn't afford to let that happen again. I was lucky this time, but luck had a funny way of running out when you needed it the most.

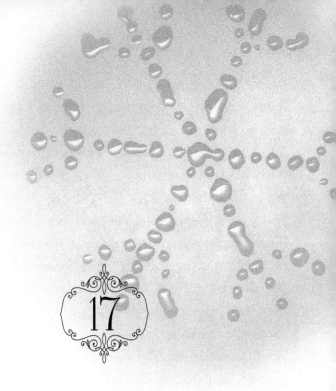

E VERY NOISE IN THE HALLWAY kept me awake. Just as slumber weighed heavily on my overstimulated mind, another sound would pull me out of it. Elijah said he took care of things and the Elites that questioned me had seemed satisfied after the mini interrogation, but I had committed a crime against the deadliest organization in the world. Easy sleep would evade me for a long time to come.

I also worried about Jasmine and Caleb. What if they didn't get far enough away? What if they were in the lock down? I would never know, because there was no way I could get back in there, and Elijah was certainly not going to march me down there. I could ask him to check, but now wasn't the best time to be calling in favors after what I pulled him into last night. However, Elijah was back and hadn't updated me on Wes, and I needed to know. Even though I didn't find him in lockdown, I needed to make sure he was okay.

Curfew wasn't lifted for another hour, so I pulled all the books from the library Jasmine and I had borrowed and flipped through the stick fighting one. The leg sweep and jab to the kidney seemed like good moves to practice, if only I had a stick. My eyes roved around the room and stopped on the closet. The pole for the clothes to hang on was just about the right length, so I popped it out of the brackets and gave it a test spin in the room. It was a little heavier than the sticks we were using in training, but that might actually be a good thing. Satisfied, I tossed it on the bed and got dressed. I would have preferred practicing in my room, out of sight of others, but the room was just too small. I did a few sets of push-ups and sit-ups before heading out with the pole.

Not many people were roaming about yet as the sun was just barely slipping up the sky, and the few that were awake headed up the hill to get breakfast. I didn't bother hiding the pole because it wasn't against the rules to practice. In fact, it was encouraged, but they didn't provide weapons for practice. I had seen people practice just the moves without weapons, but that seemed silly. I headed to the Tree of Solitude, out of sight of cameras, and spun the stick around as if I were sweeping an opponent's legs. It was awkward, and I ended up hitting myself in the face the first time, but the movement got smoother as my arm tired from the repetition. I moved on to the jab maneuver.

This move was less daunting. A half hour later my skin was wet with perspiration. I was just about to take a break when Elijah found me.

"Keeping your mind off things?" He leaned on the tree with his arms crossed.

"Are we talking again?" I swung the pole in front of me, stopping just before impact to Elijah's side.

"Impressive." He grabbed the pole and yanked it hard, causing me to stumble forward. "But you're still too weak."

I tried to yank the stick free of his grip, but he wasn't budging. "What, are we twelve? Let go," I demanded.

He tossed his end of the pole to the ground, knocking me off balance again. I dropped the pole and spread my arms out wide. "What, Elijah? Say it. Tell me again how much I screwed up." Tears pooled in my eyes as I shouted.

"You just don't get it, Abby. This is so much bigger than Jasmine and Caleb. Than any of those prisoners." He pushed off the tree and stepped toward me with his fists flailing about. "This is about you and your role in the war. They are going to make you into a weapon. *The* weapon. And you're still investing in childish notions. Grow up, Abby! Open your eyes, dammit, before you get yourself killed."

As my mind was forming a rebuttal, it sank in what he was saying. With one touch I had killed that thing outside the gate. He had disintegrated right before my eyes. I raised my hands in front of my face as everything that happened and everything Elijah said finally impacted me the way he wanted. This was bigger than my silly little plans to rescue my brother. I was in the lion's den and I was the lion.

I must have looked horrified, because Elijah grabbed my wrists gently and alarmingly asked, "What? What's wrong?"

"I … I killed someone." I shook my head. That wasn't right. I was confused. Everything I was feeling was too much. "Some*thing*." The world seemed a galaxy smaller, and my body seemed too heavy for my legs to carry. "What did I do?" I asked myself. I wasn't even sure I said it aloud. My fingers, my hands were foreign objects, separate from the rest of me. They were deadly. They were the weapons. Not me.

"Abigail, you're not making sense."

My body shook, and when I finally stole my eyes from my hands I saw that it was Elijah who was rocking me. "Outside the gate with Jasmine. We were attacked … and I killed it." I lifted my hands. "With these." My eyes darted around the grounds to ensure no one was watching. That they hadn't discovered I was dangerous, lest they might hate me even more. *Fear me.* It wasn't hate. I had been mistaken. They all feared me. My stomach flipped. I was an abomination.

"You need to sit."

Elijah guided me to the ground, and I rested against the tree. Things were still so distant, like the stars a million light years away.

"I felt something intense. A burning, but you seemed

fine when I saw you after, so I just let it go. I should have known something wasn't right. I'm sorry." Elijah looked so uncomfortable squatting in front of me, ready to run at a moment's notice. "How did you kill it?"

"Jasmine and I were practicing stick fighting, and the thing came out of nowhere. I was scared. It ran so fast that I could only see the trail it was blazing around us, and then Jasmine slowed it down enough for me to knock it with my stick, but then it grabbed my arm," I wrapped my fingers around my arm where it had grabbed me. "The bones felt like they crushed under its grip. The pain was like shockwaves of lightning through my body. But then it was the one screaming in pain, not me. It fell to the ground, screeching, and then I felt this incredible burning engulf my insides as if I were melting from the inside out." Remembering the excruciating pain sent shivers down my spine. "Then it disappeared, and so did the pain. The bones in my arm healed, too."

Elijah was hard to read most of the time, but not right now. It was clear as a bell at midnight. He was astonished. "Remarkable." He turned my arm around, checking for damage, but not even a scratch was left behind.

"Which part? That I can kill something with a touch, or that I healed?" That part was unclear to me. Almost as if he knew what I could do before I did.

"You sure you're okay?" His anger had subsided and replaced with genuine concern.

"Yeah. Physically, anyway. Mentally, I feel like I'm going a little nuts."

He let go of my arms gently and stood back, studying me.

"That's it? I'm kind of freaking out over here." He had gotten so quiet. The uneasy kind of quiet.

"I knew, Abby."

Someone else's heart had to be breaking at this point because mine was already so shattered. "How long?"

"I've always known."

And a million pieces of it explode across the sky, hoping to find peace with the stars hidden by the daylight. "How could you not tell me?" I thought of what could have happened to the Hunters. I had touched all of them. "I could have killed Wes." My voice dropped from the disappointment layered so thickly on top.

"At first I thought you could, and back then I actually hoped you would."

I should have been more shocked than I was, but I understood now the hate that Elijah had for non-humans. And I also understood how that had changed over the past few months.

"When nothing happened I assumed it was a learned gift like the rest. What I didn't count on was it being connected to fear. That's more dangerous and rare."

"That's why I was so against you coming here. I knew why they wanted you."

"It wouldn't have changed me coming here, if I knew. I

can't leave my brother lost in The Order system, but I won't break my promise. As soon as I find him, I'm out. I won't be what they want me to be."

"See, that's the mistake that is going to kill you. You really don't know what The Order is capable of. What they can do to change your mind."

I stood up, finally regaining strength in my legs. "Then, teach me, Elijah. Show me how to beat them. Make me stronger than whatever they can throw at me." I was begging, and not because I was scared, but because I wanted to end The Order. It was foretold that I would bring peace to a never-ending war. The Order equated that to non-human extinction, but it didn't have to be. The Hunters were different. Caleb was different. That gave me hope they all had the ability to change, and they deserved the right to prove it.

Elijah picked up the pole and held it for a moment, contemplating something. "You asked me to leave you alone." His voice was almost as dark as midnight on a new moon.

I swallowed hard, remembering what I had said to him in the library. I had released him. I thought I was doing him a favor. Giving him his freedom back, but that statement was reckless. If I was going to survive I needed Elijah. And a very important part of me wanted him around too, whether I was ever ready to admit that or not. "I can't take back what I said, but I can tell you that I'm sorry, and I would be grateful for your help."

He raised the stick up and his eyes followed, finally making their way to mine, and the intensity between us ripped at my chest, digging its way down, trying to find the heart that was still hidden in a flurry of pain in the sky above. Had it been there, I would have let the walls crumble, frantically climbing my way over the rubble into his arms. For the first time I was sad my heart was gone, because Elijah had a good soul. He was a strong and handsome man who would one day bring hell to its knees and heaven to the heart of someone worthy.

"We do it my way," he said, ignoring the parted seas between us.

"Of course."

"You do what I say without question."

"Yes." I nodded eagerly.

"I will get you through all the buildings, but your training won't end there. After dinner, we will train more. On the weekends, we will train all day. No wasted time."

My body flared with excitement. "Awesome."

"One last thing," he added. "You will tell me everything. No secrets. If you hear anything about your brother, I want to know. No more reckless rendezvouses."

"Full disclosure from now on." It wasn't lost on me that he was standing on the buried key he knew nothing about and that I had discovered magic that cloaked the hidden section of the library. When it was time, I would tell him.

"Great. I hope you're ready, because this is going to be the hardest year of your life." He tossed the stick to me.

"In the spirit of full disclosure, what did you find out about Wes?" He became unreadable again, the poster boy for anonymity.

"The Hunters have moved on."

"What does that mean?" I tried to find a slight twitch of his eyelid or a small shift of his body. A tell that would signal he was hiding something, but he was still. But maybe that was his tell. Stiffness.

"They moved. Most of their belongings were gone and they were nowhere to be found in town."

"So, how do I know if Wes is okay or not?"

Elijah's shoulders relaxed as he took a step toward me. "I did what I could. I can't leave you here alone. Look what happened when I was gone for just the day. We were lucky I came back when I did."

We were lucky and it was almost too convenient. A hundred questions came to mind. Why did he come down to lockdown when he did? If The Hunters were gone like he said, why was he gone for so long? Sandpoint wasn't that far from here. But I had agreed to his terms. Asking questions now would be counterproductive.

"You can't focus on your training if your mind is out there. You have to let Wes go right now. I need all of you here."

His emphasis on needing me was soft and pleading. Elijah loved me. He would do anything for me. Even die. I owed it to him to trust him. I owed it to both of us because, if I was going to wage a war against The Order, I was going to need to reach my full potential. They brought me here to win a war. They just didn't realize it would be against them.

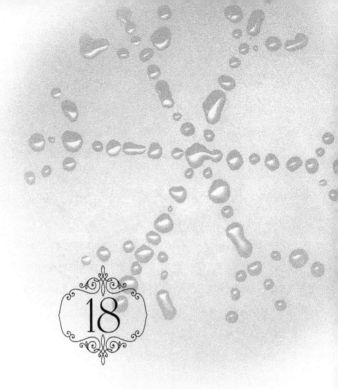

**18**

B Y THE TIME ELIJAH FINISHED with me for the day, my muscles felt like they were dripping off my bones like lava had melted them. We didn't talk about Jasmine or Caleb anymore, and he shied away from any topics involving Wes, although I still worried he was here or very nearby risking capture. I didn't blame him. He had already gone above and beyond for me. I knew when I committed to coming here I would be cutting myself off from the outside world, including my own parents. It was a risk I was willing to take to rescue my brother. Knowing the risks didn't make it any easier, but I had to push it aside. Elijah, my training, and finding my brother were the only things I should be focusing on.

When the sun rose on Monday, I was ready. I was sore

as hell, but I was going to do my best to ignore it. I rolled off the bed onto the floor and did my sit-ups and push-ups, washed up, got dressed and walked as confidently as my tight muscles would allow. Jasmine would have started today, and I would be lying to myself if I didn't admit it hurt a little that she was gone, but at least she wouldn't be Helga's next target.

Jesse fell in line next to me, affording a quick smile before fading in to the expected blank expression. He was a nice kid and I wondered what brought him here. Hopefully not something as dark as Jasmine's back story. When I looked down the line, Ebony returned a glare. The boy with white hair that had attacked me and in turn was beaten by Elijah was still absent.

Helga's hands were interlocked tightly behind her back as she walked the line to inspect us. She glared at my chucks and just as she was raising her hand, I squeezed my eyes closed bracing for impact, but when it didn't come, I opened one eye slightly to see she had walked away and Elijah stood in front of me. He looked at my shoes and shook his head, but met my surprised look with a coy smile. I stood a little taller. It was a false sense of confidence because it would be non-existent without Elijah, but I felt stronger all the same.

After we ran the instructed laps around the track, Elijah by my side silently, Helga ushered us down to the basement of Building Two. We were randomly split off into groups again. Elijah led my group, showing us different moves, and when he called me into the circle to demonstrate, my heart may have jumped slightly. He tossed me the stick and the other recruits watched closely as I avoided a crack to my head, ducking just in time. I missed the quick sweep to my feet, and I fell hard to the ground and the others reacted with excitement and taunting noises. I ignored them and hopped back to my feet, doing a slow dance with Elijah as we both tried to calculate the other's next move. A noise caught Elijah's attention for a split second, long enough for me swing and graze his arm before he jumped out of the way. A proud smile filled my face, and I caught some of the surprised looks surrounding me, but Elijah was quick. He spun with the stick, grazing my side as I fell back to avoid it, clumsily dropping my own stick. His disappointment didn't go unnoticed as he picked it up and tossed it to another recruit. I stepped back and watched as he sparred with a boy who was more his match.

After Elijah sparred with everyone, he had us spar our sticks with a punching bag until we were drenched with sweat and out of breath. A few even vomited. Had the training not ended when it did, I would have been sick, too.

"I'll meet you at the tree after dinner," Elijah instructed before he left.

I headed toward the benches, chugging water as I wrapped my head around training again tonight. I dropped my head into my hands, willing the pain away, when I heard whispers. I shouldn't have been surprised to see Ebony standing in front of me.

"Where's your bodyguard?" The way she cocked her

hip and the tone of her voice reminded me of the years I endured Natalie's mean-girl antics. "Or should we call him your boyfriend?"

A few kids laughed at her remark.

"You can call him whatever you want." I stood up right in her face, "but know that at the end of all of this you will be begging me to save your ass." I didn't wait for a response, popping my shoulder against hers as I walked away.

"We'll see who's saving who," she snapped back.

I flipped her the middle finger as I crossed the basement to the stairs. Within seconds, my head was yanked back and Ebony was on the other side of a chunk of my hair. I spun around, sweeping my leg under her feet, knocking her to the ground. She let go of my hair as I fell on top of her. I caught her fist before it made impact on my face, and I twisted it until she screamed in pain. By now everyone had gathered around us, chanting stupid crap, trying to encourage us to fight more. When silence crept over the crowd, I knew we were in trouble.

Helga pulled me off of Ebony and dragged me up the stairs without a word. I squinted at the sunlight and then ducked my chin when I saw Elijah's eyes widened with anger.

"What's this?" he demanded of Helga.

"She was fighting. You know the rules. One day in solitary."

Solitary. Where Ray was. Where Ebony said I wouldn't last a second. The recruits filed out of the basement, and

Ebony locked eyes with me, gleaming with pride. She set me up.

"It takes two people to fight," Elijah growled.

"Yes, well, it seems that Little Miss Chosen here had quite the upper hand. She broke Ebony's wrist."

When the attention was on Ebony, her evil smirk changed to feigned agony as she cradled her wrist. I wanted to call her out, but there was no point. Helga had made up her mind about the situation and to argue would only make me look weak, so I sucked it up and stayed quiet.

"See, she doesn't deny it." Helga waved the arm she was still gripping.

Elijah looked at me questioningly, but I maintained my silence.

"Fine. I'll take her." He held out his hand to Helga.

After a bit of hesitation, she handed me over and threatened the others to disperse or she would enact an early curfew. They left without a word.

"Make sure she gets there," Helga said crossly and then marched to the main building.

Before I could explain Elijah put up his hand to stop me.

"I know you didn't start it, but I'm proud you finished it. Did you really break her wrist?"

I stumbled on my thoughts for a second. He was happy I hurt her. "Uh … yeah. You're not mad?"

"Hell no. You were attacked and you reacted with precision. I can't teach instinct, Abby. You're a natural."

I shook my head and felt my cheeks flush when I saw

we were still holding hands. He dropped my hand and put a little space between us.

"It's only twenty-four hours. You think you can handle that?"

I couldn't tell if he was concerned or excited to see me rise to a challenge. "I've been alone a lot longer than that before." I shrugged my shoulders.

"It's not like being left home alone, Abby. This will be the worst hours of your life. I can try to request—"

"Stop," I cut him off. "It's bad enough I have you following me around. These kids are never going to respect me if I keep getting special treatment. Ebony set me up, so I'm going to give her what she wanted. I'm going to go to solitary and come back ready to train."

Elijah considered me for a moment and shook his head once. Then with a raised eyebrow said, "All right. Let's go."

I wish I could say I marched down to solitary fearless, but no way. I was terrified. It wasn't with the prisoners as I suspected. It was actually in the basement of the library of all places.

"Are they going to bore us to death," I teased as we walked through the doors. I couldn't help it. I made stupid jokes when I was nervous. Elijah humored me with a small smile, but hidden behind those emerald eyes was pure terror. My nerves shot right through my veins, stilling my heart.

When we stepped into the elevator, Elijah pressed his

thumb on the scanner and then took my hand in his, filling me with a calmness I didn't deserve.

"Do you feel that?" he turned to me and asked.

"Yes."

"Hold on to that. You'll need it."

The familiar feeling of the ground giving under my feet subsided as the elevator crawled to a stop. The smell hit me first, and bile immediately rose in my throat. I covered my nose and stepped out of the elevator behind Elijah, who seemed unaffected by the stench of urine and feces.

"The smell is the easy part," he informed me regretfully.

"Great," I replied, still pinching my nose.

It was set up much like the prison with a long concrete floor hallway and drain holes every twenty feet or so. Iron doors with a small square cut-out secured with bars lined the walls. I thought curious eyes would peek out, but none did, and the unusual stillness and muggy air that clung to my skin was unsettling.

Elijah stopped midway down and opened a door. "On the bright side, if you can get through this, you can get through anything."

"That's the bright side?" In the corner of the room there was a bucket, and on one of the walls there was a cot not more than a few inches off the ground with no sheets. At least the floor looked like it had been cleaned. I stepped inside and he closed the door. Only his face was visible through the barred window. I wrapped my fingers around them.

Elijah put his face as close as he could without touching the bars and whispered, "I put you across from your friend. I hope that makes this easier." With a resounding sigh he left.

"Ray?" My voice was a hissed whisper.

"Abigail? Is that you?" Her face peered at her barred window across the hall.

"Yeah," I whispered back.

"Why are you whispering?"

"I have no idea," I replied plainly. "Are you okay?"

"I've been better." She laughed once and then it faded. "Why are you down here?"

"Ebony set me up."

"I hate her."

The guilt I felt for not speaking up for Ray poked at me. "I'm sorry I let you rot down here by yourself."

"What? Don't be. This isn't my first time."

"Really?"

"Apparently, I don't learn lessons very well. What day is it?" she asked.

"Monday."

"Five more days to go? How long are you down here?"

"Twenty-four hours."

"That's not so bad. That was my sentence the first time around. My advice? Sleep as much as you can. It'll go by way faster."

I looked back at the cot. How in the hell was I going to sleep on that thing? That was obviously the point. They didn't want you to sleep through hell. They wanted you to suffer. A door down the hall slammed.

"Don't say anything," Ray whispered, panic-stricken, and then her face disappeared from the door. I followed suit and backed up to the cot and sat down. With each footstep that echoed closer, my pulse quickened. I rubbed my sweaty palms together and hoped whoever it was wouldn't stop at my door. I didn't take my eyes off of the window, waiting for the person to appear, and when I heard a lock disengage, I jumped, but it wasn't my door. Ray screamed and I ran to the door and watched as the white-uniformed woman entered her cell and slammed the door.

I had to squeeze my ears shut to drown out Ray's cries. My body shook from the physical and emotional strain. It seemed to last for hours, but in reality it might have been a short while. When the screams finally stopped and the door slammed, I thought I was next. I braced myself, rocking back and forth and counting to a hundred, but my door never opened and Ray stayed eerily silent.

"Ray?" I called for the zillionth time, but she never answered. I should have heeded her advice and tried to sleep, but I couldn't. Instead, I paced back and forth trying to wear out the nervous energy that rattled me. I couldn't even guess how much time had passed, but I was finally tired enough to lie on the cot, tucking my hands under my cheek for a makeshift pillow and closed my eyes.

My sleep was filled with screams and the woman in the white coat. Wes popped in and out and so did

Elijah. Everyone was in pain and begging me for help as I watched, helpless, because I was tied to a chair. Loud a clear the woman shoved her black eyes in my face, "Choose wisely," she warned before she walked to a row of people that consisted of everyone I ever cared for: my father and mother, my grandfather, Kendra and Jack, Wes and his family, Elijah, Jasmine and Ray, and then there was a boy and, dammit, if he didn't look like a spitting image of my grandfather when he was that age. My eyes widened with resolution and I struggled against the ropes around my wrists and ankles. I tried to scream, but nothing came out, not even a breath of air. The woman turned to me with a wicked smile, grabbed my brother out of line, and pushed him forward. Tears had fallen down his cheeks and he was shaking with terror. I struggled harder, but the ropes only got tighter. I could feel the burning of my raw skin beneath them, but I still yanked, willing the strength to come to me. When the woman raised a knife to his neck, I screamed out, this time breaking through the silence and waking me from hell.

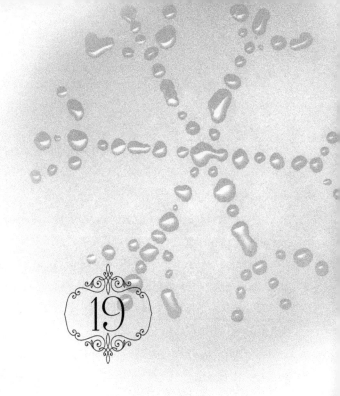

I WOKE ON THE FLOOR, DESPERATELY clinging on to my chest.
*It was just a nightmare. It wasn't real,* though the freshness
still purred against my skull. *How long had I been out?* I slid
my feet in front of me and dragged myself up, using the cot
for leverage. My body felt extremely heavy, and a steady
throbbing rolled around my head making me dizzy. By the
time I made it the door, the earth steadied. I peeked through
the bars and listened carefully for any sounds. When it
seemed like we were alone, I called out to Ray again.

"Ray?" My throat was scratchy and dry. I heard
movement from her cell and, before she spoke, I saw her
fingers wrap around the bars and then her eyes met mine.

"Are you okay?" she asked.

"Me? I should be asking you that. What did that woman do to you?"

"What woman?"

She sounded sincerely confused, as was I. Did I imagine it all?

"I heard you screaming," she added.

"I called out to you for a long time, and you didn't answer," I countered.

"I must have fallen asleep. They don't feed you much here, so I get tired easily. Why were you screaming?"

"I had a nightmare." Another door slammed and I startled, backing quickly away from the door and cowering in the corner as if I could disappear if I made myself small enough. I thought maybe I would get lucky again and the woman wouldn't bother me, but I couldn't be sure she had been here at all. How was it that I was already losing my mind? When my door clicked and opened slowly, I tucked my eyes into my knees and held my breath for whatever was to come next. Something slammed against the ground and the door locked once again. Peeking up, I saw a metal tray with water, bread, and a bowl.

After the footsteps faded, Ray shouted, "Eat it before the rats do."

Rats? I scooped up the tray quickly and placed it on the cot, my eyes searching the dark shadows for anything moving. We were given oatmeal with no spoon, so I lifted the bowl and slurped down the tasteless goop, polished off the bread, and downed the water. If the rats wanted my food they were going to have to eat through me to get it. The thought was horrifying, because what if they did? While I slept. I resolved to never close my eyes in here again.

I left the tray by the door, hoping that would give them no reason to come further into the cell, and I called out to Ray again. "Hey, Ray?"

A moment later, she peered out her bars. "Yeah?"

"Has there been anyone else in here with you?"

"I don't think so."

How could she not know? "What do you mean?"

"Well, I could have sworn I heard someone cough, but I called out and no one answered. It came from the end of the hall somewhere."

That's weird. Maybe someone else was here, but they didn't want to talk to anyone. Or maybe they were planted to spy.

"Why did you ask about a woman?"

I felt stupid telling her now. "It was nothing. I guess it was part of my nightmare." It had to be.

"What was it about?"

"Well, after the woman left you screaming in your cell, I fell asleep and then she was in my cell with everyone I've ever cared about. She told me I had to choose and then she grabbed my—one of them and held a knife to his neck. Then I woke up on the floor."

"I don't think you had a nightmare," Ray responded.

Chills crawled across my skin, and I searched the

darkness again for unwanted critters. "I woke up, so I'm pretty sure I was dreaming."

"That's not what I meant. Yes, you were sleeping, but I think you had a premonition."

The idea stuck to my ribs like the oatmeal. "Why would you say that?" I snapped concerned.

"I'm sorry. I didn't mean to upset you."

I moved away from the door. "Well, you did."

Ray didn't say anything after that, leaving me with my terrible thoughts. What if one of my gifts was telling the future? Maybe not with the precision of a Visionary, but in puzzle pieces. A gift like this could be valuable, but if that was a premonition, then someone I loved would be dying and I would be the one signing their death certificate. I shook off the thought. *It was just a nightmare.*

I couldn't be sure how much time passed and my eyelids were getting impossible to keep open, but I refused to fall asleep in this place again. I paced around the room, noticing etch marks and initials on the walls. Everyone who had been in here left their mark. How they did it was the question. There was nothing sharp in here, and nails wouldn't work on these walls.

I continued around the room, amazed at how many had been confined to this room. One person had been in here for thirty days. I couldn't imagine what they were like when they finally made it out. I circled back to the door, peeking through the bars to see if Ray was moving about, but all was quiet. I felt bad for snapping at her. Just as I opened my mouth to say I was sorry, my foot shifted and kicked the food tray. I picked it up and noticed the metal corners would be perfect for carving. I went to work on the wall, making my initials larger than the ones left before. The one tally mark looked pathetic next to the others and it was mildly amusing that I was embarrassed by it. I should be grateful I was only in here for one day. And I didn't plan on coming back.

And then I heard it. The phantom cough from down the hall. "Ray, did you hear that?"

Her eyes glowed between the bars. "Yeah, at least now I know I'm not imagining things."

"Hello?" I called out loudly.

Silence.

Another cough.

"Are you hurt?" I asked as if anybody in solitary would reply yes. I waited expectantly, but still nothing. "There is definitely someone else here."

Being invisible was my thing after Wes left town and my old clique of mean girls turned on me, but in somewhere like here I would reach out to just about anybody to not feel so alone.

A door slammed, and my gut reaction was to run onto my cot and hide, but then I thought about that cough. It didn't sound good. So I stood up straight and held my ground as the boots neared.

"Step back," a man in black fatigues demanded. He was taller than me by almost a foot and, judging by the lines at the corner of his eyes, he was almost my dad's age. "I said, step back." His fierce brown eyes met mine.

I stepped away from the door. He grabbed the tray, but before he closed the door I muttered, "That person down the hall sounds sick." He ignored me and closed the door. I latched my hands around the bars. "Please. Just check on him or her. I don't think they are well."

He turned his back and went into Ray's cell collecting her tray, too. I was relieved when he headed down the hall. I stuck my ear out the bars as far as I could, but I only heard mumbles. At least he engaged with whoever was down there. A minute later, the man stalked by with three empty trays and cups and, without a glance in mine or Ray's direction, he headed back out.

"Friendly guy." I scoffed.

"That's the most I've heard any of them say. Did you hear anything they said?"

"No. So, you never noticed them bringing food down there or picking up an empty tray?" She had been here for two full days. How could she be so oblivious?

"Honestly, I've been hiding on my cot. I wasn't really paying attention to what was going on. I just assumed since no one responded when I called out that I was alone."

"Well, we most certainly aren't."

"I have a kind of lame idea," Ray said after a few silent moments had passed. "Slide our cots up to the doors and talk. I don't know anything about you, other than you being The Chosen, of course, because everyone knows that."

I exhaled loudly. As if anyone would let me forget it. "Sure," I answered. I pulled my cot over and sat down on it.

"So, you hate being The Chosen that much?"

Her voice was muffled as it crossed the hallway, slithering through the window bars. I didn't want to sound like an ungrateful brat but, "Yeah, pretty much. I only just found about it a few months ago. Before that my life was pretty quiet and simple."

"Wait, what? Your father, a council member, and you being the fifth generation in your family to be with The Order, and he never told you?" She whistled a sound of shock and disappointment. "I am officially mind-blown."

My body burned with betrayal. From what Jasmine had told me, most of these kids knew they would be a fighter with The Order from the time they could talk. A lot of the recruits were not Specials, which I was surprised to find out. The Order did their best to acquire Specials, but most recruits were born into the world. And here I am, the single most important element of The Order, and I hadn't a clue. I knew very little about The Order of the Crest or the non-humans that were out there. I was like a kindergartner attending a high school. I was eons behind everyone else in everything.

"So, what changed his mind?" Ray asked.

When Wes came back to town. That was the pivotal turning point for me. Wes walked back into my life, which forced my dad to ask Elijah to watch over me, and then the inevitable truth about my little brother. It was an avalanche of dominos and they just kept falling. "My dad told me I had a little brother. Four years younger than me. My parents made a trade with The Order. Him for me."

"Holy sh—"

"Yeah."

"But, why would The Order agree to that? Give up The Chosen?" Ray was in a confused state of awe.

"Because they assumed he was The Chosen, not me. There's never been a female. It doesn't really matter because, in the end, they got us both, so they won." I picked at my fingers. Talking about it made me feel all sorts of things I didn't want to feel right now. Not down here. It was depressing enough without my baggage to pile on top.

"Is your boyfriend really a vampire?"

I laughed, remembering how the Hunters reacted when I called them vampires. "No, and yes. They don't call themselves vampires. They eat food and stuff." That came out as lame as it sounded. "How are you holding up without Rick?" I changed the subject to her. I hated talking about myself.

"It's hard. Especially being in here where there's nothing but time to feel sorry for yourself."

That was an epic subject change fail. Neither of us needed to be talking about the boys that got away, or went away, in both of our cases. "What generation are you?"

"Oh, first. I'm one of the gifted they picked up off the side of the road."

"The side of the road? Really?"

"Literally. I was hitchhiking."

"Did you run away?" I didn't even know how old she was, but I assumed she was close to my age.

She laughed. "Maybe if I was a year younger. No, I'm eighteen. I was determined to figure out what was wrong with me, so I left and never looked back."

I sensed an aching bitterness from her. She didn't leave because she wanted to. Not really, anyway. "They didn't understand?"

"That's an understatement. They were so scared of me they sent me off to boarding school as soon as they could. Before that, my grandmother raised me, until she died. She was the only person who didn't look at me like I was a freak."

I knew how that felt, intimately, now. "Do you mind me asking what your gift is?"

The familiar sound of a door opening interrupted us. We both knelt on our cots and peeked out. The guy from earlier marched down with a woman in a white coat. As they passed she turned to me and raised her lips into a wicked grin. It was the woman from my nightmare. I fumbled back on the cot, my heart burning like tires spinning on pavement. I held my chest, closed my eyes, and tried to steady the hyperventilating air in my lungs.

After another sound rushed down the hall I braved another look out the barred window. Army fatigues and a white coat stood on either side of a young boy who couldn't be more than thirteen or fourteen. Even from a distance I could see he was pale and underfed, but as they got closer, I caught something familiar, something so very Rose. The color of one the boy's eyes was lighter than the other. It was so very faint, but it had mesmerized me all my life because my dad had it too. But this boy's eyes were more defined. One was dark like espresso beans and the other light like an amber stone. His gaunt skin struck me next as they dragged him away.

I had just found my brother.

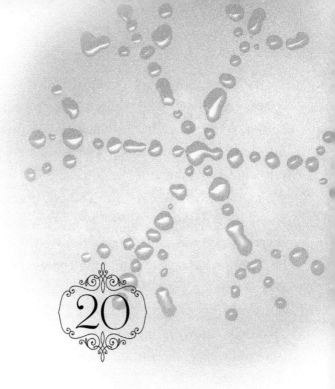

*H*OLY CRAP! PLEASE, DON'T BE imagining this. *Please.* "Ray, did you see that?" My voice was shaky. In fact, my whole body was trembling.

"The boy? Yeah. He looked really sick. I wonder how long he's been down here."

*Thirteen years.* No, it can't be. They wouldn't do that to a kid. *Yes, they would.*

"Abby, what's up?"

My fingers slid from the bars as I stumbled back a few steps. My mind was racing and my heart was aching. And then the fire started. The flares were small at first, behind a couple of ribs, but then the flames erupted, singeing my insides. The thread of fibers connecting my muscles to my brain stem were like a lit fuse of a bomb, sizzling as it ate away all sense of sanity. A scream filled the still cell, and when it finally hit me, I realized it wasn't coming from the surface of my pain. It was being pulled from deep inside my soul. I bent my neck back and opened my mouth wider, releasing it into the universe.

The cell shook and the ceiling began to crumble, showering me with concrete dust. A crack splayed out in several directions and raced across and down the walls. I had stopped screaming, but the energy pulsing from my body continued, wrecking the cell. Big chunks started to fall, and I jumped out of the way, just in time as a large piece fell, hitting the ground hard and exploding. My veins pumped with an uncontrollable fury, even as I took refuge in the corner.

"Abigail, calm down." I finally heard Ray shouting.

"I can't," I yelled back.

"You'll kill us if you don't."

I tucked my knees to my chest and covered my ears, rocking back and forth like an institutionalized whack job. *Calm down.* I slowed the rocking to a steady movement matching the slow breaths I was hoping would settle my restless mind.

"It's working. Whatever you're doing is working."

I took a peek and the cell had stopped shaking and the dust was clearing.

"What the hell was that, Abby? You could have killed us." Ray was pissed.

My cell was covered in concrete dust and rubble, and I

imagined Ray's was, too. *How did I do that?* I pushed myself up and studied the damage. All that power had come from a very dark place inside me. The same one I imagined The Order planned on using to wipe out the non-humans. I was an abomination. I was just like the monsters that ripped Elijah's mom to shreds. The Order was no better, having killed Wes' mother simply because she fell in love with the wrong person. I couldn't let The Order control me. *No one should have this much power.* It kept repeating in my head. And now that I had destroyed solitary they would know how much power I actually had. *Stupid.*

"Abby, are you okay?" Ray's irritation subsided, replaced by genuine concern.

"Yeah, but I don't think my cell is," I joked and she managed a laugh.

"Mine's not looking so great either."

A door slammed open. *Shoot.* Rushed footsteps approached our cells and a set of wicked eyes peered through my bars. It wasn't the woman in the white lab coat or the man in army fatigues. I didn't recognize the woman attached to these eyes, but they made my stomach turn. She unlocked my cell and surveyed the damage. I couldn't tell if I was in trouble or if she was riding a cheap thrill the aftermath of my tantrum had left behind.

"Come with me," she demanded with mild curiosity.

Her fingers wrapped around my arm when I failed to move and she dragged me out of the cell. I caught Ray's terrified stare before the woman yanked me down the hall.

"What about her?" I asked. She couldn't stay in that mess.

"She'll survive."

When the elevator doors opened into the library, the bright fluorescents stung my eyes and I winced, shielding them the best I could. Elijah was waiting for us.

"Get her cleaned up and back in training." She handed my arm over to Elijah and disappeared outside.

"Eli—?"

He put his finger up to stop me and pointed to a camera in the corner by the elevator. I nodded once in understanding and followed him outside. It was night. When I went to solitary, it was late afternoon, so I hadn't been down there as long as it felt.

Elijah led me to the Tree of Solitude and then lifted a wagging finger like I was a three-year-old who had just colored on the wall. "What the hell were you thinking, Abigail?"

"I—"

This time he stopped me with his palm raised as he paced slowly a few steps back and forth. "You have to stop being so careless. They can't see what you are capable of. Not to that capacity." His arm motioned to the library where I had left solitary near ruins.

I waited to try to talk again until I felt he was ready to hear me.

"Well?" He stopped directly in front of me.

"I found him, Eli."

His eyes softened when recognition hit. "Your brother?" he asked softly.

Tears pooled in my eyes. "Yes."

"Is that what all of that was about?"

I ducked my chin. "I'm sorry. I couldn't control myself."

He sighed supportively. "He was down there?"

"Yeah, and he looked like he's been down there for a while. It made me so mad to see him so sick. He looked like a skeleton, Elijah. There's got to be something you can do for him."

He shook his head. "You're mistaking how much leverage I have here, Abby. They tried to have me killed, remember? And Penelope?"

I did remember. It was hard to forget the feeling that sucked me into darkness when I thought I had lost Elijah. "What if you make a deal with the council or something?"

"Why do you think I'm glued to your side, Abby? I already played that card to protect you."

I had no idea. I just figured they wanted him watching me because I was The Chosen. "We can't just leave him like that. If you saw him, you would be horrified."

"How can you be sure it's him?"

I pointed to my eyes. "One eye is lighter than the other, like mine and my dad's. And he looked like my grandfather when he was that age. It's him, Eli." I begged for him to believe me.

He spat something under his breath. "Okay, I'll see what I can do but, in the meantime, you need to lay low and get back to training. Do what they want. They'll be more likely to entertain favors if they think you're compliant."

I nodded excitedly. "Thank you, Elijah." I jumped into his arms, hugging my cheek tightly to his chest. His heart was pounding fiercely, and when I stole a glance up, his eyes burned with something I shouldn't have seen. *Desire.* I pulled away quickly before our bond sucked me into the needs of Elijah. One kiss between us was too many. *I loved Wes.*

"You have a few hours before lineup. Try to get some rest." He took a beat to contemplate something before he gave up and walked down the hill to his building.

What he needed from me I couldn't provide. Not really, anyway. Wes was the other half of me. He always had been. When he was gone, I was lost. No matter how much I tried to fool myself into thinking otherwise, I never got over him leaving. When he came back, when he touched me, my soul ignited, and my heart mended back together. It sounded so cheesy, but there it was. He was the other half of my existence. I would never be whole without him. *Never.*

The shower felt amazing, as if I hadn't showered in months. The stream of water washed away the concrete dust that had layered thickly on my skin. Water was such a powerful element. It had the ability to cleanse so many things and it was vital to sustain life. I had taken it for granted and, now, took it down my throat in greedy gulps. *Would it cleanse the darkness from my soul?* With the power I saw the black void almost like a tunnel with no light at the end, pure darkness where evil resided. Where hatred and revenge thrived.

As I dripped down the hall back to my room, I bumped into Ebony, immediately sensing my power invade me.

"Back already?" she huffed as she went to the shared bathroom and slammed the door closed.

My shoulders relaxed, and I quickly looked around to make sure no one had witnessed what I had done. It was against the rules to use our gifts on each other. I didn't even know where it came from. It was as if something was released in solitary and was now on a rampage. I remembered what Jasmine said. *It's linked to your emotions.* I was a moody, hormonal teenager. How the hell was I going to get my emotions in check before I killed someone?

No one seemed particularly interested in my return. I became invisible again, which was where I felt most comfortable. *Emotionless.* I made it through stick fighting relatively unscathed. I was in Elijah's group, of course, but he didn't go as hard on me as before. Either he was sensing the shift in my energy through our bond or he was sympathetic to my bruised body. I couldn't remember what it felt like to not be in discomfort.

At the end of the day, I caught the glares and whispers from Ebony and her crew, but I ignored them and hurried to dinner. Eating by myself now, I felt the absence of Jasmine the most. I was a walking black plague. Was everyone else afraid of me, or did they just genuinely hate me? I met up with Elijah after dinner.

"Hey," he said carefully, his forehead creased with concern.

"I'm fine." He didn't even have to ask. "Let's just do this." I picked up one of the sticks.

"We aren't doing that today."

"Oh?" I dropped it again and crossed my arms. "What's up, Elijah? First, you take it easy on me in training, and now you don't want to work with me tonight?"

He inhaled a deep breath. "I can feel it, Abby. Your rage. It's concerning me."

"I'm angry they stole my brother and are killing him slowly? Do you blame me?" The ground shook beneath our feet as my skin became red hot.

"Abby, we need to get this under control," he said carefully.

I dropped my arms. With that simple gesture, the ground stood still again. "How?" I asked softly, resigning.

"Meditation. It's technically something you learn in Building Five, but I don't think you can wait that long."

I raised an unbelieving brow. "Meditate?"

"Yes. It will give you the right tools to control your emotions. To focus that energy when you need it most. You can't just lash out at everyone that upsets you."

I challenged him. "Why not? Ebony deserves a taste of her own bitterness and The Order deserves to die for what they are doing to my brother." The leaves on the tree rustled wildly without a hint of breeze in the air.

"It's hard to come back from the darkness, Abby. Trust me. I know."

"But it's not impossible. You seem to be doing just fine. Maybe a visitor pass to the darkness is just what I need to show these people who they are really dealing with."

"We don't even know what you are, Abby. Let's just explore the possibilities before you go Hulk smashing everything, okay?"

It was unusual but, for the first time, I could sense that Elijah was scared of me. I think that's what got me to listen. I never wanted him or anyone else I loved to be afraid of me.

We sat cross-legged knee to knee.

"Until you gain some control, I want you to absorb mine."

"What?" I was stunned. I had never tried to absorb anything before. "How?"

"Do you feel me?"

"Yes," I replied.

"Describe it."

I concentrated on the waves of energy grabbing hold of me. "Some sadness?"

He grunted, "What else? Push past the surface."

I searched deeper and found a purity so profound it made me ache with longing. "What is that?" I asked with astonishment.

"That's the pure part of me. The part I protect from

everyone. It's how I do what I do and not feel the darkness pulling me under."

"It's so beautiful."

"How does it make you feel?"

"At peace," I admitted wistfully. The only time I had ever felt like this was with Wes and yet, somehow, I had found it on my own, with Elijah's help, but it wasn't mine. It was his. "I want it." Elijah laughed, and I opened my eyes, connecting with his. "Why is that funny?"

"Because you already have it. Everyone does, but it's hard to find. Some will spend a lifetime trying to access it and never succeed."

"How did you do it?" I craved his energy that teased me like when Wes would brush his lips against mine before giving me all of him.

He adverted his glance from me. "I didn't have a choice. It was either find peace or kill until I was killed."

"I'm sorry. No one should lose their mom like you did."

"And my dad," he added.

The shift in energy was palpable. I had ruined the mood.

"It wasn't immortals that killed him." When he looked back at me, a fierceness had emerged and the purity I felt from him disappeared. "The Order had him killed," he growled.

I wished I could say I didn't believe they would do that, but I knew they would do anything if it meant getting closer to killing all the non-humans. It was ironic that, in the process, they were turning into monsters. The only comfort

I could provide Elijah right now was placing my hand on his knee. I shouldn't have been surprised when his energy instantly shifted and I could feel his purity again. "Am I…?" I didn't finish the sentence because I already knew.

"When I touched you in the forest, after the accident, that's when I found it."

His honesty poured off him like a waterfall over the edge of the world. It was his truth. *His secret*. Wes was my anchor to the light, and I was Elijah's. It was the darkest of fairytales, where not everyone could win, and someone would fall so deep you wouldn't recognize them when they returned. It was my premonition wrapped in a horrifically messy ball. I would choose who would be saved, and the others would be condemned to something far worse than death.

I was both savior and executioner.

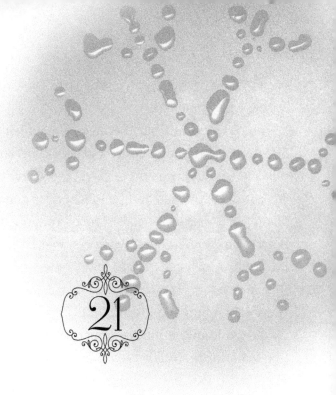

<figure>21</figure>

THE SILENCE BETWEEN ELIJAH and me was confining, like being thrown into a room with no windows or doors. I cleared my throat and broke the link that had bound us in that room. "You know, this feels a lot like the first time I met you. Super …"

"Intense," he finished my sentence.

"Close enough." Saying this was awkward probably wouldn't have been the best choice of words right now. After all, he just bared his soul to me. Literally. "How did you find out about your dad?" I could tell by the slight stretch of his back that he was contemplating whether to tell me the truth or not.

"It's not important how I found out. I believe what I've

been told, so being here, working with The Order, isn't easy for me," he grumbled.

But Elijah would stay because of me. I felt both grateful and guilty at the same time, and selfish because if he tried to leave, I would beg him to stay. "I'm sorry."

His eyes softened and he touched his hand to my knee. "Don't be. Look, we need to focus on your training. You need to be your strongest when it's time. Don't worry about me. I will do what is necessary."

Once again, his touch had bewitched me, my body leaning into him and his into mine. His green eyes were so close I could make out the amber speckles floating around like stars in the Milky Way galaxy. It felt so natural and pure, but it was only a manifestation of our bond. I could never trust the raw feelings that flowed so freely between us. *And I loved Wes.* The constant reminder replayed like a broken record.

"We need to find a source for you that isn't tied to anything physical. You need to be able to access it no matter what the circumstance. It'll be harder to find, but it will be invaluable. The universe is made up of pure untouched energy. It's the source for witches, like Jasmine, and others. Only one human has been known to tap into it."

I thought for a moment. He was referring to a state of peace and bliss. "Are you talking about the Dalai Lama?"

He shook his head. "Go back even further. Siddhartha. He was the true Buddha."

I had heard of Siddhartha before in my philosophy

class, but it was so brief I didn't remember much past the fact that he was on a quest of enlightenment, somehow accomplished it, and then became known as Buddha.

"It was only when Siddhartha went on his own did he reach the core of his inner being. He found it while meditating under a *ficus religiosa* in India."

"Are you suggesting that I go to India and sit under a ficus tree?" Elijah's laugh was a welcome break in the tension. I even joined him, because it did sound ridiculous.

He raised a pointed finger. "You're under one."

I lifted my chin and looked at the Tree of Solitude with a new pair of lenses. "Seriously?"

"Yep. A *ficus religiosa.* The Order has been waiting for you, Abigail, far before you were even born. This tree was planted as a seed over a century ago."

I had always thought it was a strange looking tree, out of place here. It looked like a bonsai tree with its twisted up mess of a trunk, but it was so massive and I had never seen one so big before. "How is it thriving here? I thought those types of trees hated the cold?"

"Magic," he answered simply.

*Of course.* "And here I thought it was just a weird looking oak tree."

"Definitely not."

"So if they believe this tree is going to help me find the core of who I am, the Chosen, then why aren't they monitoring it with cameras?"

"They can't."

"Magic," I answered my own question.

"That and they have superstitious beliefs that anything modern, or not natural, will affect its purity. And your dad knew it because he was in the Inner Circle, so he used it to his advantage."

"Wow." My head shook in disbelief at all the things out there that I could never have imagined.

"It's also why they don't question when you disappear from the cameras over here. They want you here."

It made me feel slightly dirty doing something The Order favored. "What you're saying is this is *my* tree?"

"In a nutshell, yes, it was brought here for the Chosens. This will be your source. Once you find it, you won't need anything or anyone to access your purity."

The pressure of it all made my stomach turn. What if I failed? "If I reach Nirvana, wouldn't it be going against enlightenment by murdering?"

"Nirvana is pure, non-humans are not. They are tainted by the supernatural, which has been long believed to be rooted in evil."

"Pure humans," I added finally understanding what The Order was trying to do and why they had failed over the centuries. They needed pure light to cleanse the darkness. They needed me. Anxious tingles immediately raced through me and I jumped up. "I can't, then. I can't reach nirvana. I'll become a murderer."

"You'll become a purifier," an unfamiliar voice announced.

Elijah jumped up as I spun around to face our eavesdropper. I didn't recognize him, but by the vexed look on Elijah's face, he did. He was a tall grey-haired man with a white mustache and tanned skin. He covered his thin frame with a long black trench coat, his hands tucked in the pockets.

"Don't be so alarmed. I'm only observing."

I looked to Elijah quizzically.

"Observing what?" Elijah asked carefully.

"The facility. It's been a long time since I've walked the grounds, and I thought today would be a wonderful time. The sun is shining, and everyone seems to be enjoying the last days before snowfall." He looked to me. "Are you enjoying yourself, Miss Rose?" His eyebrow rose suspiciously.

"I guess?" How could anyone say they were enjoying getting their asses kicked every day?

The man looked over to Elijah. "Is something the matter?"

Elijah shook his head, "No, sir."

He studied us both curiously and cracked a small smile. "Splendid," he said more cheerfully as he clapped his hands together once dramatically and strolled away. Elijah and I stood stiffly, watching him, and then spoke once he was out of earshot.

"What was that?" I inquired.

"Or who?" He looked troubled.

"It kind of seemed like you knew him."

"I'm familiar with his outline."

"His what?"

Elijah snapped out of whatever trance he had been stuck in and clarified. "It's hard to explain, but I'll try. Have you heard of blind people being able to see vibrations of sound?"

I was a little embarrassed to admit I knew nothing about blind people so I just shrugged my shoulders.

"I see sound waves in the dark, and I know that man from a council meeting. They stay hidden in shadows like the tribunal, but I have memorized all of them."

Imagining Elijah with such an ability was hard to wrap my head around. "And you are sure he's one of them?" The man chatted with some recruits a little ways away.

"Positive. Each person has a unique vibration and color."

I wondered what I looked like to him. It made me a little self-conscious but mostly intrigued. "Is it normal for them to just walk around like this?"

"Not at all, but notice how he didn't introduce himself? He's still taking a huge risk. It doesn't take a genius to figure it out."

The man twisted toward us and smiled. "He can't hear us, can he?" If Elijah could see in the dark, there was no reason not to believe this man could hear from long distances.

"If he could, then he would know that you've reached nirvana."

I rolled my head to him and was about to say something

when he gave me a look that said to be quiet. He was watching to see if the man reacted, but he made no indication that he had heard. "I don't like this." I suddenly felt more exposed than before, which I thought was impossible.

"The tree is a dead zone for everything. The magic will shield us, remember? Let's stay close to it when we talk from now on."

I nodded. I was ready to pitch a tent under the tree, if it meant I would be invisible.

"That's probably why they sent a council member out. You've been spending a lot of time at the tree and it puts you off the grid."

All of the compiling truths about this place were overwhelming. "I think I need to go to bed." My head was hurting and I just needed to lie down. I took a few steps when Elijah grabbed my hand.

"Abigail, I know all of this has been a lot, but you need to figure out a way to deal with all of it so we can get to work."

His voice was kind, but urgent. "I know how important this all is. The gravity of all of this is not lost on me. But I'd be lying if I said it wasn't affecting me. I'll find a way, though." I gave him a reassuring smile and headed down to Building Two. It was still an hour before curfew, so the grounds were busy, and the building hallway was deserted. I just wanted to wash up and go to bed. I grabbed my clothes and toiletries from my room and stepped back in the hallway only to be face-to-face with the council member we saw at the tree. I dropped my stuff, not expecting to be confronted in the hallway.

"I'm sorry. I didn't mean to frighten you."

He bent down and gathered my things while I stood frozen in fear. *What a warrior.* I did an internal eye roll. When he handed everything over, I took them without saying a word. What the hell was I supposed to say? Stalk much?

"How are you getting along, Miss Rose?" He clasped his hands in front of him and straightened his spine.

"Aside from being thrown in solitary? Fabulous," I replied sharply.

"Ah, yes. You made quite a mess for us to clean up."

I scrunched in guilt. "Is Ray okay?" I asked since we were on the subject about solitary.

"Your friend is fine. She was moved to another location while we clean up. Now, tell me, how are you feeling?" He dragged out *feeling* to emphasize the subliminal context of his question.

"I'm a little angry and very tired," I lifted my bathroom stash, "which is why I was trying to go to bed early."

"I see." He seemed disappointed. "Then I will be on my way."

As he turned to leave, I grabbed his arm to stop him. "Wait…" I dropped it immediately when my hand burned. I tried not to react, coughing instead to cover up what I had just felt in case he knew that I could feel when someone wasn't human.

"Yes?" he asked with a curious but seemingly unknowing eyebrow.

I almost forgot what I was going to ask him. My heart pounded so hard I was afraid my voice would shake when I spoke, but it didn't. "When I was in solitary there was a very sick boy. Is he okay?"

He studied me for a moment and then said, "He is recovering in the basement infirmary."

Remembering how dire his situation was returned the heat to my insides. I wanted to make them all pay. "Can I visit him?"

He squared his body to me again and smiled, but it wasn't kindness that radiated from his mouth, it was evil. "You are quite the sympathizer, aren't you? I have a proposition for you."

I didn't like where this was going. They knew he was my brother, but I couldn't let on that I knew. When I didn't respond, he continued.

"I'll let you visit the little boy if you tell me where our little friend Jasmine got off to."

He knew I had let her escape, which meant they all knew. The nausea roiled in my stomach and fear weakened my muscles.

He leaned down, his eyes lined up with mine, and with a growl behind his words he said, "I want her back. Do you take us for fools? You can't hide from us. We know everything that happens here. Everything. Break the rules again and it will be Elijah who suffers. We know he helped cover up your little escape, giving us every authority to punish him how we see fit. Remember that."

My hands were shaking by the time he stood up and walked down the hallway.

He turned around and added, "As for the boy, I will let you see him as a sign of good faith to show you we are all on the same side."

I jumped when the door slammed, leaving me alone in the hallway once again. I needed to warn Elijah that he had been made, and also tell him that the council member was not human. I rubbed my tingling hand and hoped that the man didn't feel what I had.

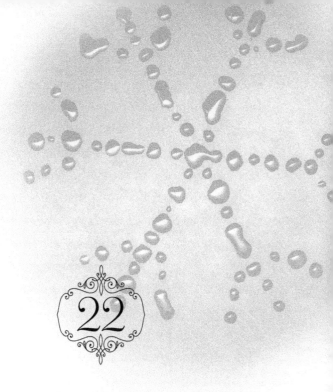

I ABANDONED MY BATHROOM stash to try to find Elijah, buzzing his building an annoyingly amount of times to no avail. I knew the man was watching me from somewhere, but it wasn't like he told me I couldn't tell anyone he had confronted me in my building. No one would flinch at it anyway. We endured a lot worse here.

After about thirty minutes of running around the grounds like a mental escapee, I washed up and slipped into bed, not that I could fall asleep. My brain was too full of promised threats. They knew I had helped Jasmine and Caleb escape, and they didn't reprimand me or throw me in solitary again for it. Yet, they had punished me for the petty fight with Ebony. That was in front of a crowd, though. They had no choice. No one else knew I was involved in Jasmine's escape. I needed to be more cautious about everything and trust no one. Elijah was my only exception.

When I finally fell asleep, I dreamt about Jasmine and Caleb. It was a good dream. They had made it away from the facility and were in hiding somewhere far away from everyone. It was the only thing that gave me peace the next several weeks as I trained hard to get through Building Two. Elijah didn't say much about the council members knowing I had helped Jasmine and Caleb escape and that he helped cover it up. I knew he was worried, but there wasn't much either of us could do about it. We were volunteer prisoners. Elijah was here to protect me, and I was here for my brother.

The tall man had promised I could visit him, but I hadn't heard a peep until a week into Building Three when he stood at the edge of the pool, surprising me as I popped my head out of the water after doing a strenuous amount of laps. Elijah was close by, watching the exchange carefully.

"Miss Rose, I see you have no trouble with swimming." He smiled, bearing slightly stained teeth and a silver crown. He was wearing his long trench coat again with his hands comfortably tucked in the pockets.

My fingers gripped on to the side of the pool as I caught my breath. It was a great excuse for remaining silent, too.

"I promised you a visit with the boy. Would now be a bad time?" he challenged.

I looked around apprehensively as the others watched us. No matter what I did, I couldn't avoid being the center of attention. "It's perfect. I just need a minute to get dressed."

"I'll be waiting outside," he said as he walked away.

I pushed myself out of the pool, grabbing my towel off the bench and quickly drying off, avoiding eye contact with the spectators.

"What did he want?" Elijah stood anxiously in front of me.

"To bring me to my brother," I responded as I wrapped the towel around myself and walked to the locker room.

Elijah stayed close on my heels. "Are you sure you're ready for that?"

I spun around, surprised by his question and a little angry. "Ready?" I lowered my voice when the sharpness of my tone attracted some active listeners close by. "Eli, this is what I've been waiting for, playing along so I can find him." He took my elbow and moved me to a deserted corner.

Elijah let go and scrubbed his face.

"What's wrong?" My excitement was quickly fading as I watched Elijah's normally calm exterior turn stiff.

"Your brother has been with The Order his whole life, Abby. They are his family. It's likely he doesn't even know he has a family outside of that."

"So? I'll tell him. I'll tell him everything." I was getting agitated. I needed to get dressed and get outside before the man changed his mind.

"Abigail, you aren't thinking straight. If you tell him everything, you are going to shock his mental state into who knows what. You can't just erase his whole life with one revelation. He might not even believe you or want to believe you. He could be a basket case for all you know or The Order could have planted him here to control you more. There are too many variables, and we are going in completely blind." The panic had risen in his voice.

"I understand what you're saying but, in the end, he's still my brother." I took his hand in mine, feeling the immediate buzz tingle up my arm. "I promise I'll be careful. I'll feel him out first and see where it takes me. Okay?"

His eyes softened as he nodded. Before he released me, he squeezed my hand then stepped out of the way.

"Thank you," I said as I rushed into the locker room. I dressed quickly in my orange uniform and red chucks, and pulled my wet hair back into a messy knot. As I rushed by the pool, I felt the stares, but didn't address them. I would never win with the other recruits, so I stopped trying.

Ray grabbed me just before I flew out the door. "Where are you going?"

"Hey." I wasn't sure what to tell her. When she got out of solitary she had pretty much avoided me. This was the first time she had talked to me directly. "I have to go."

"Be careful," she said as I slipped out of the building.

She looked worried. I thought she was mad at me for getting her locked up in the first place, but maybe she was just traumatized by whatever they did to her, because I hadn't seen her interacting with anybody unless she had to. Now I felt like a jerk for being so wrapped up in my round-the-clock training that I hadn't made more of an effort to check in with her.

The man stood with his back to me as I approached slowly. It was a cloudy day, the threat of the first winter storm approaching. From what I had heard, it wasn't a particularly big one, but the chilly breeze still made me shiver.

"Walk beside me," he demanded, evenly-toned.

I did as I was I told, but it was hard for my shorter legs to keep up even with his slow pace. I followed him down the hill to where the unmarked building was hidden behind Building Four where I had discovered Elijah was still alive. It was one of the best days of my life, and my body shivered again, this time because of the kiss we shared after our reunion.

The man scanned his thumb and the door unlocked. I remembered the unassuming entry with only an elevator. He pressed the button to open the elevator doors and stepped in first. I rushed in and stood as far from him as possible.

"I don't bite despite what others might say."

"Nobody says anything. I don't even know who you are." My stomach tightened. I knew he wasn't human because it burned when I touched him previously, so it could be entirely possible that he did bite.

"Shall we rid the elephant in the elevator? I *am* human." He looked down at the hand that had touched him.

A million questions jumped around my mind, but I couldn't decide which one I should ask first.

"I am a gifted individual much like your friend, Jasmine."

"So, you're a witch." It made sense now. When Jasmine had touched me I had hurt her, but I had thought it was because she got in between me and the non-human.

"Yes." He smiled proudly. "I yield the power of the elements, and I have for almost a century now." He looked old, but not a hundred years old. "My gift affords me more time than humans. If your friend had stayed, she would have learned how to harness her youth, as well." He lifted his chin sharply, facing the elevator door.

Before I could respond, the doors opened and we were in the infirmary. He stopped outside of the bathroom. I already knew what to do so I rushed in, put on the blue scrubs and rejoined him in the hallway. "How come you don't need to wear this?" I waved at my sea of blue.

"Because I am not going any farther. I will be waiting for you here." He dipped his head once and then raised his eyes past me. The woman from solitary was coming toward us, and I suddenly felt safer with the man. "She will bite." He bent down and whispered in my ear with a tinge of humor in his voice.

"Follow me," the woman said with an unfriendly tone.

She ushered me by several rooms. The doors were open, but the curtains were pulled across the room so I couldn't see who inhabited each one. The only sounds that filled the space were my booties against the cold tile floor and the beeps of hospital machines. She stopped in front of a door and said, "You have ten minutes," and continued down the hall.

It wasn't until now that reality hit me. Just behind the curtain was my little brother. Tears were already pooling in my eyes, and I wondered how I would get through this without breaking down.

"Hello?" a young, weak voice called out gently at first. "I know you're there," he added brusquely.

I inched my way into the room and around the curtain. I wished I could close the door, but the camera at the corner of the ceiling confirmed there would be no privacy anyway. My brother was layered under white hospital sheets, but he wasn't attached to any machines. On the bed next to him a book was open and upside down to hold his place. It made me smile knowing he enjoyed something I did. I fixated on his unusual eye trait that ran in our family, and only when he cleared his throat did I say something.

"Hi." I waved a lazy hand. Not the first thing I imagined saying to him the first time we met. It was much more profound when it played out in my head.

"Hey." His eyebrows came together tightly in confusion. "Why are you here?"

He seemed more annoyed than grateful to have company. "I was in solitary with you. I told them how sick you sounded."

He crossed his arms in front of his chest. "Yeah, so?"

Not the friendliest kid on the planet, but I knew it was just a defense, because it was also very much like me, too.

"I was worried." I took a step toward the bed, running my finger along the sheet near his feet.

He raised his arms and stretched them out like a bird getting ready for flight. "As you can see, I'm fine."

There was something hidden deep within his words. A sadness I was also familiar with. He was putting up a front, and I wondered how much it had to do with the camera. I walked around the bed and stood close to his head, my thighs leaning against the mattress and my head blocking the view of the camera. "Is that better?" His eyes wandered to where the camera was and nodded. My instincts were right. "Is there audio?"

"No."

"Are you sure?"

"Yes. One day I was screaming for help and no one came. Not until I threw myself out of bed so they could see I needed them."

The thought of him being ignored when he needed someone made my skin heat with anger. "You would think they'd have a button to press like in hospitals."

"You would think," he said sharply. "Now, who are you, and why are you here?" He eyed me suspiciously. "And why would they let you in a high security building?"

Where did I begin? I wanted to spill the truth like a knocked over glass of water, but I couldn't. I didn't know where his mental state was or if he was put in my path by The Order on purpose. "Are you here against your will?"

He laughed, and it sounded so much older than his

thirteen years, but he did look better. His face was fuller and his eyes were clear of the red spider-like veins. "Right now it would appear so."

I huffed in frustration. "I want to help."

His eyes scanned the room. "I am being helped."

"Why are you being so difficult? I don't have much time."

"Why do you care?" he snapped back.

I bit back the urge to say too much. He wasn't very forthcoming with … well, anything. "Why were you in solitary?"

"Same reason you were. I broke the rules."

"How long were you down there?"

His body shifted under the sheets. "I don't know." He let his wall down ever so slightly. His voice was strained and he turned away from me.

I placed a hand on his shoulder and he turned back to me. He squinted when he looked back at me, studying my eyes with more fervor than before. "One of your eyes is lighter than the other."

"Just like yours," I confirmed, one side of my mouth lifting, satisfied with the confirmation that we had to be related.

I wasn't sure if he quite understood what that meant, because the woman came rushing back into the room, interrupting us. She looked up at the camera and then back to us.

"Time's up."

"You said ten minutes," I protested, but she didn't budge.

"I didn't catch your name." I was still at his side.

"Asher."

"I'm Abigail. Abigail Rose." I watched for some sort of reaction that might hint that he knew who I was or what I might be to him, but he didn't even blink.

"Now," the woman barked.

"I'll see you around." I didn't really know if I'd ever see him again, but I was determined to find a way. I wouldn't let this be the only time I saw my brother. I trailed the woman out of the room, but just before I stepped out, Asher called after me.

"Hey, Abigail?"

I twisted quickly toward him. "Yeah?"

"I *will* see you around."

He said it with such conviction I knew he had a plan. It might have had something to do with why he was in solitary in the first place, and it left me with renewed hope.

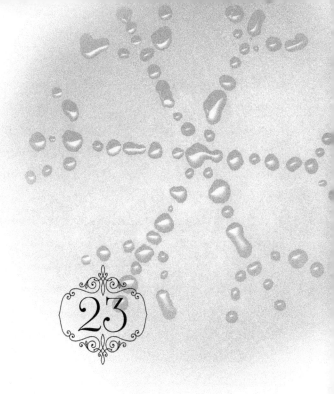

## 23

THE MAN WAS WAITING FOR me at the elevator. "Did you find what you were looking for?" He pressed the button and asked without bothering to look in my direction.

"Maybe." He couldn't possibly expect me to trust him. I had no intention of telling him anything.

We stepped into the elevator and remained silent on the way up. I figured we were done, so I rushed out when the door opened.

"I need Jasmine back," he called before I made it to the double doors.

I stopped and turned back to him. "I honestly don't know where she is."

With each step he took toward me my heart leapt, and

when he stopped just a step away, I felt a wave of dizziness from his fury.

"You touched her, so you can find her," he hissed.

Was he saying I could track her like Elijah could with me? "I ... I've never done that. I don't know how." And now my hands were shaking, but not because I was afraid of him, but because I feared he was right and I would put Jasmine and Caleb in danger.

"Good thing you know someone who can teach you," he spat. "You have two weeks. There's a special meeting she needs to attend." He walked outside and left me to ponder how the hell I was going to get out of this one.

I rushed back to the pool, but Elijah wasn't there, so I raced up the hill to the tree. He was pacing and talking under his breath. When he looked up at me, relief washed away the worry that had plagued him.

"Are you okay?" He closed the distance between us, pulling me close to the tree and hugging me tightly. I felt safe in his arms. I was starting to fear I might die at the facility.

"I'm fine."

He pulled me away, keeping his hands securely on my shoulders. "But there's something. What is it?"

I sat down at the base of the tree. "For starters, my brother's name is Asher."

"Happy," Elijah commented.

"Huh?"

"His name means happy. Fitting, I guess."

"How so?" I asked curiously.

"Your name means joy. And both of your names start with A."

It made me wonder if my dad had named him before he turned him over, but he would have told me. It would have made finding my brother a whole lot less complicated. It's not like I could ask my dad or the council about it, so I left it alone. "He looks much better, but there was a camera in his room, so we couldn't really talk. He noticed my eyes, though, so I'm hoping he'll put it all together." I pulled at the hem of my orange uniform.

"What aren't you telling me?" He squatted so that he was eye level.

"They want Jasmine back, and the man seemed determined." He was more than determined, but I didn't want to worry Elijah. He did enough of that. "He said that I could find her." I peered up slightly to gauge his reaction. He seemed less than thrilled.

"Like, track her?" He seemed to consider the possibility.

"He seemed pretty positive that I could. What am I, Elijah? Do I have no limits?" It scared me to think I had so much power and no idea how it worked or how to control it.

He pinched the bridge of his nose and suddenly looked ten years older.

"There's more," I admitted.

He sighed. "Of course, there is."

"He gave me two weeks to retrieve her. He said there's

some big meeting she needs to be at." His hand dropped from his face, and his eyes widened in understanding. "You know something."

"Nothing you need to be concerned about."

"Like hell I don't. Jasmine is my friend. If I bring her back and that puts her in danger, then it's definitely my concern." I was fuming. "No secrets, remember?"

"Right." He shook his head once. "Twice a year, the leaders of the each state and country come here for a summit. One in January and one in July."

"Why would they need Jasmine at a summit meeting?"

"I don't know." Elijah rubbed his chin. "They are closed meetings, and I've never heard of recruits being invited. Unless …"

"What?" My muscles seized up.

"Unless she's on trial for something."

"Like helping an immortal escape?" *Then wouldn't I be guilty, too?*

"I don't think so. They would handle that like the tribunal with Penelope. It has to be something bigger that would affect The Order's security. What do you know about her? Where she comes from and her powers?"

I shook my head, trying to think of anything spectacular. "Not much. She suspected her father was a visionary like her and that's what made him go crazy and kill her mom."

"She's a Visionary?" His voiced pitched high.

"You didn't know that?"

"No, I didn't. I thought she was just a witch." He

frowned. "Something must have happened to the current Visionary."

"What does that mean?"

He stood up. "It means they need her or else we are going to war blind. I hate to say this, but the man is right. You need to bring her back. We don't stand a chance without her."

"So now we want to go to war for The Order?" I pulled my knees into my chest, wrapping the guilt securely around my body like plastic wrap around a vegetable. How could I do that to her? She was only thirteen and just wanted a normal life. And I was the one who pushed her to go.

Elijah knelt back down. "We won't be fighting for the same reasons as The Order." He placed a hand on my knee. "I know you care for her, but she won't be in danger here. They will protect her at all costs. *We* will protect her." His words were soft and comforting.

I knew very little about this war except that I was an integral part of it. And so was Jasmine. I trusted Elijah, and I knew we would both do what it took to keep her safe. "Okay," I agreed. "Show me how to find her."

He sat down across from me in meditative form, so I did the same. "Do you remember when you might have bonded with Jasmine?"

I nodded. "When we were outside the gates and the non-human attacked us. She accidentally touched me when I was … when I killed it. I hurt her."

"What did you feel from her when that happened?"

There was so much going on, and I was so upset, it was hard to separate the two events. "Lonely," I said sadly. "She felt alone and scared."

I could see he empathized with me. "That is the source of your bond. Close your eyes and imagine it's a rope. Follow it until you reach her on the other end."

Inside my thoughts, a rope was tied snuggly around my waist, the other end out of sight. The darkness around me faded into a street of high-rise buildings. It was cold and wet, but still light out.

"Do you see anything?" Elijah's words joined me in the open space inside my head.

I nodded. "I'm in a city, and it's raining."

"Do you see any street signs?"

I walked down the pavement until I reached a corner, but the sign was blurry and I couldn't read it. I kept walking, unable to make out any words on the buildings either. "I can't read anything. All the words are blurry or jumbled."

"That's normal. You're new at this. It takes time to learn to see everything clearly. Focus on the things you do know. You are in a major city with high-rise buildings. What else do you see?"

Tents appeared along the sidewalks, glistening in the rain. A woman in damp clothes pushed a shopping cart slowly down the street. "I think I'm in a homeless community." I followed the woman until I was standing outside of what appeared to be an abandoned building. The broken windows were boarded up, and the door was cracked open. I pulled the door open and went inside. It was dark and the carpet was old and dirty. "Why can't I smell anything?"

"You aren't really there. The only sense will be sight."

When I opened the door, I realized I didn't feel the push on my fingers. Not having sensations was somewhat disconcerting. I continued down a hallway. It looked like this place used to be an office building. A woman cradled a baby in a small room with a trash bag spilling clothes on the floor and a mattress pushed against the far wall. I could tell the baby was crying by the way she rocked it in her arms. As I continued down the hall I noticed some doors were closed to rooms while others were open and occupied. These must have been the lucky ones, having some privacy and security.

There was a set of stairs, so I climbed them although it felt more like I was floating. When I reached the top I saw more offices, but a large metal door with a sign stole my attention. It appeared to be a roof access door. I went through it and up the stairs to the open air of the gloomy day. It looked to have been under construction before it was abandoned. Unfinished studs and plastic sheeting made up an enclosed area. I pulled the plastic aside and walked deeper inside. It was surprisingly sheltered inside, and the space was large. I followed a flickering light and found Jasmine and Caleb standing next to a fire set inside a metal trash can.

"I found them," I announced. "They are in an abandoned

building on the roof." Jasmine smiled as Caleb's body shook with laughter. They were happy.

"She went home," Elijah stated.

I opened my eyes, squinting against the harsh light of the day. "How do you know?"

"Because that's where I found her."

Recognition sank in like a boulder in water. "You were the one who took her?"

"I helped gather recruits. She was one of them. I didn't know it was Jasmine, though. She was lying in a pool of blood, and she was dirty. She was unrecognizable." He stood up.

"Where are you going?"

"To Los Angeles."

I jumped up. "Just like that?"

"Yeah. I need to get there before they move on."

"What are you going to do with Caleb?" The council man hadn't said anything about him.

Elijah thought for a moment and said, "I'll leave him. I won't hurt him. I promise."

"He's not just going to let you take her. They have a bond, Elijah."

He shrugged. "That will make it more difficult, but I have to bring her back. I'll make him understand."

"Okay."

"Okay? That's it? No arguing?"

He seemed almost surprised. "Be careful," is all I said and he left quickly down to his building. All I could do was

I hope I had done that right thing and that Jasmine would forgive me.

I stayed at the tree for a while trying to get back to Jasmine and Caleb, but the scenery only kept fading in and out. It almost seemed as if Elijah's presence increased my power. Or maybe it just gave me more confidence? My head dropped to the ground where I had buried the key and the charm. I hadn't tried to go back to the library since the incident with Ray, and now that I knew they were watching every move I made, I wasn't so sure it was smart to bother. But maybe if I knew when the summit was, they would be so distracted I could find a way. It seemed like a good plan any way.

"Abigail?" Ray had quietly made her way over.

"Ray, hi." My voice was unsure. This was the first time we had been in contact outside of the training. I was too much of a coward to confront her after everything that happened.

"Can I sit with you?"

"Please." I smiled.

Words escaped us for a few moments, but then she broke the silence.

"I need to tell you something." She fumbled nervously with her fingers.

"Me, too." I wanted to apologize so many times, but I didn't know how.

"Can I go first?" she pleaded softly.

I nodded. I was surprised when a tear fell from her eye. "What's wrong?"

"I lied to you in solitary. That woman did come into my cell and she did things to me, to my head. It hurt so much." She folded an arm over her stomach, grasping the other one tightly.

It looked as if she was reliving the whole nightmare. "Why did you lie?"

"They made me. They wanted to scare you into obedience."

"Oh." They were using the others to keep me under control even if it meant hurting them. My body weakened slightly, thinking how far they would go to make me do their bidding. "I'm so sorry, Ray. I had no idea they would do that."

"I know, Abby. It's not your fault. I was just in the wrong place at the wrong time."

*With me*, I thought. I was a plague on others. They were smart to keep their distance and ostracize me. "What about the dream I had? Did you lie about that, too? That it could be a vision?"

She shook her head. "No. I wish it wasn't true, but I really think it was a vision."

Her eyes met mine with such grief I wanted to run away. I could never choose which of my friends and family to save. I wouldn't. "You're risking a lot by telling me all this."

She looked up at the tree. "I know what this tree is. I know they can't see or hear me."

"How did you know?" I was under the impression it was The Order's best kept secret.

"It's my gift. I can read thoughts."

When I realized she was talking about *my* thoughts, I shifted uncomfortably. "Oh." I swallowed hard.

"I promise I won't tell anyone about you and Elijah."

My heart stopped beating for just a fraction of a second. "What do you mean?"

"I know how you feel about each other. Underneath all the chaos and rules. It's ok. It's not my secret to shed."

My mind raced through all the thoughts I had about Elijah. They conflicted and collided with my feelings for Wes and, most of the time, it was such a jumbled knot of strings I didn't know what I really felt, but somehow Ray had seen through it all and understood.

"I …" my voice choked on the revelation and I started again. "I can't talk about that."

"And I don't expect you to. It's none of my business, and I wish I could control it better. That's why I'm here. All my life it's felt like a migraine of complaints and anger and pain. I could barely get out of bed most days. And then they found me and told me they could teach me how to control it through discipline. And it's working. It's not as bad as it used to be."

The way she was talking reminded me of what my father had said about The Order before their motives changed. It was a sanctuary and a place where those who were different could not only learn to survive, but thrive with their gifts. It all sounded so magical. It killed me to think that if we destroyed The Order all those kids would be alone again, running from life rather than embracing it like Elijah had done after his father was killed.

"Thank you," I said with confidence.

"For what?" Her confusion was more than warranted.

"For reminding me that some things are worth saving." Elijah and I had talked about destroying The Order, but it didn't need to be destroyed. It needed to revisit its roots. The council members needed to be reminded of why The Order was founded and how much good it had done over the centuries. The Order of the Crest needed to be reborn, and the summit was the perfect opportunity to make them all see that.

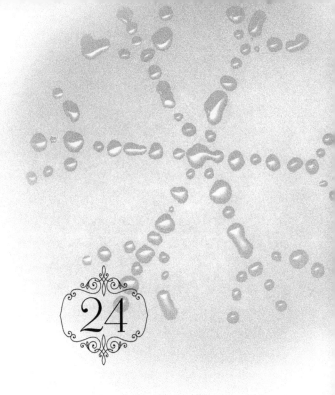

24

IWASN'T SURE WHAT I EXPECTED when Elijah left to find Jasmine, but when a few days turned into a week, and then another week with the summit only a day out, I began to worry. I tried to find Elijah like I had found Jasmine, using our bond as a guide, but he was somehow blocking me. Like he didn't want me to see him. I asked around, but no one knew anything. Even Jack was in the dark. I made it through Building Three and was now wearing yellow for Building Four. My eyes were practically glazed over with every horrible scenario imaginable about what could have possibly happened to Elijah, when he stepped into the wrestling ring. I almost stepped out of line to jump in his arms when I remembered I was surrounded by several dozen peers. I jostled enough that those close to me took notice. I stiffened up again and tried to wipe the exuberance from my face.

Elijah demonstrated several moves and paired us off to practice. I was disappointed when he didn't pair off with me and, instead, seemed to be avoiding me altogether. Did something go wrong and he was afraid to tell me? Was Jasmine hurt? It was nearly impossible to concentrate, and my partner, whom I hadn't met before, bested me several times.

"Are you even trying?" she asked.

I jumped up, glaring back. "I'm a little distracted today."

"We all noticed." She looked over to Elijah who was helping another pair.

Had I really been that obvious? "He's my mentor. Nothing more."

She rolled her eyes. "Whatever, just pick up the heat. I can't get better without a challenge."

I grabbed her around the neck, flipping her over and pinning her to the ground. "Was that enough of a challenge?" I smirked and then let her free.

Another day gone, and the summit was tomorrow. I had latched on to Jack while Elijah was gone, soaking up any information he had. The leaders were arriving tonight after curfew so they would go unnoticed. They had already announced at lineup that the main building was off limits tomorrow, but gave no explanation. Some speculated while others could care less. Jack seemed pumped about it and was hoping to get an invite to sit in on it. He said that some

Potentials were invited, but it was limited. I doubted he would be after Elijah told me Jack was just there because of me. They didn't seem too interested in him outside of that.

Elijah hung around the training area while everyone vacated, so I waited until it was just the two of us. He was standing on the wrestling mat now.

"If you are going to interrogate me, then you have to train," he said as he waved me to the center.

As soon as I reached him he grabbed my arm, twisted it behind my back, and pinned me on my stomach. "Seriously, Elijah?" I struggled to get free, but he held his grip and leaned in. The warmth of his breath on the back of my neck sent memories of our kiss down my spine.

"Always be prepared to fight," he whispered and loosened his grip.

He sat back, and I flipped over and sat facing him. My eyes lingered on his lips for a moment before I shook off the intimacy and began to grill him. "Did you find her? Is she okay? What about Caleb?"

He put his hands up. "Whoa, slow down, Champ. She's fine and she came willingly. Caleb wasn't there, so I assume he'll be lurking around the facility shortly."

I sighed with relief and then leaned over and slapped him. My hand stung from the impact, but I was mostly shocked at what I had just done. He froze for a second and then shook it off.

"I guess I had that coming."

"Elijah, you were gone for nearly two weeks. What took

you so long? You have no idea the things I was imagining."

A smile crept on his face. "You were worried about me," he said smugly.

My face scrunched awkwardly as I tried to discredit his comment. "What, no. Yes, but mostly about Jasmine." All the recent comments about Elijah and me were making me squirm with unease. I thought I had gotten over this feeling around him, but it was skirting just below the surface this whole time.

"Aww, come on, just admit that you were worried about me and then we can move on." He winked.

Now he was just messing with me intentionally. "Fine, I was worried, about all of you. Now tell me why you went underground for so long."

"Not here. Go eat dinner and I'll meet you at the tree in thirty."

I shrugged in disapproval, but what he had to say was obviously meant for my ears only, so I agreed. I ate dinner quickly, but he wasn't as swift, making the anxiety in my stomach build until I finally saw him walking up the hill.

"What took you so long?" I chastised him when he was close enough to hear me.

He looked down at his watch. "I'm right on time."

I grabbed his arm and pulled him close to the tree. "So?"

He laughed at my impatience. "It took me a day to get to her, and then I scoped things out for another day to pinpoint Caleb's routine. When he left to fetch dinner, I swooped in. I told her everything I knew and that I suspected the current

Visionary was deceased and she was needed. She agreed reluctantly, left a note for Caleb, and then we headed back."

The timeline didn't match up. "That accounts for two days, Elijah. You were gone for two weeks!"

He sighed amusingly. "I couldn't just bring her back without knowing the whole picture, so we went searching for her dad."

"What? Why? He was an awful man." It made me sick just imagining Jasmine having to face her mother's killer again.

"Are you going to let me finish?" He raised an eyebrow.

"Sorry." I shut my mouth and knotted my fingers together, letting them bear the brunt of my distress.

"Her father was a Visionary and a full generation ahead of Jasmine. She shouldn't have been up next, unless he was dead, which he was. We spent a week trying to find out how, but didn't come up with much except for rumors by pals he hung around. He was buried in an unmarked grave. No one wanted to front the money for a stone."

"What were the rumors?" I asked carefully, not sure if I was allowed to interject.

"That he was murdered for killing Jasmine's mom. Some sort of crime of passion. They said her father suspected she was seeing someone and that's why he went off the handle. Said he had been seeing visions of her with a man, a man who sounded a lot like our very own tall, thin council man who's been hassling you."

It made total sense. The man was a witch and was acting

very protective over the Visionaries. If he had been around for over a century, he could very well be a Keeper of some sort. I had read about them in one of The Order books. "A Keeper," I shared.

Elijah looked mildly amused. "You've been reading."

"I love reading," I defended my intelligence.

"Oh, I know."

His words made me blush and reminded me that before we first met, he had been assigned by my father to watch me. I just didn't realize how closely. "What else do you know about me?" The coy smile that lit his face made me raise my hands and shake them wildly. "Never mind. Don't answer that." I needed to get Elijah out of my head before I completely lost sight of Wes. *I loved Wes.*

He chuckled, then continued, "Yes, the man is a Keeper, and his name is Samuel. That was as much as I could discover without the library, so I need to head there after this and try to find out more about him."

"Aren't there other Visionaries?"

"No, not like Jasmine's family. Just like you, Abby, there are many gifted humans out there, but you're the only Chosen. There are many witches, but her family carries the Visionary gift."

"The other Chosens weren't related to me, though." The look he gave me made me think otherwise. "I couldn't find anything about the origins of the other Chosens."

"And you won't. It's their most guarded secret. Only those in The Order know who you are, but any members joining after a Chosen's death won't know who they were. If our enemies were to discover that it's a generational gift, they would be inclined to wipe the map of all of you down to the furthest removed cousin."

I knew I had relatives on both sides, but my parents lost touch with them when I was little. The last time I saw them was at a large family reunion my mother organized before she was pregnant with my brother. "I remember some of their faces, but I was so young." It coincided with my memory wipe of the pregnancy. "There were a lot of them. I can't remember how I was related to all of them, but my grandmother's younger brother on my father's side took an interest in me at the reunion. He and my grandfather told me stories that I thought were fictional and repeatedly told me I was special. Do you think they knew I was the One and not a future sibling?" "They must have." He raked his hands through his hair as if he was contemplating telling me something. "There's more."

I sighed. "Isn't there always?" I said half-heartedly.

"Do you remember Polly?"

A memory of her handing me the charm on the bus when I was younger flashed in my head and then another memory of her here at the facility. She hadn't aged a day. "Elijah," I squealed loud enough for him the cringe. "Sorry," I said excitedly. "I completely forgot to tell you that Polly is the woman who gave me that resurrection charm on the bus." In the process of telling him my discovery, I had grabbed both of his arms and was shaking him wildly. I was disappointed that he didn't reciprocate the same excitement. In fact, he seemed way too complacent, as if he already knew the truth. I let go and stepped back. "No, uh-uh. Seriously, Eli? You knew?"

This time when he raked his fingers through his hair it was out of guilt, and his expression wore it shamelessly. "There are so many lies and secrets built up over the years it's hard to remember which ones I've shared with you."

I crossed my arms and popped a hip. "Spill," I demanded.

"Polly is your great-grandmother on your father's side. Your father's side carries the gifted genes. Your mother's side does not."

"So we are all Chosens?" I was completely confused.

"No. Your grandmother's little brother, Ethan, was until he passed away five years ago. That's when the magic awoke in you and when your grandfather started pushing your father to get you involved with The Order."

"Then, how does Polly look like she could be my grandmother?" The council man popped in my head, and I answered my own question. "She's a witch."

Elijah nodded. "Yes, and her son, Ethan, gave her the charm to pass on to you well before he died. He was very sick for a long time and hadn't been able to actively work with The Order, which is what prompted them to take your father's deal regarding Asher. They were desperate to groom the next Chosen. They were completely blindsided when they realized he was just a witch like the others in your family. That's when your grandfather approached them about you, and the rest is pretty much history."

As mush disbelief I had absorbed over the months, there was still plenty to blow me away, like Asher being a witch. "Didn't my father think that this would have been useful information for me to have before I came here? The lack of communication between all of us really sucks."

"I guess he just figured you'd find things out when you needed to."

"Just so I'm clear. My whole family on my dad's side is either witches or were Chosens, no one in my family knows about my little brother aside from my father and present company, and Polly is my great-grandmother who controls her aging process. Did I miss anything?"

"Nope. I think you got it all."

But there was something else. Something that had been eating at me ever since my father told me about my memory wipe. "Elijah, do you know who wiped my memory?"

A fear I had never seen in Elijah burned brightly, and he didn't need to tell me because I already knew. It was him. Rage consumed me, and my fist flew out and collided with his cheek. Pain surged from my knuckles up my wrist and through my arm. Elijah's head jerked to the side, and he stumbled with the force. It should have been enough, but it wasn't. I launched every ounce of strength into my shoulder and crashed into his stomach, bringing him to the ground. Leaves shook free of the tree and rained down on us as I straddled him and punched him passionately in the sides, the shoulders, the face. My insides burned hotter and hotter with each impact, my power consuming me, but I couldn't stop myself. I was in too deep now. I trusted Elijah, loved him even, and he had wiped away the only memories I had of my little brother and then lied to me about it.

Hundreds of ignored wishes poured into my fists as they pounded him. And, all the while, he didn't fight back. He didn't even crouch away in fear or pain. He opened his body up for me almost challenging me to do my worst because he deserved it. Every hit represented a lie, and every tear that dropped from my chin, a betrayal. When I was too tired to throw another punch and Elijah's face was bloodied and swollen, I fell into his chest, his arms wrapping around me tightly, and I sobbed, broken on the inside as much as I had broken him on the outside.

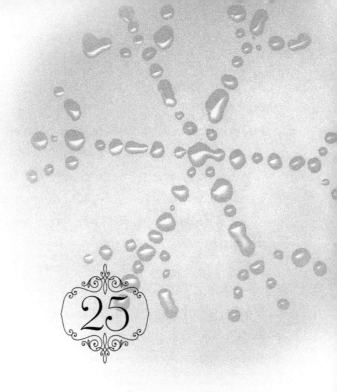

I SAT AT THE EDGE OF ELIJAH's double bed, my eyes still stinging and my body exhausted. His room was triple the size of the ones I had been accustomed to, and it was a room you'd find in a five star resort. Original artworks from over the centuries hung on the walls, and luxurious furniture was perfectly placed around the room. I was surprised he didn't have his own fireplace.

Elijah slipped out of his en-suite bathroom, pulling a clean shirt over his head, concealing the lines of hard work etched into his abdomen. I turned away quickly not needing any more reasons to be attracted to this man.

"I'm sorry I ruined your shirt." I had sobbed on his shirt until it was soaked with tears and snot. Not my proudest moment.

"It's not ruined," he reassured me gently. "Are you feeling better?"

I shrugged my shoulders and walked over to the paintings. "Is this an original Renoir?"

"Probably. I never paid much attention to it."

I moved my head side to side, awestruck. "It's even more spectacular in person. I've only seen it in my art history book."

"He was an Order member, along with many other famous people."

It was small for me to think the members were just ordinary folk going about their boring lives relatively unnoticed when, in fact, some were doing extraordinary things.

"Back then, The Order was civilized and revolved around virtue. It was an honor to be a member."

"And now?"

"I sometimes wonder if anyone of them would have joined if they knew what it would become." His eyes had fixated on the painting and then dropped away, disappointed, and he sat on the bed next to me. "You need to let go. All of it."

He was referring to my multiple breakdowns since I found out about The Order and my place in it. "I know."

"Everyone you know has lied to you and kept secrets. Most likely there are so many more that I don't even know, but you can't let it affect you like this. Not anymore. You're not a kid anymore, so you need to stop acting like one."

"Wow, don't sugarcoat it or anything." I frowned.

"We can't afford it. You've been showing progress, and I see your small acts of rebellion." He looked to the red Chucks dangling off the side of the bed. "But that's all they are, *acts* of rebellion."

I let it really sink in this time. The betrayals I felt were real, but immature. I lacked the world experience to realize that reality was full of deceit, and I was not an exception. When my father built up walls and became less easy to talk to, I hated him for it. I wondered why he would do that to the two people who loved him the most, making me and my mom feel like we had done something wrong, but I get it now. It was to protect himself out here, outside of the safety of our house. It was because of love that he guarded himself.

I looked over to Elijah, admiring the wisdom his twenty years projected. "I understand."

A storm had rolled in, along with the leaders for the Summit. The light tapping of drops on Elijah's window were soothing. There had been a few smaller storms over the last month, but this one promised to pack a winter punch.

"I should go. It's almost curfew." Ever since Jasmine's escape, they had instated room checks every night.

"I'll walk you." He stood up, but I waved him off.

"I'll be fine. No need for us both to get soaked." I paused just before I stepped out of his room and turned back to him. "Are you invited to the Summit?"

"I am."

"Will you tell me what they decide for Jasmine?" My

gut told me she would be ok because she was protected like myself, but that didn't necessarily mean good treatment.

"Of course."

"Thanks, Elijah." I flashed a weak but appreciative smile and left.

It was freezing once I stepped outside, no longer surrounded by the warmth of the fireplace in the common area of Elijah's building, instantly making me regret leaving my uniform sweatshirt on my bed after training. It wasn't this cold earlier. The storm had approached with frightening speed almost as if the universe knew the power that was descending on us tonight. I ran into the rain and up to Building Four. My corner room had a window that faced the main building up the hill. I planned on staying up just to chance a glance at the leaders' arrival. The darkness and the distance from the building would make it impossible to make out their features, but my curiosity would keep me from sleep anyway.

At first, the shadows came only a few at a time, but as the night grew darker, they arrived in packs, making it hard to differentiate one from the other, melding together like a canvas of watercolors. I didn't realize there were so many, and I wondered how many of them were prominent figures in the world.

The thunder overtook the night and, at some point, I had fallen back on my bed. I woke groggy and huddled in a ball. The night chill had crept through the glass and blanketed me. I snatched up my watch. It was an hour before the alarm would sound for morning training, and my body was begging to go back to sleep, but thoughts of the summit swam feverishly in my head. Just as I stood, stretching away the funky position I had slept in, a light knock sounded on my door. I unlocked it and was confused as to why Elijah was here so early.

"What's up?" I looked down the hall to see if he was accompanied by anyone. He was alone.

"They want you at the summit."

"What?" I exclaimed too loudly for the early morning quiet.

Elijah pushed his way into my room and closed the door. "They didn't tell me why, only to retrieve you."

The familiar tingle of nervous energy buzzed through me. I wanted to know what the summit was and who the leaders were. I needed to make sure Jasmine was good, but I never imagined I would be attending the occasion.

"Get dressed and meet me outside in ten."

He tried to hide the worry, but we were bonded. I knew he feared for me, but as I sat up last night, I thought hard about what he said. I wasn't a little girl anymore. My days of self-pity were over. It was time to be brave and find peace with the uncertainty.

Elijah waited just inside the doors, the storm raging outside. It wasn't quite cold enough for the fluffy snowflakes, but cold enough for pellets of hail.

"It's not letting up anytime soon, is it?" I asked as I stood next to him, admiring Mother Nature's wrath. I had always liked stormy days, but I hadn't experienced something so intense in a very long time.

"She's definitely pissed," he added as his eyes looked me up and down. "Ditching the old Chucks?"

I looked at my bright white uniform shoes indignantly. "I figured this wasn't the best time to ruffle feathers."

"There's hope for you after all," he teased.

When we stepped outside, Elijah grabbed a large umbrella that was leaning up against the building and opened it over us. The grass was already mushy from the relentless down pour, so we stuck to the path. As if the weather wasn't ominous enough, the silence between us added to it. We were both apprehensive as we approached the main building. Tawny buzzed us in and raced over to grab the umbrella. The first and only time I met her, she was confident and poised and a whole lot snotty. Now she was wound tightly.

"They are gathering in the Summit Hall," she announced and raced away like a mouse skittering across a room.

I followed Elijah quietly to the elevator, unconsciously grabbing his hand and interlacing my fingers in his. It was the Tribunal all over again, only I hoped this went better. No Penelopes on trial or fathers being banished. He squeezed lightly as we entered the elevator. I hadn't noticed a panel of buttons the last time I was in here for the Tribunal. The elevator had descended on its own, so I assumed there was only one floor, but then Elijah opened a hidden panel and pressed SH, Summit Hall.

"What should I expect?" I snaked my other arm around his while the other hand gripped his fingers tighter.

"I wish I knew. Going in blind in any situation is disconcerting."

Bright lights and a rush of voices met us on the other side of the elevator doors. It was a stark contrast to the tribunal where everything was dim and silent.

"I thought the identities of the leaders and council members were a secret?" I was whispering close to his side, but even at a normal level no one would be able to hear me with how rambunctious the voices were that carried down the hall.

He didn't need to answer my question because, as soon as we approached the curtained entrance to the hall, a masked figure stepped from the shadows and waved us inside. My eyes darted around the room from a red sparkly ball gown to a white tuxedo and then to so many plain black masks that the people adorned. It covered the entirety of their face accept for the eyes and nostrils. I felt completely exposed without a mask.

"Why didn't we get one?" My heart thumped lightly against my chest, releasing nerves throughout. My fingers wished to shake, but they dug into Elijah even more.

"Because we are not a secret to them as they are to us."

More delicately designed ball gowns swished around the room with colorfully pressed tuxedos. It was an oddity to have such formality at the facility, such decadence.

"Is this really a thing? It's a Masquerade Ball, not a

summit." I drank in the heads that turned toward us as the masked figures took knowledge that we were present. I rubbed the goosebumps from my skin and made myself stand strong and confident. When the room finally settled into a silence only the eye of a storm could protect, the Keeper appeared from the crowd and approached us. He wasn't wearing a mask either.

"I owe you two a thank you for bringing our Jasmine home safely. The council was very pleased. So pleased they will let it slide that the immortal is still loose."

His eyes burned me with intensity. "Where is she?" I fumed.

"I'm right here." Jasmine stepped from behind the man. Her smile was big, but her eyes spoke of loneliness.

"Jasmine!" My hands dropped from Elijah and I pulled her into a strong hug.

She hugged me back. "I missed you, too, but you're crushing me." She chuckled.

I released my grip, but didn't let go. "I'm sorry. I just …" I pulled her away and examined every part of her. "Are you hurt?"

"Not even a little. I'm good. I miss Caleb, but I know he's safe. Am I the only one who feels like they walked on stage with no pants?" Jasmine's eyes scanned the room.

"It's not comforting, that's for sure. I'm sorry about your father." He was a monster in his own right, but he was still her family.

"I made peace with it. Maybe he'll be a better person in the next life."

It astounded me how strong she was. You could only tell she was thirteen by her physical appearance. Inside she could be as old as the Keeper standing next to her.

A soft bell rang three times and the conversation ceased immediately. Ball gowns and tuxedos walked purposefully to the perimeter of the expansive room while the four of us stood motionless until the Keeper spoke.

"You three get to sit in the middle since you are our esteemed guests." His arm moved fluidly through the air and stopped on three chairs that had been placed in the center while we were distracted.

The feeling of nakedness increased ten-fold. Now, we would be on display, too. I took Elijah in one hand and Jasmine's in the other. *We are stronger in numbers.* Jasmine's hand trembled while Elijah's was strained. I wish I could say I was the neutral one in the middle, I was far from it, but I faked confidence well as we stalked to the chairs. A whisper could carry across the room it had become so quiet.

Once we took our seats, the Keeper stood next to us with his hands linked casually behind his back. He was waiting as were we. All of us at the mercy of this room.

"Welcome, Elijah, Abigail, and Jasmine. It's a great honor to have you join us. It's not very often we entertain guests."

None of us knew where the feminine voice was coming

from. Our heads moved back and forth, trying to pinpoint the person.

She continued, "As you know, for the safety of the leaders and the high council members our identities must remain a secret to you." She paused and remained hidden. "You are simply here today to be recognized by all who hold the code of The Order of the Crest above all else. Jasmine, will you please stand?"

Jasmine looked over to me tensely and then stood.

"Please join me in recognizing our new resident Visionary."

Applause filled the room, the sudden break in silence making me cringe.

"You may sit," she directed. "Elijah, will you please stand?" He didn't even hesitate. "Some of you have already had the pleasure of working with Elijah, but now he takes on a new role. He will be assisting and guiding Abigail through her new life with The Order of the Crest, ensuring her safety and her loyalty."

Elijah's fist balled at the last word. *Loyalty.* I shifted uncomfortably, not ready to be recognized by a bunch of people I not only didn't know, but couldn't see. So much for trust.

"Thank you, Elijah. You may sit. And lastly, but certainly not least, Abigail, will you please stand?"

I wanted to refuse, but my defiance would only hurt the ones I cared about, and I would never let that happen again. I inhaled a deep, soothing breath and stood.

"We have waited a long time for Abigail to join us and lead us into the next generation of The Order. We have been without a Chosen for far too long, and Abigail isn't just any Chosen. She is *the* Chosen that was foretold to finally end the war with non-humans. Abigail will bring peace to our world and the purity of human life."

The applause was deafening this time, hammering against my ear drums. Our eyes wandered the crowd, bodies shaking with excitement, except one. Elijah's eyes had fixated on her, too. Was it possible that not everyone agreed with the new Order of the Crest?

Once the crowd settled into silence again, the woman spoke again. "Thank you, for being here today," she addressed us directly. "You may go."

That was it? I looked from Elijah to Jasmine, confused.

"I will walk you out," the Keeper informed us.

Gowns and tuxedos filled the center once again, drifting about as if all of this was completely normal. Except for one. The woman who stood motionless amongst a zoo of animals. She was trying not to draw attention as she neared, her body pointed toward Elijah. Was she going to hurt him? I didn't see anything in her hands, but one was balled in a tight fist as if ready to attack. My heart raced as she got closer and the Keeper got farther away as Jasmine followed him out.

"What's wrong?" Elijah asked as his eyes scanned the chaos and then zeroed in on the woman. "Go. I'll take care of this."

"Are you sure?"

"No one is dumb enough to get out of line at a summit."

I nodded once and headed toward Jasmine and the Keeper, but when I glanced back at Elijah, I caught the woman slip him a piece of paper and disappear in the crowd again. Before Elijah turned back around, I caught up with Jasmine. By the time we made it to the hallway, Elijah was with us again as if he were never missing. The Keeper didn't seem to notice, and I couldn't be more grateful when the elevator opened and we spilled into the lobby of the main building. The Keeper left us and we all walked out into the storm together.

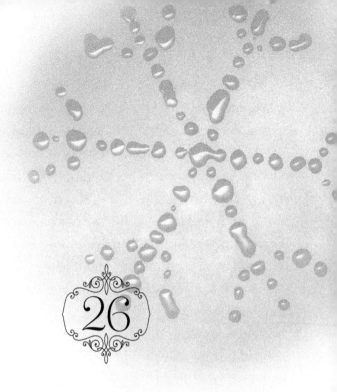

S OFT WHITE SNOW FELL IN place of the harsh hail that
pummeled us on our way into the Summit. We weren't
in there long, but the shift in weather was inevitable just
as the shift in perception. I imagined all the leaders to be
stiff and dressed in attire similar to the black army fatigues
the Elites wore, and was perplexed when I was faced with
shimmering ball gowns and colorful tuxedos. I was further
shocked when one Elite had slipped Elijah something when
they thought no one was watching, but I was. My gut told
me there was something strange about the way she fixated
on us.

"I guess back to it, then?" Jasmine looked to Elijah for
the answer as we stood outside, watching the white layer
the ground.

Before he could answer, the Keeper turned and barked at Jasmine to follow. Her shoulders slouched and her wide eyes slanted in disappointment. As she bid goodbye, one side of her mouth shaped into a sideways smile, and she reluctantly left to catch up to him, the white of the snow starkly contrasting the glossy sheen of her black hair. I didn't know when I would see her again, and it left me feeling a little empty. Elijah sensed my mood decline and wrapped an arm around my shoulder.

"You'll see her again. At least you know where she is and that she's safe."

"For now. Our safety is a ticking time bomb. Once we've fulfilled our mission, it will blow up, leaving pieces of our legacy all over this land." Elijah's body started to shake, so I glanced over to see what was going on. His face was plastered with a guilty smile, and he was trying hard not to fill the air with his laughter. "Are you laughing at me?"

His mouth opened and with his words spilled the laughter he was holding in. "You have to admit that was a bit dramatic."

"Are you serious right now?" I elbowed him in the side, and his arm dropped from my shoulder as he soothed the jab, but he only laughed harder.

"I'm sorry, Abs. I can't stop."

I let out a frustrated gurgle, but his laughter was contagious and I ended up joining him. "I hate you," I said with a huge smile and started down to Building Four. Behind me, I could hear Elijah catching his breath and choking back the last of his hysterics. When he appeared beside me again, I mustered the courage to ask about the exchange inside. He had promised he would stop lying, and I hoped he would tell the truth.

"I saw that woman hand you something."

Before he said anything, he grabbed my arm and dragged me to our tree. I stumbled along, excited he wasn't going to keep the truth from me. As soon as we were safe from prying eyes and ears, he opened his fist and unfolded a piece of paper.

"She handed me this, but I haven't read it yet."

"Do you know her?"

"Yes. I met her just before I came back. She's an Order leader in the Seattle sector." He flattened out the paper and read it aloud. "We leave just after midnight tonight, so if you are going to make your move, now is the time." He stared at the paper for a few more beats and raised his eyes to mine.

"What move?" The worry in my stomach churned.

"After our kiss, I went to the council and asked them to let me watch over you during your training."

My fingers tingled and my cheeks burned at the memory of that kiss. It was desperate and passionate, but it was wrong. I needed comfort and intimacy, and Elijah ended up being my target.

"They agreed and I left that night to find your father. I wanted to make sure he knew I was doing all it took to keep you safe."

My heart skittered at the mention of my dad. "How was he? Is he okay? And my mom?" The questions came out quickly.

"They left your home to be safe, but I found your father at your grandfather's home. We decided to seek out other Order members to see if they knew about the coming war." He shook his head.

"And?" I urged him to continue.

"They're all oblivious to the Puritan mission. They knew they were eliminating non-humans, but they didn't realize that gifted humans would be next. Half of The Order is made up of gifted humans now."

I chewed on my fingers nervously. "Did they believe you? What did they say?"

He ripped the paper into tiny pieces, bent down, and dug a hole. He put the papers in it and replaced the dirt. He rubbed his hands together to clean them. "It took some convincing, but that note affirms they do. Now, we need to convince the others."

Overwhelming sense of recognition traveled through my body, along with a rush of excitement. "Is my dad coming tonight?"

"He is, but you can't see him, Abby. It's too risky."

"What? No way. I'm a part of this, and I barely got to say goodbye to him." It had been months since I saw or heard his voice. "Please, Eli. It'll help me get through the rest of this."

He watched me for a moment, possibly weighing the

consequences of his choice. "You have to stay hidden behind me, and you can only speak to your dad. No one else." His finger waved as he spoke, and scrubbed his face hard as If he had made the biggest mistake of his life.

I jumped up and down excitedly, warming up my frozen muscles. The snow was falling steadily, and the chill was making itself noticed the longer we stood outside.

"Go to your training. I need to prepare for tonight. I'll meet you at your room just before midnight."

My smile was so wide my cheeks ached and my lips cracked. I was going to get to hug my dad tonight. I mentally clapped and rushed off to training. I took down all of my wrestling opponents, securing my move to Building Five. The program was a year, but I was flying through the buildings. Not that I was the first to do so, but I wondered what they would do with me in the remaining months, or would they release me early, but I already knew the answer to that. They would never release their biggest weapon. I knew the ending to this chapter. I would be running for my life.

I had hoped I would see Jasmine at lunch or dinner, but it seemed the man was keeping her to himself, so I sat at out building's table and ate silently with the rest of my building mates. Most ignored me as they had always done, but a few curious glances would fall on me from time to time. I wasn't an enigma anymore, and some had even become less afraid to befriend me, but they still kept their distance for the most part. In high school, this would bother me, but here, it didn't seem to matter. We were all prepping for a war, not finals.

I tried to read in my room while midnight slowly approached. It's what I had done while Elijah was gone looking for Jasmine, and it was the only thing I enjoyed after training. Every so often I would jog the path and hear the laughter and shouts come from the recreational buildings, but I didn't have a desire to join them. Part of the reason was not wanting to ruin their fun by entering the picture because, inevitably, the room would go quiet, and there would be awkward silence until I left.

When the knock finally sounded on my door, I swung it open with so much energy I almost lost the door out of my hand before it crashed into the wall.

"You ready?" Elijah asked as his eyes rolled down my body.

"Yes!" I looked down at my jeans, t-shirt, and my grandfather's bomber jacket I had arrived here in. "I thought it would make me stand out a little less?"

"Good idea."

He was wearing dark jeans and a plain black hoodie, and damn if it didn't look good on him. I had gotten so used to seeing him in a black uniform this look tugged at my angsty desires a little too much.

"What?" he asked in response to my gawking.

I turned away quickly and busied my fingers, pulling my hair up in a top knot. Elijah brushed pass me and my heart beat just a little harder. He pushed my pillow under the sheets and messed them up to look as if I were sleeping.

"Just in case," he said as he stood back to admire his work. "Let's go."

Elijah walked out first, making sure no one was wandering about. I clung to his sweatshirt like a four-year-old scared to leave her mother's side. He didn't seem to mind, though, so I clutched on and let him lead. Once we were out of the building, we kept to the shadows as close to the perimeter wall as possible and headed down to the back entrance Jasmine had taken me through. Elijah scanned us through the gate and, before I knew it, we were locked out and standing in the darkness of a large tree. There were several inches of snow on the ground now, and I was glad I had chosen my black army boots over my Chucks. I only wished I had gloves. I tucked my fingers into the bomber jacket and tried to control my shivers.

"It's cold tonight," Elijah filled the snowy silence.

My body was stiff as the chill wrapped its way around each bone in my body while Elijah seemed unaffected. "Is controlling your body temperature one of your superpowers?" He seemed to have so many gifts.

He chuckled. "No, I'm just used to it. Stakeouts occur in all types of weather."

When my body transitioned from shivers to bona fide convulsions, Elijah pulled me into his chest and wrapped his arms around me, rubbing my back to get me warm. The faint scent of shaving cream and spice filled my senses as I inhaled deeply, letting the familiarity coat me. Elijah instantly made me feel safe and warm. I could never imagine a world where we weren't close.

The sound of boots crunching through the snow drew our attention, and when my dad's figure came into view, my heart sang with joy, but when I saw he was followed by Penelope, it burned with fear and confusion.

"What's she doing here?" both my dad and I asked in unison.

We came together in a tight circle.

"I wanted to see you," I said tensely as my eyes jumped from my dad to Penelope and back. I had instinctively grabbed on to Elijah's hand when we separated, but my dad's gaze had me take a step away from Elijah, dropping his hand in the process.

My dad stepped to me and hugged me tightly. "You're crushing me." I laughed.

He let go and pulled back, smiling proudly. "Your mother and I miss you so much. You look good. You're getting stronger." He squeezed my biceps before letting go.

"How is she?" I wanted to know everything.

"She's good. We rented a little cabin in the woods until things settle down."

It was a reminder how much all of our lives had changed because of The Order. "Dad, I found him." Tears were already filling my eyes, and my dad's matched within seconds.

"Is he okay? Does he know who you are?" The urgency

in his voice spoke volumes to the guilt he had been carrying all these years.

"We didn't get a chance to talk much, but I think he knows I'm family." I didn't know how much of the truth to tell him. I was afraid it would break him to hear his son was near death and imprisoned horribly.

"We are going to get him out of there. I promise you that," he said with so much conviction that I couldn't help but believe him.

"I know." I smiled weakly as a few tears fell.

"I hate to break this up, but we need to be going," Penelope interrupted.

My dad answered my inquisitive look. "One of us will explain later."

Elijah took the lead, followed by me, my dad, and Penelope bringing up the rear. The beauty of snowflakes lightly covering the forest was quickly overshadowed by dark figures stomping through the woods. Chills raced through me and nerves gripped my stomach. There were only four of us and what seem liked hundreds of them. Why in the world would they listen to us?

Someone within the dark figures shouted, "Stop," loudly and the crunching of the snow immediately ceased. The forest froze as if it knew danger was imminent, but the snow fell just the same. I clutched on to Elijah's sweatshirt as a figure approached us.

"Elijah," a woman's voice broke the levels of eeriness that had built.

"Lorna," Elijah answered.

"They will give you five minutes. Better make it count." She turned and we followed.

I let go of him and straightened my back, hoping confidence would follow. I was too afraid to look back, but I could hear my dad and Penelope's footsteps follow. The dark figures were courtesy of long, black-hooded robes. A bit dramatic, but effective.

Elijah stepped to the center and addressed them. "Thank you for hearing me out. I am Elijah Winters—"

"We know who you are." A hooded man took a stand next to Lorna. "Meeting with us behind The Order's back is treachery. We could all be punished."

"By who?" Elijah challenged. "We make up The Order, not the council members. They have shifted course from the true mission of The Order of the Crest. They no longer seek peace, but retribution. They want purity, and all of those among us that are gifted, including myself, will be eliminated."

A crowd of whispers jumped around the forest as The Order leaders considered Elijah's accusation.

"Where's your proof?" the man responded.

Elijah turned and waved to Penelope who stepped forward. "This is Penelope."

Seething murmurs flew between the leaders.

"She's a traitor," the man said, "and so is he." His glare pierced the night sky and fixated on my dad.

"Let them speak," Elijah urged.

The crowd quieted and Penelope spoke. "There's a list of gifted humans, Specials. My family was on it. The Order killed my parents and my brother and then used *me* to track Elijah to kill him. They were priming me to be a killer. I had nothing to lose after I lost my family. I was out for revenge, because The Order told me it was non-humans that had killed them, but when I found out they were behind it, I bargained my freedom and then I ran."

"It's your word against theirs," Lorna added.

I could see Penelope's mouth curve up in a wide smile. "I memorized the list." And then she started naming all of the Specials, including Lorna and even the man standing next to her, Alden. Hushed gasps resounded as each was outed and proof had been provided.

"That list is sacred, yet they share it with you?" Alden spat in disgust.

"I'm not the only one. There's a whole building devoted to the cause, and they all know who you are, where you live."

I shot a look to my dad who seemed just as surprised as I was.

A less confident Alden spoke again. "Let's say you are telling the truth. What do you propose we do about it? The council members have powerful magic at their disposal."

He had to be referring to Jasmine and the Keeper who watches over her. Without thinking, I stepped forward. "Because you have me."

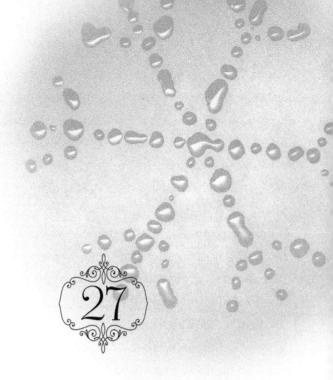

# 27

Elijah turned to me, seething. "Abby," he hissed.

I knew he wanted to keep me out of this as much as possible, but they were failing at convincing the group, and if we were going to stop a war that could possibly spill over into the human world, we needed them. I stood beside Elijah and continued. "My power is stronger than whatever they have." I tried to sound confident, but no matter how much power brewed below the surface of my skin, it was meaningless if I didn't learn to control it. It was enough to stir up whispers, though.

"And you have learned how to control it?" Alden questioned as if he read my mind, which I knew wasn't out of the realm of possibility.

There was a good chance somewhere in this group there

was a Detector, so to lie would only hurt our pleas. "Not entirely." Whispers turned to disapproving grumbles and head shakes of disapproval. "But I'm learning quick. I was able to find the witch with only one lesson."

Alden seemed impressed, but not yet swayed. "Projecting is far easier than manipulating your energy to kill."

So he knew about my abilities, which meant that it was likely the other leaders knew as well. I swallowed hard. I was about to admit something that could land me in solitary again. "I already have killed."

I could see Elijah's fists ball while Penelope and my dad gasped in horror, or shock, I couldn't be sure.

"Go on," Alden pressed.

"I went outside the facility walls to train when a non-human caught me off guard." I continued as the group shared words and looks. "I was scared, and when it grabbed me, an overwhelming energy burned in my chest and transferred to it through our touch. Then it…disintegrated."

"That only proves you're emotional. It shows no control," he pointed out.

I couldn't argue that, because I was far from mastering it.

"We have been working every night. She will be ready by the next Summit," Elijah stated confidently. "We have to act soon. Once they see Abigail has reached her full potential they will start the war."

Alden thought for a moment, his eyes shifting around

the four of us. He didn't seem to care what the other leaders thought, as he hadn't even spared them a glance. His eyes bore on me once again.

"Do you understand what is weighing on you, little girl?" His eyes slanted tautly.

What he was really asking was if I understood that all of their lives depended on me. I stood tall and answered, "Yes. I *will* be ready."

Now, Alden turned to the leaders and gathered them close as they spoke in quick, hushed whispers. Nervous energy buzzed through me, but I refused to shift or even clench my fists. They needed to see my confidence. They needed me to be strong. When he finally turned back to us, my chest sizzled from holding my breath for so long.

"We strike on the day of the final trial," he announced with no intention of allowing a rebuttal.

Elijah's face hardened, but he agreed. As Alden turned to leave, so did we, remaining quiet until we reached the gate.

"I understand where their head is, but the trials will be attended by everyone in the facility. We are taking for granted the loyalty of the recruits to The Order," my dad stated plainly.

"The only other options would have been a complete blind attack or on the day of the summit, but they didn't give us a choice, and we *need* their backing. The day of trials it will have to be," Elijah replied.

"I can reach out to the others in my group that were

trained to kill and try to get them on board. We all have special gifts, so I think once I explain why those people are on those lists they will be more likely to join us," Penelope contributed.

What I was about to say was not going to go over well, but desperate times, right? "What about the Hunters? Wes could reach out to non-humans he trusts and they could—"

"Absolutely not," Elijah and my dad spat simultaneously.

"But—"

"It's out of the question, Abigail. If the non-humans get wind of this, they can plan their own attack and come at us when we are most vulnerable. This has to stay an inside job."

After a meeting time and place was established with Penelope and my dad, Elijah and I went back inside the facility. He walked me to my building just after one in the morning. We stayed in the shadows for a few minutes longer.

"Are you nervous?" he asked me.

Biting my lip was enough of an answer for him.

"You'll be ready for the final trial, and when the moment is right, we will strike and get you and your brother out of here."

"Is there any way you can check on Asher? Make sure he's getting better? He needs to be strong when all hell breaks loose." Asher was so frail when I last saw him in the hospital.

"I will try," he promises as he squeezes my shoulders and heads back down the hill.

Even now, his stroll was assured and strong when everything is up in the air. Where would we end up after the trial? Would we all survive? It seemed unlikely that casualties wouldn't accumulate. We were taking on The Order of the Crest, an organization that has been protecting humans from non-humans for hundreds of years. To underestimate that power would no doubt fate us all to the underground.

THE REST OF the weekend was uneventful and Jasmine was still in hiding. I was hoping that today I would run into her because it was Monday, and she was still fully immersed in the training program, unless they were training her privately. As I stood in lineup, I searched the other lineups, and when I saw her long jet-black hair at Building Four, I smiled to myself. This would give me a chance to tell her about the plan.

I wasn't disappointed when Elijah walked in front of the line, dressed in all black, and inspected us. We had already started meditation, so I was ahead of the others when we filed down into the basement and sat on yoga mats. I was more comfortable under my tree, but I quickly settled into the breathing exercises. Elijah was very thorough and made his way to each recruit, whispering instructions in their ears. When he came to me, his warm breath seemed to travel through every part of me. It took all the control in the world not to shudder. When he was this close, our bond was inescapable. I yearned for more, but also fought hard against my urges, remembering how deeply I cared for Wes. *Six more months.*

"I spoke to the council and requested to be Asher's private trainer, and they agreed," he whispered.

My head turned to him instinctively, and water pooled in my eyes. My heart could burst with happiness. Elijah had made it happen. If we were alone, I could have kissed him, and the thought caused me tilt my head away just a fraction. "Thank you, Elijah. I owe you so much." I knew Asher would be ready for the fight now. Elijah would make sure of it.

"Thank me when this all over and we are still alive." He stood up and continued around the room.

My nightmare from solitary haunted me on repeat. I wanted to believe we would all survive this, but the vision of me having to choose affirmed we wouldn't.

After training was complete for the day, I lurked around Building Four, hoping to run into Jasmine. Ray walked by with Ebony and a few other girls. I waved weakly, and she only responded with a quick half-smile before tucking her head. We had cleared things up, but being around me had gotten her thrown into solitary and tortured. Avoiding me was for the best. It just made me long to find Jasmine that much more.

"Abigail!" Jasmine screeched excitedly as she popped through the basement door.

"Jasmine." I pulled her into a tight hug. When I pushed away, I searched for her Keeper. "Is he with you?"

"Bart, no? He disappeared after the Summit."

"Bart? I did not picture that at all." I snorted as I laughed.

"Technically, it's Bartholomew, but it irritated him so much when I called him Bart, so it stuck."

It was nice seeing her in good spirits. I felt a little more secure with a friend by my side again. We walked up the hill to dinner. "Why did you go back somewhere you knew The Order could find you?"

"I had a premonition that they found me, so I didn't really think it mattered where I went. Being there allowed me to control the situation and make sure Caleb was out of harm's way."

"Smart." No one gave Jasmine enough credit, me included.

"I felt you there. Projecting," she admitted sheepishly.

"Really? That's so cool. I didn't even know I could do it." I stopped walking when it dawned on me that she knew I was the one responsible for her return. "I'm sorry. I betrayed you."

She turned back. "Abigail, you had no choice. I felt how uneasy you were. I would have said something, but I didn't want Caleb to know. Honestly, it gave me time to say goodbye and send him off."

"Won't he come looking for you?"

"No," she said sadly. "I left him a note telling him I needed to find my family and to let me go." Jasmine tried to hide the loss she was feeling by turning her head swiftly and ducking her chin.

"I'm really sorry, but something big is being planned, and you might not be separated for as long as you think."

"Really?" Her big brown eyes brightened through her lashes.

"I'll tell you after dinner. At the tree."

She smiled, and things didn't seem as daunting knowing I could bring her some relief.

We ate in record time. We couldn't sit together because we weren't in the same building anymore, and her yellow uniform against my green didn't allow for mingling during meals. It was a lame rule. I shot at glance over to her at the table and we both shot up, attracting strange looks from others in close proximity. I wasn't in the mood to try to play it off, so I grabbed my trash just as Jasmine did and we speed walked out the door, laughing once the chill hit our cheeks. We raced to the tree and huddled close to one another by the trunk.

"So, what's going on?" she asked through her chattering teeth.

I filled her in on everything that had happened after the Summit and the plan for the day of the final trials. I expected her to be cautious, but when she returned a horrified expression, my stomach churned uneasily.

"What's the matter?" I studied her eyes as she searched for the right words, which only made me more anxious.

"I had a another premonition last night. I thought it was just a bad dream, but now it makes sense."

Her body was shaking terribly, so I wrapped my arm around her shoulders and squeezed her to my body. I couldn't tell if my own shivering was from the below freezing temperature or for what she was about to tell me.

"It was your final trial and you had to face something, someone. It was a blur, but I could feel its energy and it was angry and dark. You had to choose: a life to live and a life to take."

The chill that sliced through my heart was not from the bitter cold outside. It was my vision. She had seen it too, confirming my sense that we would be carrying someone's death on our shoulders for the rest of our lives. Or, at least, I would be.

"I'm sorry, Abby. I didn't mean to upset you."

"I know, but there's no way to stop what's going to happen at the trials. With or without a rebellion, I will be faced with my worst fear. I saw it too when I was in solitary. I thought it was just a nightmare. I mean, I hoped it was, but it was the same as yours. I'll have to choose. Have you ever witnessed a premonition not come true, or change?" I asked, hopeful with all my heart.

"No." She shook her head solemnly.

"I didn't think so." And now, for the next five months, I got to carry around with me a horrible fate that I had no control over. I swallowed back the fear that etched itself in my throat and hoped I would make the right choice, for everyone's sake.

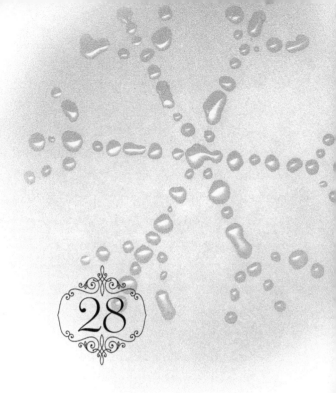

## 28

THE REST OF MY TRAINING SEEMED to fly by in a blur. I went through the rainbow of uniform colors, passing all of the buildings within a month. The intensity of the training increased after meditation and seemed to be more tailored to our individual gifts. Building Six, we were split off with others that possessed similar gifts and were assigned a Potential to work with us. When Ebony and the white-haired boy who had attacked me in Building Two were put with me, I thought someone had made a mistake, but it turns out we can manipulate energy in some way. Ebony and the others' was more superficial than mine, only controlling the way things felt around a person, while I could disintegrate a non-human with one touch. Of course, they didn't bring in a non-human to work with, so I worked on controlling small levels of energy like the others.

Building Seven was a little more intimidating for me. I never thought I was afraid of heights until they asked me to jump off a two-story building, with only a net to catch me below. I wasn't the only one to hesitate upon jumping, which was mildly comforting, but as the height increased, the panic set in and the dizziness was overpowering. My heart beat so fast and hard I was convinced I would die of a heart attack mid-air, but as the net gave way under my weight, reassuring that I had survived yet another fall, it calmed back down. By the third week of jumping onto different things, such as large trash containers full of foam, and pick-up trucks loaded with blankets, I became more comfortable, but wished to the stars that I would never be in a situation that had me jumping for my life, because the odds of something soft breaking my fall were pretty low.

Ray was assigned to me for Building Eight. At first, it was awkward between us. She didn't know how to act, and I didn't know how to respond, so we exchanged sheepish looks and awkward, one-word sentences, which worked, because we were boxing most of the time anyway. Ray was a skilled fighter, and I knew I would learn a lot from her. I also suspected Elijah paired her with me because she would do the least damage, seeing how we were somewhat connected because of solitary, although her right hooks to my temple might beg to differ. By the end of the first week, she was opening up to me more. She had received a letter from Rick, an Elite on a mission now. He didn't say much, but she knew he was alive, and it lit this spark in her eyes I hadn't seen before. It was something I imagined would happen when I finally met Wes at the bridge after the trials. A piece of me was missing without him.

Building Nine just plain sucked. There was an all-out battle between the recruits. The entire building was set up like rat maze, where we crawled through air ducts, ran up flights of stairs, and hid from threats. The object was to find a flag that represented a human who had been kidnapped by a non-human. We wore vests and carried laser guns. Black was designated as humans and red as non-humans, and contact fighting was allowed. Every recruit, including those who hated me, now had permission to kick my ass without consequence, and they didn't hesitate, but I had gotten stronger and I would even say I wasn't half bad at one-on-one combat now. I only sported a few bruises at the end of each week. We switched between human and non-human roles each day and were encouraged to kill as many non-humans as possible when wearing the black vests. The winner was given a pass to visit their family for the weekend.

The nervous buzz in my stomach started in Building Ten where I was now subjected to wearing my least favorite color: brown. I think I looked like a poop emoji minus the stupid smile. I cringed at the pink from the last building, but it did make for a good laugh on the guys. Brown was just degrading, and the poop jokes lasted the entire month.

It was now April. The buds were blossoming, and tulips were pushing through the ground, but it also meant we were only two months from the final trials of Building Twelve. Each building's purpose was to prepare us for the finals, but The Order had kept the trial itself a guarded secret. Recruits spent countless conversations discussing what it could be, but the situation that I feared the most was having to face a non-human. My ability to control my gifts was near perfect, but I hadn't been given a chance to test the one that mattered most. If I learned anything from my encounter with the non-human creature, from outside the gates with Jasmine, was that my emotions could get the best of me under pressure. While all the training had focused on dealing with stressful situations, that one would be the hardest to overcome. Building Ten was a more in-depth weapons training. We learned to use everything the armory vault had to offer, from Tasers to archery and sword fighting. Everyone went away each day with a new slice or burn mark. Someone had even been impaled. Ten was the most strenuous of all the buildings because we also ran five miles a day and did a few hours of weight training. When they announced we were headed to Building Eleven, I dropped to the floor and thanked the grass, until I realized the end was so close, and the day of my vision was even closer.

I was grateful for the gray uniform of Building Eleven, but equally confused when the Potentials marched us outside of the gates instead of to Building Eleven. Elijah stood next to five other Potentials all wearing black uniforms. The recruits stood in line formation appearing as a sea of gray that blended into the rocky terrain and thick forest.

One of the Potentials stepped forward. "Your final month will be spent outside, putting all of your training to work. Real-life situations will be set up each day, and you will need to work together or individually, as you see fit, to survive or save others. Your watches have GPS and sensors that will monitor vitals. If you are in a life or death situation that you can't get out of, push the top button and you will be extracted. Are there any questions?"

"Yes, sir."

Of course, Ebony had a question.

"You may proceed, recruit."

"Are we going to be living out here for the month?" she asked evenly.

I hadn't even thought of that. I just assumed we would go back to our rooms each night, and I wasn't the only one who thought that. I saw the nervous shifts of bodies on either side of me.

"Yes. You will need to find shelter and provisions. Tools and food have been hidden all around the five mile radius. The shelter supplies are limited, however, so some of you may need to be resourceful or learn to share. Food provisions will be replenished daily."

The weather was pleasant during the day in May, but the nights were still chilly. My first priority was going to be finding shelter and starting a fire. We had learned basic survival skills in the last building. Now, I understood why all the recruits had been instructed to wear sweatshirts.

Elijah stepped forward. "This will be as close to a mission as it will get without being the real thing for you. The five miles is secured by a fence that is heavily guarded. If you reach a gate, do not engage with the Elite guards, and move on. All means of survival are acceptable to a point. You are not to kill or permanently maim another recruit, but combat may be necessary in some situations. There are cameras throughout that will be watching carefully, but we will only intervene if you press the button. Is that understood?"

In unison we all responded, "Yes, sir."

I should have been more scared, but all of the training we had undergone had built up my confidence. I could barely remember the person I was when I came here—the frightened and frail Abigail Rose. She used to ride on the outside but now burrowed deeply beneath the surface.

"Good luck," Elijah finished.

The Potentials stood obediently at attention in front of us with no other instructions for us while me and the rest of the recruits shifted restlessly wondering what to do next, but I did know what this was. It had begun, and I'll be damned if I wasn't going to be the first one out, so I ran, and within seconds I heard the pounding of shoes on the ground behind me. I launched into the forest off to the right, dodging branches, maneuvering around rock formations, and jumping over storm debris. Five miles might seem large, but there were twenty-four other recruits vying for the same provisions. A blinding light from the sun's reflection on the ground caught my eye as I ran. I stopped to investigate and found it was a machete. I had nowhere to anchor it so I carried it and used it to break through unruly trees and overgrown bushes. I heard voices close behind, but I had managed to get enough of a start that they hadn't reached me, yet.

I was elated when I came across a small makeshift shelter under a tree, but it was exposed to the elements, and my gut was telling me I needed to find something well-hidden, so I continued. When I heard celebrations behind me, I knew they had found what I left behind. I ran deeper, zigzagging my way to throw anyone off my trail. I wasn't the best at covering up my tracks, so speed was my strength.

An hour had passed, and I still hadn't found a shelter I deemed worthy enough, but when my breath became labored and my legs burned from the constant exertion, I knew as I reached a stream I should take a break.

I cupped my hand under the frigid water and splashed my face, welcoming the relief it brought to my sticky face. The coolness worked itself into every pore, releasing the heat. I cupped some more and drank it down. As I squatted, listening to the slow-moving creek, I scanned the area. There were several rock formations a couple of stories high. If one had an opening large enough for me I could dwell in it. I quickly cupped another handful of water, savoring the hydration it replenished and then made my way to the first formation. There were small crevices, but nothing big enough for a person. As I went around to the others, I was losing faith, but then the second to the last formation had a fairly large opening hidden behind a thick set of bushes. I crunched through them, my sweatshirt taking the scrapes rather than my bare skin, and crawled into it. The first few steps were discouraging because of the low ceiling height of the rock, but then it opened up into a large space and there were several crevices up above that enough light shined through, which could also serve well as ventilation for a fire.

I spun around slowly, smiling at my first victory. I placed the machete down and went back out of the cave, listening carefully for movement or voices. The creek seemed to go on for a while so people wouldn't need to congregate here for water, but there was no avoiding them altogether. When I was sure there was no one around, I gathered kindling and large branches. Once I piled those in the cave, I used the machete to chop down thicker pieces of wood. I could have survived without it, but it was definitely making my job easier.

Once my pile was large enough to get me through the night, I gathered up the thinner pieces of branches and began shredding them to create a kindling pile. It took some time, but I knew if I made a good pile, then the actual fire starting would be less work. I grabbed a split piece of wood and used the machete to make a notch for my spindle stick and then I got to work on whittling my spindle. Once I was satisfied with the point, I placed the nest on the split wood at the end of the notch and then built my fire area, placing the kindling at the bottom and creating a teepee structure with the wood.

I stepped back to admire everything I had accomplished on my own. My watch confirmed half the day had passed, and I hadn't run into any other recruits. I wasn't sure if the isolation was a blessing or a curse. People were stronger in numbers, so now that I was confident in my shelter and fire, I needed to venture out for provisions and see where others have ended up. We started the day as allies, but I wondered how long that would last when desperation set in.

As I followed the creek I quickly came across a group of recruits hanging out. One was the burly guy who won the rat maze challenge, Jackson. I was proud to admit that I knew all of the recruits' names now. They stopped talking when they noticed me walking over. A small, thin girl named Brielle and a strong girl named Tony joined him with three other boys, Vick, Brian, and Chase. They seemed to be quite comfortable until I interrupted.

"Hey," I offered first.

"Hey," Jackson replied with a friendly smile.

"Did you guys find anything?" I asked innocently.

"There's a large tree fort up there." Chase pointed up to a tree a few yards away. "Figured we'd all share. You're welcome to join us."

I considered it, but I knew a group this large was a target. "Thanks," was all I said, not giving them an answer either way. "Any food around?"

"We were just getting ready to search," Tony answered

as they all started to push off the ground lazily as if they were back at home hanging with a bunch of friends during summer break by a lake. No sense of urgency radiated from any of them, except maybe Brielle. She definitely seemed on edge.

Everyone paired off instinctively, Brielle and Jackson coming with me. We set off in three different directions— Tony went with Vick and Brian with Chase. We were to meet up at the fort in a few hours. It was agreed that provisions would be shared equally. I led them down the creek near my shelter to ensure no one from the other groups accidentally stumbled upon it. We went a little deeper into the forest, finding food in holes of trees, hollow tree stumps, and rock formations. We had gathered bananas, bread, and dried jerky. We were pretty pleased with our haul and, combined with the others, we definitely had enough rations to go around and last us a few days. Maybe being in a large group wasn't so bad.

We stayed in the fort until sunset, sharing stories of how we came to the facility and funny experiences while training. Here they treated me like an equal, and it finally seemed like people were accepting me. The day had gone so smoothly until a voice came from below, and everyone suddenly realized their food rations could be at risk.

"What do we do?" Vick asked. "I don't want to share my food, and the fort is pretty crowded now."

The voice called out again. It was female and, if I wasn't mistaken, it sounded like Ray. "I'll go down," I volunteered.

I gathered my food, stuffing the bananas into my sweatshirt pouch pocket, pushing the jerky into my waistband, and stuffing the wrapped bread down the front of my shirt. I climbed down the ladder and sure enough it was Ray.

"Abigail, am I glad to see you. I've been lost all day and have only come across a bunch of bananas. Is anyone else up there?"

"Jackson, Vick, Brian, Chase, Brielle, and Tony." The woods were quiet, so I was fairly certain she was alone and hadn't been followed.

"Can I come up?" Her head tilted up to the fort.

I knew they would turn her away, but I couldn't just leave her alone. My instincts had been nagging at me all day that their group was too large. "Actually, follow me." A safer option, and I wouldn't be alone.

I didn't say goodbye to the other group. I doubted they would miss me much and, hopefully, they would be grateful I led someone astray. Every so often I would stop and listen to the forest and try to pinpoint any unnatural sounds, but found none.

"Did you run into anyone else?" I asked Ray as we stomped down the creek.

"A few, but the majority headed to the center when you took off. I figured I would try to follow you since you seemed to know what you were doing, but you were so fast. I couldn't keep up, and then I lost track of you altogether."

"They must have all found shelter and food. It's been pretty quiet over here."

"Where are we going? Aren't you with the others?"

I stopped by the hidden cave opening. "Actually, no, I was alone and found a shelter. I stumbled across them when I went out looking for food. I pulled out the bread and lifted my shirt to show the jerky.

"Oh, wow. You scored." Her words were salivating with hunger.

"I'd be happy to share my food and shelter with you, but we need to keep the location a secret, okay?"

"Of course. Thank you so much."

I stuffed the bread back down and dropped my shirt. After another careful scan of the area, I led her into the cave.

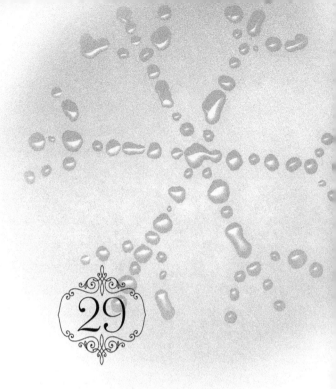

## 29

"**W**OW, THIS PLACE IS PERFECT and you already have everything for a fire."

Ray looked around rather surprised, which I took slight offense to. Did all of these people think I was useless?

"Yeah, it was nothing." I placed the food on a pile of green leaves I had pulled from the branches and got started on the fire, placing the kindling nest on top of the notched wood at the end where I would be rubbing the spindle in hopes of a quick spark. Ray walked around the cave while I got busy. Despite the chill of the night creeping in through the cracks of the cave, sweat had begun beading on my skin from the tireless motion. Ray and I switched off and, finally, my third time around a spark ignited the nest and we had our fire.

Ray peeked out of the cave. "I don't hear anyone, and the sun has set. I think we're safe for the night."

I knew having a fire, even in a cave, could draw unwanted attention. The smoke was ventilating out the top and was a direct signal to where we were, but I had to assume there were several other fires across the five miles. I was just hoping ours was the least conspicuous.

"We should look for sleeping bags or blankets tomorrow," Ray said as she pulled her hood over her head and gathered leaves in a pile for a pillow.

"Yeah, this isn't the most comfortable," I agreed. At least the ground was fine dirt inside the cave. Outside, the terrain was rough. We were in a rocky area of the forest, and while the run into the sanctioned area was flat for the most part through dense trees, where I ended up by the creek was at the base of a steep rocky mountain. We had become skilled rock climbers, but I wasn't certain their intention was for us to climb up it. At least climbing was an option if we got in a tough spot.

I watched the light of the flames dance off Ray's face. She sat across from me with her hood tight around her face and her knees tight to her chest. She seemed so much more relaxed when I met her in the library, but ever since our stay in solitary she remained on edge. Her body was twisted in a tight pretzel, engaging all of her muscles.

"Ray, can I ask you something?" Her eyes moved from the hypnotization of the dancing fire to me. "In the library you said you could see the magic hiding the missing section of books, but you said your gift was reading minds. Do you have more than one gift?"

Her knees fell apart into a more relaxed crossed sitting position and she rested her hands in her lap. "I lied. I couldn't see it directly. I saw it in your thoughts."

"That's impressive. So, it's not just words you hear? You see thoughts, too."

"It's pretty overwhelming. I wish it were just one or the other. It gets so crowded in my head with my own thoughts fighting for attention."

"I can't imagine." I tried to focus my mind on trivial things. I didn't like that I was in tight quarters with someone who could probably read me better than I could read myself.

"I can control it now, so don't worry. I'm not reading your thoughts."

"I appreciate that. Thanks." I tossed another log on the fire and then gathered the remaining leaves for my own pillow. "I'll take the first shift."

"Are you sure?"

The circles under Ray's eyes were dark and I could see her bloodshot eyes through the fire. "I'm not tired yet. I'll wake you in four hours." I checked the time on my watch. It was almost ten.

She lay down close to the fire and fell asleep almost immediately. I lied when I told her I wasn't tired, but I had a hard time trusting that she wouldn't fall asleep on her watch if she didn't get some rest first. I passed the time by stripping off fine, long pieces of the branches to use for weaving a basket that we could carry water in, so we didn't have to expose ourselves right outside of the cave too frequently.

When it was my turn to sleep, my eyes were barely slits, heavy from being awake too long and stinging from the steady stream of smoke. Ray looked somewhat refreshed after a quick walk to the creek for water. Her face glistened under the glow as my eyes closed and I let the crackling embers lull me to sleep. I wasn't ready to wake up when my body started shaking violently. Prying my eyes open wasn't easy, but when Ray looked back at me, eyes filled with terror, adrenaline shot through me, and I sat up straight, wide-eyed.

"What's wrong?" I looked at my watch. It was just past four in the morning. I grumbled at only getting two hours of sleep.

"I heard someone calling for help. They sound like they're hurt. What do we do?"

Things were still foggy, but I tried to process the situation rationally. They could either be trying to lure people to them, so they could steal their shelter or rations; or they could actually be in trouble, but that's what the watch was for. They could be extracted at any time. My head turned to the cave opening when another shout filled the silence.

"Dammit," I cursed under my breath and stood up, grabbing the machete.

"So, we're going?" Ray chewed on her fingers.

"You can stay if you want. Make sure no one finds

the cave. I have this." I raised the machete. We had been training for this for over nine months, so her apprehension was disconcerting. She wasn't ready for the trials.

She nodded once, and I headed out of the cave. The moon was nearly full, providing enough light to survey the surroundings and catch glimmers off the soft waves rolling down the creek. This time when I heard the cry for help I recognized the voice. It was Jackson. How could a boy of his size get himself into trouble he couldn't fight his way out of? And where the heck were the others?

His voice came from the south, so I headed blindly in that direction being light with my footsteps. His next shout was close, maybe a hundred yards, so I whisper-shouted to him. "Jackson, I'm coming. Stop shouting." I gritted my teeth. The whole forest knew he was in trouble by now.

"Abigail?"

My chest growled deeply. "Shhh." What part of being quiet did he not understand? I swear they should have taught Common Sense 101 in one of the buildings.

I crept up slowly, peering through the trees before I approached Jackson. I listened for a minute to see if anyone else was making their way to him, but I only caught sounds of baby birds in nests and rustling of leaves from the slight breeze. Jackson was hanging upside down from a large branch, a rope tied around his ankle. I rolled my eyes in disbelief. How could he get himself trapped on the first day?

The tree I was hiding behind reached over to the tree Jackson was hanging from and made for a better access point to cutting him down. Climbing with a machete would be impossible without maiming myself. I needed to cover the blade. "I'm coming, Jackson," I reassured him so he wouldn't cry out again. I pulled some large leaves from the branches and covered the blade. Using a long thin branch I wrapped it around the leaves and blade and tied a secure knot. I tucked it into my sweatshirt and climbed the tree, wincing from the scratches of the bark on my palms. Being up high gave me a good vantage point and everything seemed to be clear.

A thick, sturdy branch reached over to the other tree and I scooted carefully across it, my stomach dropping every time the branch dipped from my weight. I wouldn't die from the fall unless I landed on the machete. Not a pleasing image right now. Jackson jostled to look up at me, causing my branch to bounce.

"Stop moving," I hissed.

"Sorry," he whispered.

Once I reached his tree, I pulled the machete out, unwrapped the leaves, and chopped through the rope. Jackson landed on the ground with a loud thud and grunt.

"A little warning would have been nice," he grumbled as he rubbed the back of his head.

"Sorry." I shrugged my shoulders and giggled to myself. The bigger they are, the harder they fall. "Watch out. I'm going to drop the machete so I can climb down." I dropped it off to the right of him and was about to climb down when a low rumbling that sounded a lot like a growl rushed through the forest.

"What was that?" Jackson asked.

"I don't know. Let me go up and get a better look." Jackson grabbed the machete and pushed his back up against the tree trunk.

I climbed up a few more branches and looked around. Movement to the east several hundred yards away shook the forest awake. Birds flew from nests and branches cracked. What the hell was it? Another snarl filled the night silence, making me flinch. It was coming faster than I hoped I could climb down and warn Jackson, so I shouted, "Jackson, run!"

"What? I can't. I think my ankle is broken."

I held my breath in attempt to steady my racing heart, my mind begging me to stay up here where it was safe, but my instincts telling me that I was Jackson's only hope. I launched myself down the tree and landed next to him just as the thing jumped through the trees, its hot breath visible as white smoke against the chill of the night and its golden eyes glowing brighter than the sun.

"Is that a werewolf?" I asked dumbly. Of course, it was. It had to be. It lifted its lips high, revealing its razor sharp teeth.

"Why would they let a werewolf loose?" Jackson lifted the machete but released a low grunt when he shifted weight onto his hurt leg.

They wouldn't. "Get back." I stepped in front of Jackson.

The creature dug its paw into the ground and let out a deep breath, readying to pounce.

"What? I'm bigger than you."

"This is not the time to debate whether size matters. This is what I do." I kept my eyes trained on the beast's, feeling the ebb and flow of its energy when it inhaled and exhaled, looking for the shift that would warn me of its attack. When an irregular pulse vibrated, I grabbed the machete from Jackson and swung in the air, making contact in the crook of its neck. It screamed loudly, but it didn't alter its intention as it shook its head violently to release the machete from its muscle. My flesh tore easily under its claws, and the pain was blinding. *The watch*, I thought as black spots bubbled in front of me, but I couldn't reach it, and I couldn't speak to tell Jackson. Maybe the leaders were right to not put their faith in me.

A burning sensation exploded in between each muscle, tendon, and bone in my body and I screamed out as the last of my pain tolerance diminished, and when I fell to the ground, I wondered how long it would be until I died, but then numbness doused the fire spreading through me, followed by a comforting warmth like tanning under the sun at the lake with Kendra.

"Abigail, are you all right?"

It was Jackson's voice and not Kendra's that greeted me on the other side of my daydream. It took several blinks for my vision to clear and see Jackson hovering above me. I smiled weakly.

"That didn't go exactly as planned."

He released a reserved chuckle and fell back on his butt. "If I didn't see it with my own eyes...I heard what you could do, but no one actually believed it."

*Well, that was just awesome,* I thought sarcastically.

"And your wounds...they're gone," he added, mystified.

I looked down at my arms that the beast had made mincemeat of only moments ago. All that remained were thin, smooth, silvery scars. The first of many scars I imagined I would accumulate.

"How about that," I stated, pleased. Did this mean I couldn't be killed? That would make me indispensable for sure, but wouldn't it also make me immortal? Was my gift turning me into the very thing The Order feared? Is this what they were trying to prevent? The evolution of immortality?

Bouncing lights through the trees and commanding voices cleared the thoughts away as we were safely surrounded by black uniforms and one pissed off Elijah.

"What the hell happened here?" Elijah fumed as he marched over and knelt beside me, taking in the scars left behind by the attack.

"You tell us. I thought you had this place secured?" Tingles trailed from his thumb as they caressed the silvery scars gently, and my breath hitched slightly from the sensation.

"It must have come from the mountain range near your shelter."

I cocked my head curiously until I remembered that

they had planted cameras everywhere. They must have seen the whole attack.

"Vanished?" he asked.

I nodded. "Just like the non-human. What took you so long to get here?"

"We were here in two minutes," he stated plainly.

Had it really only been two minutes? It felt like so much more, but I guess when everything runs through your memory in slow motion it would.

"There has never been a breach before. I take full responsibility," he continued.

"Eli, I'm fine. Jackson broke his ankle from your little trap, but other than that—"

"What trap?" Elijah stood and addressed Jackson.

Jackson lifted the cut rope off the ground. "Stepped in it and was hanging from my ankle until Abigail cut me down."

Elijah's jaw clenched, but he didn't say another word. It was obvious this was not set up by the team. Then, who did it and why? I knew when it was a bad time to ask questions and this was definitely one of those times, so I kept quiet as Elijah called for a full extraction and marched us out of the forest.

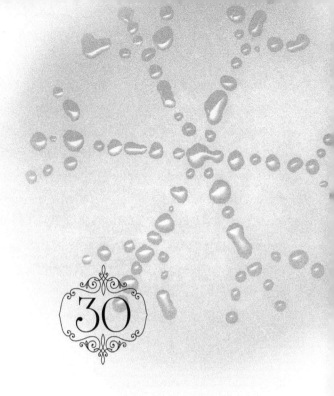

THE ONLY SOUNDS THAT FILLED our march out of the forest were the crunch of sticks under our boots, and the early morning songs of awakening birds. The dark sky lightened with soft hues of blue as the sun readied itself to warm another summer day. I was at the front of the line while Jackson was carried out on a stretcher in the rear. Black uniformed Potentials walked on either side of the line, carrying assault rifles, and I imagined many other concealed weapons.

What happened to Jackson and me was not an accident, and the possibility for another attack was highly plausible.

Once back within the facility gates, everyone scattered for the day awaiting new instructions for Building Eleven in the morning. Elijah and I meandered instinctively to the tree where we could talk open and freely.

"I'm sorry you were put in danger." Elijah's eyes drifted shamefully from me to something off in the distance.

His first thought was my safety rather than what had gone horribly wrong. That couldn't be right. Not when there were so many other lives at stake. Mine shouldn't be the most important. "Unless you set the trap, then you have nothing to apologize for." There was a bit of sass curling around the hard edges of my words.

The morning dew settled into the pockets of silence between us.

"When you killed the werewolf, was it like when you killed the non-human? Did it hurt?"

I thought about the two events and also thought about the time I touched Jasmine and the other witch that watched over her now. It was also then I remembered the boat with Wes where we shared our first kiss. I fell ill quickly, but I didn't connect it to my gift back then because I knew nothing of it. It was my first interaction with something otherworldly, so I had nothing to compare to, but now it made sense. I was so nervous that night because I was still reeling from Wes' sudden return and the heartbreak he had dusted over two years of my life. My emotions had been unchecked, so when we touched so intimately, it was as if I had an adverse reaction to him, but never again after that one time. Only an intense bond between us remained, much like the one I shared with Elijah. I wondered how similar the two bonds were: fabricated and misguided.

Elijah stared at me as he waited for my reply to his question. "No, not at all. I still felt the energy transfer, but it didn't feel the same. It was hot and powerful, but it's as if the pain was muted like a quick push of a television remote."

His lips curled into the first smile I had seen in days. "Then you're ready for the trials."

"You think?" I wish I was assured as he was.

"I know," he said softly.

From what I'd heard, the trials could be anything from our training. Our test could be a sport or an event, physical or psychological. They were tailored specifically to our weaknesses, so everyone's experience would be different, challenging. I was lightyears from the person I was when I came here, but I still harbored many weaknesses, so I couldn't even imagine what they would have in store for me, and Elijah was none the wiser either.

"How's Asher's training coming?"

"He's a fighter just like his sister."

"I wish I could see him." There would be a dull ache slithering in my chest until we were permanently reunited.

"One more month and this will all be over."

That was the plan anyway. The leaders would take the fight directly to the hub of The Order, here on the day of trials. My trial. I couldn't imagine us failing, having all the leaders backing us, but there were still the recruits, Potentials, and the Elites who were fiercely loyal to The Order. The leaders understood the way The Order worked better than anyone. They knew when Penelope called their names that they had been issued a death sentence. The others would need convincing or they would surely die, too.

The next morning, all the recruits from the failed outdoor training exercise were assigned to rotational training for the remainder of the month. We wouldn't be living in an assimilated reality. We would work on sharpening and honing our skills. It was tiresome, day in and day out, and we still didn't have any answers about the attack. Elijah had stopped training me after dinner when he began working with Asher, so I spent the evenings in the library, gathering books on The Order and taking meticulous notes. The more time I spent in the library the stronger the pull became to the magically cloaked section *F*. Ray had mentioned only a key could break the magic, but I had been too afraid to try the key my grandfather left me. What if it sounded all sorts of silent alarms and a band of Elites surrounded me, hauling me off to solitary again, or worse? With the fight on the horizon, being low-key was pivotal, but when it was over, I would come back and see what they have hidden away so carefully.

The weeks passed quickly with still no answers about the attack and The Order have taken extra precautions to secure the area, but have left it off limits. I had another theory, but it would take a certain kind of finesse to get the truth.

"Are you crazy?" Jackson choked through stolen breaths

as the weight of my shoe crushed his Adam's apple. His hands wrapped around my foot in an attempt to pry it off.

So, maybe finesse wasn't the right word. I meant brute force. "Admit that you and your little team set that trap."

He struggled to get free, but I only pressed harder.

"How the hell would we pull that off?" he squeaked.

"I will crush your neck, Jackson." My voice was calm and deadly.

When terror registered in his eyes as the rest of the oxygen seeped from his lips, he finally gave up. "Fine, I'll tell you."

I knew it. I released my foothold and gave him a moment to gather himself as he bent over his lap choking for air.

"Spill." I crossed my arms over my body, standing over him. I had taken down the strongest recruit at the facility. It was a proud moment.

"We needed to know if you were really capable of destroying those things. It's our asses on the line out there."

I wasn't shocked by their lack of faith in me. I had never been given any indication otherwise, but to get a creature on facility grounds was damn near impossible. "How did you do it? How did you get it here?"

He looked around as if afraid someone would hear him. "The tall guy that follows Jasmine around."

"Why the hell would Bart help you losers with anything?" Things weren't adding up.

"You have it backward. He came to *us*. He said the council had sent him, and it was a secret test. We only went along with it because he promised no one would be in any real danger. We were all curious to see your gift in action."

Words swirled in a frenzy of hurricane force winds in my head. Bart was up to something and I doubt the council had a clue. "Don't tell anyone we talked about this." I hovered my foot over his throat again in warning.

"I won't. I value my life."

I wasn't sure if he was referring to my idle threat or of the witch.

As I turned to leave, he added, "For what it's worth, we all trust you now. With our lives."

It shouldn't be worth a damn to me after what they pulled, but this meant a lot. This war wasn't about sides. All lives mattered, and I was hoping to save as many as possible.

I found Elijah running the track that evening with the look of a man deep in thought. I stood on the edge of the path and waited for him to notice me. It was hard not to appreciate the flexing of his muscles as they pumped him toward me, and I squatted down and pretended to adjust my shoelaces to hide the affect that burst inside me.

"Hey, what are you doing out here? It's almost curfew."

He pulled his shirt up to wipe the sweat that rolled down his hairline, gifting me a brief look at his waistline, the veins popping under the pressure of the workout. I, again, tried to focus my eyes elsewhere.

"It was Bart, the Keeper. He set up the attack with Jackson."

Fury immediately raged in his eyes like a swarm of bees protecting their hive. "Tell me."

"There isn't much to tell. Jackson said the witch approached him with the council's blessing to test my gift before the trials."

His jaw clicked as he clenched his jaw. "Then the council lied to me."

"Or Bart has his own agenda."

He shook his head. "I don't think so. They are testing you early, which probably means they have other intentions for your final trial."

"What do you mean?"

"You know the trials can be physical or mental. They wouldn't waste the final trial on your psychological strength if they weren't confident in your physical ability."

My brief stint in solitary drummed to the surface. They had attacked me psychologically, and while it wasn't the worst someone could endure, it certainly wasn't pleasant. I shuttered at the thought of what they could manifest for a final trial. "Should I be worried?"

"Always. You should never feel comfortable. Not with your gift. They will strike when your guard is the lowest."

That was my worst fear. Over the months, I had become physically stronger, my skills that of a professional, and my control was infinitely better, but it would never be enough to make me confident going into these trials.

When I fell asleep the night before my trials, the only

words that floated through my head were those of my grandfather's before he died.

"Weakness comes from love, and strength comes from the soul. You cannot have one without the other. When the soul is lost, so is the love."

I couldn't remember the rest, and hadn't thought of my grandfather's words since he spoke them, but for some reason they had been dug out of the dark sea of foggy memories and spoke loudly as if my grandfather was standing before me now, alive and healthy. These words meant something, so I let them repeat over and over again until sleep became so heavy that blackness gave me peace for one more night.

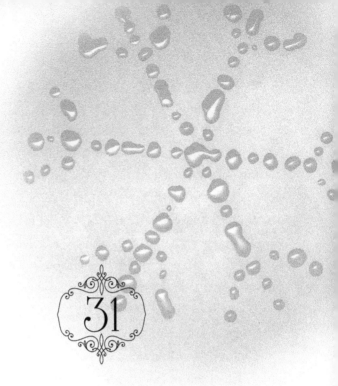

MY GRANDFATHER'S WORDS RESONATED like a bad omen, if one believed in that kind of thing, which I kind of did now. With monsters and witches roaming the earth, it would be dangerous to ignore signs, especially when a low hum similar to that of an electrical wire buzzed through me almost constantly now. The intensity varied with situations, but it was always there warning me that my days of comfort were long gone.

The morning of the final trials had come and, as I lay in bed, I thought of Kendra and how much I missed her. She was always the better person in stressful situations, whether it was a trigonometry test or fending off a false rumor started by the mean girls. Kendra was the epitome of grace no matter what the conflict, she knew just what to say to me to get me through it. My eyes stung realizing I may never get a chance to see her again.

Before the knock sounded on my door, I could hear footsteps shuffling nervously up and down the hall, recruits getting ready for the trials. Our numbers had dwindled down to twenty and I was the last trial. Elijah arranged it to accommodate the rebellion that was set to attack at the end, or intervene if my trial went sideways. It meant that I had to sit with a nauseating feeling rumbling in my stomach all day as I sat through trial after trial, seeing how bad things could be for my own. If Elijah hadn't set me up to go last I would have assumed the council did it just to torture me.

The door creaked open slowly and Jasmine's lava locks greeted me before her apprehensive eyes. "Hey," she said weakly, biting on her lip.

"Hey." Pulling myself up seemed harder today, doomed almost. Was it another omen or just my nerves getting the best of me?

"A lot of nervous people out there." She closed the door behind her, building a barrier between us and the chaos.

I had reverted back to picking at the skin around my fingernails, a habit I had lost over the months as my confidence built. Today I was lacking in that. This could be the last time I saw Jasmine or even the last day I lived depending on how things went. It was also my last chance to warn her about the rebellion. I begged Elijah to give me permission, but he was afraid that somehow Bart, the witch who followed her relentlessly, was bonded to her and would find out. The guilt had been eating me alive because not warning her meant she was at more of a risk than necessary.

"I know what's bothering you."

I peered up to her both relieved and concerned. "Oh, yeah?"

"Visionary, remember?" She pointed to herself.

She knew I had been keeping this from her. She must hate me.

"I'm not mad. I understand how dangerous this kind of knowledge is. When I had the vision the first time, I was scared Bart would find a way to extract it from me, so I shielded it with magic only a Visionary could break."

I leaned forward urgently. "I'm so sorry. I wanted to tell you, but—"

"I get it." She raised her hand to stop me. "I didn't like what I saw, Abby." Her eyelids pushed together for a moment, and when she looked at me again, her eyes were darker.

"What did you see just now?" Did I even want to know? Would it change the course of the rebellion? It was too late to stop it, but going in with a peek into the future could save lives.

She sat cross-legged on the bed, her chin dipped low, so her eyes were hidden from view. "Blood, pain," she said slowly and then added, "you," as her water-filled eyes found mine.

Chills raced across my skin. "What about me?"

Her head shook slowly, telling me I didn't want to

know. "It's just a blur of images. I don't see things clearly. Emotions are stronger. I feel them in stereo." She paused. "Your heart…I feel it break."

Her vision gave more meaning to my grandfather's words, but I still didn't understand them fully.

"That could mean anything." Was I asking a question or reassuring her? I couldn't differentiate. Everything was a pile of weeds and rocks, muddying my thoughts.

"Whatever is going to happen is going to be bad. For you," she warned.

"I know." It was a truth I had come to terms with that night in the woods standing across from the leaders. My fate was bound to the dissolution of the current Order of the Crest, good or bad. "You should go, Jasmine. Find Caleb. In less than twelve hours this place is going to be a war zone."

"I can't." She took my hand and held it. "I'm the only one who can save you."

My heart anchored to the sea floor, the final bubbles of air rising to the surface while it suffocated in the dust. Her revelation made it impossible to breathe, to swallow, to think. Her fate was in turn tied to mine. "How?" Swallowing the lump down did nothing to hold back tears that now ran down my cheeks.

"I don't know exactly, but I do know I need to be there, or you will be lost."

I zoned in on the word *lost*, matching it to my grandfather's words. Everything was winding together carefully, but I couldn't see the final outcome. It was maddening to have so many pieces and not be able to put it all together.

"I can save myself, Jas. You can't be there tonight. You have to leave." I wouldn't let her sacrifice herself to save me. I was stronger than anyone here. Stronger than her.

"You know that I can change the future, Abby, even if I leave. Somehow, I will be there to save you."

Not if I could help it. I might not be able to save everyone, but I would save her. "I'm sorry, Jasmine."

"Don't be."

I apologized again when I hugged her goodbye, but it wasn't because of what she thought she had to do, but because of what I was about to do to keep her safe.

I dressed quickly and snuck out of Building Twelve. Everyone else was too anxious about the trials to pay much attention to me as I slipped out and ran up to my tree. I sat cross-legged at the base of the tree and steadied my breathing, letting the morning chill fade from my skin and the unstable energy flow from my body.

I could feel Caleb's sadness before I could see him. It was pulsing strongly, leading me to his location. He was squatting on a thick tree branch overlooking the facility. He was here for Jasmine. I thought it would be hard to get him here in time, but he had been stalking her all along.

My projection floated up to the branch and sat next to him. I hadn't tried to physically reach out to anyone yet, but I needed to try. The first time my fingers reached for him, they slid right through, but after several more tries, he flinched, and I knew he felt me.

"Who's there?"

His iridescent eyes looked over to where I was perched, and I willed him to be able to see me.

"Abigail? How?"

"Caleb, can you really see me?" This was easier than I had imagined.

"Yes, I see you, but barely. You're like a ghost." He brushed his brown hair from his ashen face. "What's wrong? Is Jasmine in trouble?"

"Not yet, but she will be. You need to get her out of here before the sun drops."

"How? I've been trying for months to get inside."

"The back gate will be unlocked in a few hours. I will make sure she's there just before noon. Take her as far from here as you can." My projection began to fade. "Alright?" I needed confirmation.

"Yeah, I'll be there. Thank you."

Elijah shook me awake. "What are you doing?"

"Saving someone," I said but didn't give a further explanation. He would be livid if he knew that I had just set free the only person who could save me.

The day sped by in a blur of instructions by Elijah, and the other recruit's trials. Some faced non-humans that had been starved, while others faced their families. One had to complete a puzzle while another had to run a time-sensitive maze. It was such an odd mixture of events that there was no predicting what they had in store for me.

I dropped Jasmine's sleeping body off at the gate and watched with relief as Caleb stole her away. She would never forgive me for slipping sleeping herbs into her drink at lunch that I stole from her room, but it didn't matter, because she was safe. I had already saved one person.

Everyone had passed their trials, some bloodied and bruised, but the standing ovation of the council after each one earned them a spot as a Potential.

I stood behind the gates of the large circular arena, pacing as I waited for my name to be called. The stadium seats rose steep and high to accommodate the council, leaders, recruits, Potentials, and Elites. Each trial took time to set up and break down, so when the arena was left empty for me with only the dust of the ground and the threatening clouds above, the low warning buzz in my veins built up strength.

"Are you ready?" Elijah asked as he strolled to me and wrapped his arms around my body.

"No," I confessed.

He nuzzled his nose into my hair just behind my near, inhaling deeply and exhaling softly, as his lips rounded my cheek and grazed my lips. My body blazed with our connection and the sudden urge to feel his lips on mine stole away the nerves. We pressed together feeling the finality of our embrace, the loss of some of those around us, and the uncertainty the future would bring upon us all. The tingle of our touch remained as we pulled away.

I should have told him I loved him. I should have told him I always had, but my loyalty to Wes choked the life from the truth.

I was in love with two boys.

His calloused fingers brushed through my hair and he leaned in, kissing my cheek, leaving me with the words I didn't have the courage to utter, "I love you, Abigail."

The automatic gate retracted. As it closed with me on the other side, I watched Elijah walk out with a blade in hand. In a matter of minutes, this place would explode with screams and chaos and our lives will be forever changed.

When I spun around to face the center, my ears pulsed with adrenaline, the shouts of the crowd fading in and out with the pounding of my heart. Closing my eyes, I worked on slowing down my breathing and centering my energy. As I stepped toward the center, the voices hushed. I found Jack in the sea of black uniformed Potentials and Elites, excitedly showing me a thumbs-up. It was nice to see that the carefree brother of my best friend still remained even after all the dark truths he had learned about this world.

The recruits were grouped together by building, and I easily found Ray who adorned a mixture of fear and optimism for me. I was surprised when Jackson and several others smiled and cheered for me. I had managed to win them over, something I never thought possible, and yet, I had also put their lives in imminent danger. Many gestures of goodwill accompanied the body language of all the recruits, and it truly warmed me that they believed in me.

The twelve council members were seated at the northern side of the arena, wearing deep red cloaks with hoods that carefully hid their identities beneath. They sat stiffly, awaiting my fate to play out.

The leaders were hidden in shadows on the east side of the arena. Their body language was more telling, with unsettled feet and heads moving side to side, awaiting the signal that would throw us into battle.

Intuitively, I knew my final trial would not be easy. I knew it would tear me into so many pieces it would be impossible to be whole again. I felt it in my grandfather's words and I saw it through my vision, but what I didn't expect was for it to shred all hopes I had for a future with Wes, because what they dragged across the red tinted dirt was not the Wes that held my hand on the swing set in the playground, or the Wes who swept me from the rushing river that nearly swallowed me before he disappeared for two years, or the Wes that held me close under the blanket of the stars on the charred cliff that overlooked Sandpoint. The Wes that fell to the ground, shackled, starved and broken, bearing his fangs and growling with insatiable hunger, was not the Wes that stood on the bridge in the redwood forest, promising a year could never change his connection to me.

The pure soul that glowed underneath his iridescent eyes was gone, replaced by a furious frenzy of chaos and evil. And when he snapped at me, a dog on a leash just out of reach of its prey, I knew something had gone very wrong, and our plan was about to fall apart.

I stepped farther away, my hands shaking and my heart ripping from my chest. This couldn't be real. Wes couldn't be here in this arena right now. Elijah would have told me if he was here. This was a trick. They were using magic to assimilate this. This wasn't real, I kept repeating in my head as my eyes jumped around at all the faces in the stadium, some horrified, others excited. Were they seeing the same thing as me? Was this a trick for only me, or were they experiencing, too?

The gate opened again and out came Polly first, wide-eyed and confused. When her eyes stretched across the arena to meet mine her expression darkened, my heart sinking further to that bottomless sea. Then, golden streaks of sunlight spilled over the face of my best friend, and I heard Jack scream from his seat, clawing over the recruits in front of him until restrained by his peers. His shouts reached down my throat and tugged on my soul, but what came next flung me over the edge of my worst nightmares. My thirteen-year-old brother, stronger than I last saw him, but doused in unfathomable fear, stumbled in behind.

I blinked rapidly, trying to make the illusion vanish, to wash the projections from my mind, but they only became more vivid as my loved ones came closer. They weren't shackled like Wes. There was nowhere for them to run. We were trapped within the tall concrete walls and iron gate, and I was living the vision that had been haunting me since solitary.

A booming voice spoke through the speakers, echoing off the concrete and bouncing in the air. "Release him."

The drumming in my chest deepened as the shackles fell from Wes' arms and legs. He stretched his back and the frenzied hunger locked its eyes on me. Polly, Kendra, and Asher fell back against the concrete wall, Polly standing in front of them protectively.

"Wes," I begged softly.

His lips upturned, the small break in the clouds allowing the sun to glisten off of his white teeth. The night of the accident billowed in the space between us, blood red spilling into the iridescence completely filling his eyes. Black was anger, iridescent was pure, and red was soulless.

A booming half-crazed laugh escaped him, filling the arena. "Yes?"

Was he toying with me? I still wasn't convinced this was real. That *he* was real. "What did they do to you?" I kept my voice even, strong.

"Why don't you ask your boyfriend Elijah?"

*No.* He was lying. Elijah would never hurt anyone I cared for. Not unless...he had no choice. "Wes, you can fight this. Whatever they did to you, don't let them win."

He let out another bone-chilling laugh. "Why would I fight my true nature? Don't you see, I'm free now? All they had to do was release my soul." He waved his arms out as if thanking the universe for his new-found freedom.

And that's when my grandfather's words spun around me frantically, coming together as clear as day. *Weakness comes from love, and strength comes from the soul. You cannot have one without the other. When the soul is lost, so is the love.*

There was nothing left to love. Wes' soul was gone, and all that remained was a vessel inhabited by a creature born of darkness and decay. I could have fallen to the ground with how shattered I felt, life with less meaning, and the world tilted off its axis, but I still had people to protect, people that relied on me. People I loved.

Everything happened so fast I couldn't say what came first: the teeth that ripped out Asher's throat, or the arrow that took out a council member and had him falling to his death on the arena floor. I felt the scream in my ears before I registered it coming from me as I raced to Asher's side. Polly was restraining Wes with magic while Kendra cried in a heap on the floor, Asher's blood soaking into the dirt around her.

I flung myself over him, rocking his head in my lap as I whispered to hold on for just one more second as I pulled the Resurrection charm from my pocket and held it tightly to his chest. I had dug up the charm and key from the tree roots when I projected out to Caleb. I didn't know if I'd have a chance to retrieve them once the fight broke out, and I was relieved that I had listened to my instincts.

The fight blew up around us, bodies falling to the ground, guns firing, arrows flying. Commands barked across the arena and chaos broke out. I had to get us out of here.

"Polly, we need to go," I shouted.

Her body was shaking under the struggle of maintaining the magic, and I knew she didn't have much time before her energy was depleted and Wes would continue his attack on us.

"Go. I'll hold him off as long as I can."

I looked down at Asher's still, lifeless body and Kendra rocking frantically against the wall. I didn't want to leave Polly behind, but I didn't have any other choice. I scooped Asher up in my arms and kicked Kendra's foot. "We need to get out of here." Her bright red cheeks and swollen eyes peered up through the thick lashes I had always envied and she nodded, scraping herself off the ground and following me to the gate, only it was still locked and Polly no longer held Wes back.

No one could have predicted what came next, Jasmine appearing out of thin air next to Polly, mixing their magic to keep Wes from killing us all, but Wes being a hybrid was stronger than both of their magic combined and ripped out their throats, taking the life of my best friend and great-grandmother right in front of me. I squeezed the charm tighter to Asher's chest as their deaths tore through me like a Samurai sword, taking my humanity in one fell swoop. A fury I had never felt raged through every limb, every muscle, every vein and I laid my brother's body carefully to the ground, instructing Kendra to hold the charm over his heart.

I launched myself toward Wes with a madness only a person who had felt extreme loss could understand. This was what the council wanted. For me to kill Wes and, although they were all meeting their own deaths at this very moment, I knew it was my only recourse. I had to kill Wes. But when I faced his soulless red eyes, all I could see was a halo of iridescence surrounding his body. Was it just a trick of the light, or was it a sign that he could be saved?

In my moment of indecision, I had given him the opportunity to attack, and as his fingers wrapped around my neck, crushing my windpipe as he lifted me off the ground. I knew I had made a mistake. The only sensation I felt after my eyes closed was a weightlessness much like floating, only the burden of life and death, love and hate, had also been released, and…

I had finally found peace.

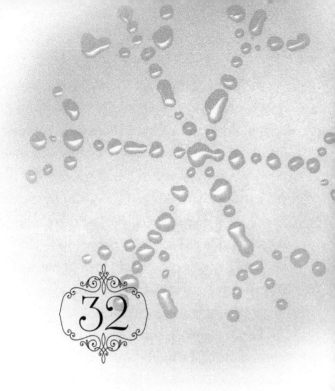

## ELIJAH

ITHOUGHT I HAD PREPARED myself for every scenario the council could throw at Abigail. I knew they would probably have her face Wes and give her an ultimatum to kill him, but I never imagined they would brainwash him and feed her and the others to him. A lion's den full of sheep. Abigail was strong, but to kill someone you loved, whether a beast or not, was an impossibility for even the inhumane. There was a time when I wouldn't have been able to pull the trigger, and if faced with a dark version of Abigail, I knew I would have made the same choice she did when Wes wrapped his claws around her neck.

I was almost too late. I cursed myself as I forced the gate

open, yelling for Kendra to take Asher somewhere safe as I flew by. Just as I was about to take Wes out, a blinding flash of light exploded between them, and Abigail dropped to the ground like a pile of bricks. Wes had vanished altogether. If Abigail's gift worked as it had previously, Wes was dead.

I dropped to Abigail's side and checked her bruised neck for a pulse. It was faint, but there. The bruises already began to fade as I scooped her up and held her to my chest, keeping track of the soft rhythm of her heart. We were far from danger as the war was in full swing above us. I needed to get everyone to a safe place.

Kendra and Asher were hidden in a shadow against the outside of the arena wall. I rushed over, placing Abigail down carefully next to her brother.

"Is she..." Kendra couldn't say what she was thinking, though.

"No, but we aren't safe here."

A shrill sound captivated our attention. "Dragons," I shared as I looked to the sky.

"What? There are dragons, too?" Kendra screeched, her face a mess of smeared mascara and snot.

"They either broke out of the prison, or the rebellion was leaked to the non-humans. Either way, it's not good. We need to get as far away from the facility as possible."

Kendra shot up, confused and still half delirious. "I don't think I can carry him," she declared frantically.

The charm was still on Asher's chest and his throat had healed. Only dried blood remained. I leaned over his chest and caught wind of a faint heartbeat, so I pocketed the charm and scooped both on either shoulder. "Let's go," I barked.

Kendra stayed close behind me as we slid from one shadow to the next. The sun had set, and twilight would soon fade with the new moon. Darkness would be our only friend tonight. We stuck to the perimeter as we made our way to the back gate. I stopped one building away from the armory, where not only were the weapons I wanted but also a prison full of tortured non-humans.

"Why did we stop?" Kendra whispered over my shoulder.

"I need to get weapons." I placed Asher and Abigail carefully on the ground and turned to Kendra. I felt sorry for her. Her world had been split wide open, and everything she thought she knew was false. Her blue eyes looked like an ocean in the midst of turmoil, waves crashing against a rocky cliff and spilling over onto the land. I wasn't good at comforting people but touch always seemed to help, so I placed my hands gently on her shoulders and gave her instructions. "I need you to stay here with them while I retrieve weapons. You're their only hope, so stay hidden and quiet."

She nodded slowly, but obediently. I gave her the hunting knife from my boot. "Aim for the heart or the throat."

"Okay," she barely choked out as she took the knife.

It was a bad idea leaving her alone. I needed to be quick.

I raced down to the armory. It was quiet here. The fighting was contained to the arena so far. I scanned my hand and slipped inside, rushing down the hall as the lights flickered on and off, and straight to the door to the prison. It was still secured, so if any of prisoners got out, it was through the tunnel. I grabbed a black duffel and filled it with weapons quickly—Tasers and darts, guns, more knives, poison grenades—anything I could fit in the bag. I slung it over my shoulder and rushed back out.

When a girl's scream reached me coming from the direction of where I left Kendra, I shot over to the building where I found Caleb and Jack circling each other only feet from Kendra, Abigail, and Asher.

"Where is she?" Caleb growled, his eyes black as night.

"Who?" Jack asked sharply.

"Caleb, Jack, stop," I commanded. They both acknowledged me, but they remained rigid and on alert.

"Where's Jasmine?" Caleb hissed.

If I told him the truth now, he could lose all sense of rationale, and attack. We didn't need a fight right now. We needed to get out of here.

"She—" Jack began.

"We don't know," I cut him off quickly. "The fight broke out after she appeared."

Jack gave me a questioning glance, but didn't refute my confession.

"Where?" Caleb asked less offensively.

"The arena," I pointed to the far end of the facility. The

arena had been built just outside of the facility off to the side near the entrance.

Caleb didn't hesitate as he raced in that direction. "We have only a few minutes before he discovers her dead body. Let's go."

Jack ran to Kendra's side, checking her for injuries.

"Carry Asher," I demanded as I scooped up Abigail. They followed behind as I led them out the back entrance and through the woods.

"We aren't going to get very far carrying them," Jack whisper-shouted.

"I know." It was a ten-mile hike to the road, and the cars were too close to the facility to risk stealing right now, but I knew where we could wait it out, and it was only about three miles away.

The sounds of the war faded in and out as gunshots bounced off the mountains that surrounded us. The plan was for me and Abigail to fight alongside the leaders, but things soured quickly. My only thought was getting her to safety. There would be repercussions when the dust settled.

I knew we were close once we reached the creek.

"Where are we going?" Kendra pleaded, out of breath.

"It's not much farther," I assured her. "And it will keep us safe until we can get to a car."

Once we reached the rocky alcove at the base of the mountain, I pushed aside the brush that hid away the cave and ushered everyone in.

"Someone's been living here." Kendra's panicked eyes

worked their way around the cave, noticing the pillows made of leaves, the fire pit and stacks of wood.

"It was Abigail's safe place." I didn't elaborate.

We placed Abigail and Asher side-by-side, their breathing still shallow.

"Are they going to be okay?" Kendra had her knees pulled to her chest and watched warily. Jack sat next to his sister, putting his arm around her shoulders.

I sat next to Abigail, keeping track of the rise and fall of her chest. "I don't know," I admitted. She had never been knocked unconscious before. I had no idea what was happening. Asher would likely be awake in a few hours. At least that's how long it took for me to raise from the dead with the charm.

"What the hell is going on?" Kendra asked her brother. "Where are we, and why did Wes attack Abigail? What happened to him?"

Understandably, she had a lot of questions, and I was grateful that Jack was here to fill in the blanks, because I had no desire to coddle a child right now. Not while the only person I've ever been able to love was on the brink of death. If Abigail died, I would never be the same. My humanity would fall six feet under with her, and I would kill every damn non-human, supernatural thing out there. Good or bad, they would all die in her name.

Though it was summer, the nights were still cold. I didn't want to risk a fire, so I gathered more leaves to cover Abigail and Asher as Jack and Kendra huddled close for body heat. I was used to the cold and days without sleep, so I remained next to Abigail, watching and listening throughout the night.

When the sun rose, I used a woven basket to carry water back from the creek and we passed it around.

"How was it out there?" Jack inquired.

"Quiet."

"Do you think the fight is over?"

"Maybe." It was too soon for all of us to traipse through the woods back to the facility, but in a few hours, I would need to go and assess the situation. Neither Abigail nor Asher was awake yet, and as the hours passed, I became more worried.

"Why aren't they waking?" Tears fell down Kendra's tanned skin.

"I don't know," I growled. Something wasn't right.

My head jerked to a rustling just outside the cave. I hopped up, taking the knife from my boot and stalking over to the entrance quietly, holding up my finger to my lips in Jack and Kendra's direction. Jack stood slowly, retrieving his own knife and walked to the entrance across from me. When the sunlight spilled in, I jumped in front of the entrance to block the intruder. Ray screamed, putting her hands up defensively.

"It's just me," she rambled off quickly.

"What are you doing here?" I wasn't ready to put the knife down, so I held it steady at her neck.

"The same as you, escaping."

"Were you followed?"

"I don't think so. I covered my tracks and made a few loops in different directions." She looked past me. "Oh, my God, is that Abigail? Is she okay?"

I put the knife down and let her walk by. "I'm going to do a perimeter check. Watch her," I said to Jack and then slipped out. The sun was bright today, not having to contend with any impeding summer storms. I walked around the creek and through the woods, listening for unnatural sounds and also for the war that was miles away. Only small creatures roamed about, gathering food and stretching their legs. Birds flew about their business, and squirrels raced up tree trunks. Just standing here you would never know what happened only hours ago. The world was on the brink of a startling reality, and I couldn't say at this very moment that we had done the right thing.

When I got back to the cave, Ray was comforting Kendra while Jack stood alert by the entrance.

"Did she say anything?"

"Not much. She said it was chaos. No one knew what side to fight on. She barely got out."

"Dammit! I need to get back there." I looked over at Abigail's lifeless body. Could I really leave her here unguarded? Jack had gone through training, but his instincts were lacking, and Ray barely passed her final trial.

"I know you don't trust my ability, but trust that I will do anything to keep my sister safe. I won't let anyone get to them."

Jack's eyes burned with a soldier's truth, but what was out there could tear him to shreds before he even lifted his knife.

Kendra cried out and we both spun around ready to fight when Caleb and Jasmine appeared next to Abigail and Asher.

"How?" I asked as I approached cautiously.

Jasmine's dark hair flowed like a river over her shoulders as she turned to me. "I told her I was the only one who could save her."

"But I saw Wes rip your throat out along with Polly's?"

Caleb's eyes flared. He didn't know.

"I was projecting, so I could help Polly." Her eyes fell solemnly. "I failed."

"Well, where the hell have you been, then?" I clenched my jaw, trying to hold back the anger that had been building.

"Watch your tone," Caleb warned.

"It's okay, Caleb. He's angry." She turned back to me. "Projecting on the level is not easy. It takes a lot of energy. I just barely woke and came straight here." She looked back down to Abigail.

"Why won't they wake up?" I asked sincerely, calming the storm that never seemed to fully dissipate within me.

"She's linked to the charm, so until she wakes, Asher won't. She is also linked to Wes. Abigail told me about the night of the accident. I didn't put it all together until now. He became a hybrid that night and their blood mixed, so their energy resides as one. The only way she will wake is if we bring him back, too."

A stillness bestowed the cave like nothing I had ever felt.

"Do it!" Once Abigail was back, I could deal with Wes.

"I don't know how or where he will come back," Jasmine warned. "He could manifest right here in this cave."

"I don't care," I barked. "Wake her up."

Caleb stepped forward protectively. "She is not your witch to command."

"Don't threaten me." The veins in my temple pulsed and my jaw ached under the continual stress. I was three seconds from ripping this monster's head off.

"Enough," Kendra shouted, startling everyone. "Can you save my best friend?" she asked Jasmine softly.

"Yes." Jasmine nodded.

"Then, please, save her."

Jasmine nodded once in agreement. "I don't know where Wes will manifest."

"Ray, take Kendra into the woods. There's a tree house—"

"Yes, I know where it is."

"Stay there until we find you."

She nodded and led Kendra out of the cave.

"Ready?" I asked Caleb and Jack.

Jack lifted his knife and Caleb crouched in a low fighting position. I stood closest to Jasmine. "Let's resurrect some people."

Jasmine knelt between Abigail and Asher, placed one hand on each of their chests, dipped her head, and began whispering words rapidly. The temperature in the cave dropped so low we could see our breath, and a moment later, a warm glow beneath her hands lit up Abigail and Asher's chests. Jack, Caleb, and I stiffened, primed for a fight when a bright flash of light blinded me, black spots impairing my vision.

"Jasmine?" Caleb yelled.

No response.

"I can't see," Jack whined.

"Shut up," I snapped. I blinked feverishly, finally seeing pockets of the cave through the dissipating spots. Jasmine was lying on the floor, unmoving, with Abigail and Asher. I scanned the cave, satisfied only when there were no signs of Wes.

Caleb fell to Jasmine's side, rocking her in his arms. "She's not breathing."

I rushed to Abigail, worried that I might find the same, but her heartbeat was stronger than ever, as was Asher's, but they still weren't awake. I crawled to Jasmine.

"Put her down." No one was dying on my watch. I pressed on her chest thirty times and blew two breaths into her lungs. I checked for a pulse, but still nothing. I was about to do another round when Abigail's legs started to move.

"I'll take over," Caleb offered.

"You have to be careful. With your strength you could

break her ribs." I didn't wait for a response as I moved over to Abigail. Asher was also beginning to stir.

As she lifted her head, I helped her sit up. "Hey." Emotions I had locked away when I thought I had lost her came rushing through me, and I did nothing to wipe away the tears that fell.

"What happened?" She blinked and brushed her hand along her throat where Wes had crushed it.

"You fought hard. Jasmine saved you."

She looked over to Caleb who was still working on Jasmine. "She's gone," Abigail said plainly.

"No, we can save her," Caleb growled, but it had lost its edge as the grief penetrated.

"No, you can't. She came to me just now. She said to tell you thank you and that she's at peace. She's with her mom."

Abigail's words were spoken like an angel had touched her lips. She didn't cry for her friend or yell in rage. She truly believed her friend was in a better place.

Caleb stopped his compressions, crying over Jasmine's lifeless body. Abigail had told me once about their bond. I knew the pain he was feeling because I glimpsed it when I thought Abigail was gone.

Asher sat up, rubbing his eyes, and then grabbed his throat frantically. "What's going on? Where am I? Are we dead?"

"No, brother, we are very much alive." She smiled and waited until what she said registered.

"Brother?"

"Yes." She nodded in affirmation and then reached out and wrapped her arms around him. He was hesitant at first but gave in, his body settling into hers comfortably.

We stood in front of the dirt mound that marked Jasmine's grave. Abigail gathered wildflowers from the forest blanketing the mound with whites, purples, and blues. We stood silent for a long while until the sun began to set on another day. Abigail stayed, so I did, too.

"Thank you," she said, breaking a long quiet that had settled over the evening.

"I killed your friend," I responded. It was the truth, after all. I didn't care what the consequences were as long as Abigail lived.

"She knew. She said it was her destiny. Jasmine doesn't blame you."

Something felt off about Abigail since she came back. She spoke evenly and without emotion, but most notably, I couldn't *feel* her anymore. It was as if Jasmine was only able to bring back a part of Abigail.

"He's not dead," she continued with her eyes focused past me out the cave.

There was no anger or sadness, just words spoken as if it didn't matter.

"I know. Jasmine warned us that bringing you back would also bring Wes back."

Abigail walked away without another word, leaving me to wonder what happened to her when she died and would she ever be the same again.

When I joined the others, they must have sensed whatever I had with Abigail because the energy was off as we stood awkwardly outside of the cave.

Jack leaned over. "Is Abigail okay?"

I watched her sadly as she sat cross-legged on the ground in a meditative state. "I don't know," I replied truthfully.

Her eyes popped open. "It's done. The war is over, and the Order has been dismantled. The non-humans escaped, but not before setting the facility on fire. We have to go back. There's something I need."

She had projected so easily I didn't even realize it. *When had she gotten so much control over her powers?* "It's too dangerous."

She stood up and announced, "Then stay behind. I don't care. Either way, I'm going."

The old Abigail would have sounded fierce with her proclamation, but this one sounded flat, as if it didn't matter if anyone accompanied her. As if none of us meant anything to her.

"Like hell you're going alone," I snapped.

"Fine. Come on, but don't get in my way."

Kendra whimpered quietly in Jack's arms.

"I'll go with Abigail. The rest of you find a road and follow it until you get to a town. Go home," I suggested calmly.

"What about me?" Asher asked. "The facility *was* my home."

Abigail strolled up to him, placed her hand on his cheek,

and closed her eyes. A moment later, she said, "That's your home now."

Asher's eyes filled with something that looked like gratefulness.

Abigail strolled away and started through the forest back to the facility without so much as a goodbye to the others. Reluctantly, after making sure everyone else would be okay, I jogged after her.

"Abigail, you're being reckless." I grabbed her arm to stop her, but it didn't even slow her down. She could have dragged me across the forest and not even broken a sweat. "What the hell happened to you?"

She stopped and spun around. "Isn't this what you wanted for me? Strength, confidence, control? Well, now I have it, so stop questioning where it came from."

She continued on toward the facility. All I could do was follow and see what would happen next. Clearly, Abigail wasn't herself, and in this state she was lethal.

I had hoped to stake out the perimeter before charging into the facility, but Abigail had other plans. She headed straight for the library. There was smoke coming from behind the building, likely a grass fire, while most of the other buildings were a smoldering pile of rubble. It was odd the library was left untouched.

"It's the magic," Abigail answered a question I hadn't even asked.

"Are you reading my mind?"

"Unfortunately." She rolled her eyes as she turned

back to answer. "You're very broody in there. You need to lighten up."

Too shocked for words, I didn't respond and continued to follow her inside the library.

She stopped in front of a stack of books, pulling a key from her pocket. It was identical to the one around my neck.

Right when I thought about the key, her eyes darted to my chest, and she was trying to grab for it, but as fast as she suddenly was, I was still faster. I grabbed her wrist. "What are you doing?"

"My grandfather gave me this key, and it opens something in a cloaked room behind this stack of books. Let me see yours," she demanded.

I knew better than to feed into this obsession, but I was just as curious to know why her grandfather and my father had identical keys. "Play nice," I warned as I let go of her wrist. She put her arms up in surrender and took a step back. I pulled the necklace over my head and showed her the key that dangled from it.

"Remarkable." She studied it with determined fascination.

When she tried to take a swipe at it, I pulled it away. "That's not playing nice," I wagged my finger at her.

"Whatever. Just bring it over here." She moved back to a stack of books against a wall.

By the looks of it, she was seeing something I wasn't, but once I got closer with the key, the stack of books faded and a room appeared in a foggy haze.

"Holy—"

"Told you." She smiled, beguiled. "Let me have it." She put out her palm with her key in it.

Magic was dangerous, and a secret room hidden within the facility couldn't lead to good things. I placed my key next to the other one and they both immediately glowed, and then a burst of energy blew outward, knocking us back a few steps. The haze disappeared, leaving a clear path into the room.

Abigail laughed.

"What the hell is so funny?"

"This whole time I was looking at the key, literally, like, to open a locked door or something. All along we had the keys, and once placed together, they broke the magic. Whoever made these keys was a genius."

"But how did your grandfather and my father end up with them?"

"I don't know. Maybe my grandfather created these. My bloodline is full of witches, after all."

"Okay, that explains how you got one, but my father didn't know anything about you or the Order of the Crest until we joined." Then a memory flashed in my head. I had seen the key once when I was a little boy. My mother was rifling through some drawers. She was making a lot of noise, so I ran in to check on her. That's when I saw the key drop from a pile of papers.

"Your mom," Abigail confirmed as she relived the memory with me.

"Will you stop doing that?" I demanded, annoyed at her new gift.

"Don't you see, Elijah? That's why they took your mom. They knew she had one of these keys."

I didn't want to believe it, but it made sense. "Let's just find out what fortune cookies these keys broke."

We stepped into the hallway, and the entrance immediately closed behind us. "Hope this wasn't a one way ticket," I grumbled.

The hall turned out to be a small room, and at the far end was a stone altar with a single sheet of paper on it. Abigail picked it up and read it to herself. I couldn't make out the words from where I was.

"What is it?" I asked after a few moments.

"It's a spell," she replied in a dazed stupor.

"For what?"

She turned slowly with the paper still in hand. "Eternal life."

"Like, immortals?" It didn't make sense, because they could create more immortals so easily.

Her head shook slowly. "No. Eternal life as a human."

My heart forgot how to beat, and words failed me. The ramifications of eternal life would be catastrophic. The scenarios raced through my thoughts. "Abigail, there is a reason why this spell was locked away in a hidden room, cloaked with magic, and the keys separated. No one was supposed to find this."

She looked up, unconvinced. "But what if we were

meant to find this? What if those keys were just waiting for us to be born and to come together? With this, we would never have to see a loved one die again. There would be no more grief."

Her eyes were filled with a blind faith in something she didn't truly understand. "Abigail, I know you're hurting because of Jasmine, but you can't keep that spell. There are too many things that could go wrong with it. And if it got into the wrong hands..."

"I'm not leaving it, Elijah. Fate brought us together to find this. I'm not turning my back on it."

I couldn't let her leave with that spell. I launched at her, but she anticipated my move and dodged me. As soon as she was close enough to the exit, it opened. She still held both keys.

"Abigail," I yelled. The foggy haze was manifesting around the entrance already. She turned around on the other side and faced me. *She wouldn't lock me in here*, I thought, but then she turned away and the walls closed me in. I pounded and shouted, hoping she would come to her senses and let me out, but she didn't.

# Acknowledgements

I was tempted to tell you how this series came about and the love/hate relationship that still lingers, but I'll save that for the last book, Midnight Hunter. Instead I'll tell you about how this series almost never came to completion. I almost shelved it because of the lack of interest (or lack of audience reach). It's hard to write a book that no one wants to read even if I do write for myself. I was ready to move on to a new story when I decided to put Midnight Rose on Wattpad. Wow, did it ever take off. If it wasn't for Wattpad highlighting it as a Hot New Story and then a few months later as a Featured Story, I'm not sure where it would be. So many amazing Wattpad readers have embraced the story and the characters and it has inspired me to continue the series, which I'm so grateful for. It really has been a fun world to explore and the characters keep growing in so many ways that it keeps me excited. So thank you to all of my readers, but especially to the Wattpad readers.

A special thanks to my team who rallied to my side to help me get this book ready for publishing when I had no money to offer them. You truly are amazing ladies and you'll never understand how much it has meant to me. Catherine Jones, you are my story notes rock star. Without your advice and beautiful manipulation of my words the story would not be as full as it is. Paige Smith, you have been my editor since day one and it killed me to the core that I couldn't afford you for this book, but then when you offered to read through it for free, I about cried more buckets then Abigail. One day, Paige. One day. And to the newest person on my team, Jodie Tarleton, your final look and comments helped round out the final product. To all of you ladies, thank you from the bottom of my heart.

For the readers who have continued to follow my writing journey, you keep me on social media and publishing, so thank you for the support, even when I go MIA.

And always to my family. My husband is my champion on my good and bad days and I probably would have quit publishing a long time ago without his encouragement.

Write every day. Read every day. Make a plan. Believe in yourself. Only you can accomplish your goals.

# About the Author

DANI HART graduated from the University of Southern California with a degree in Theatre and a concentration in Screenwriting. To find other books by this author, please visit her website, danihartbooks.com